Cimmerian Wandering

Tales of the Pandaus

Cimmerian Wandering

Tales of the Pandaus

ISBN/EAN: 9783337174217

Printed in Europe, USA, Canada, Australia, Japan

Cover: Foto ©Andreas Hilbeck / pixelio.de

More available books at **www.hansebooks.com**

To

आ. आ. आ.,

my Companion

in many of the localities mentioned,

I dedicate

the following little work.

❧Preface❧

A WORD of explanation is due to the Reader of the following "Tales of the Pandaus." They have no claim whatever to be considered exact reproductions of Hindú fable, as they have in fact little or no foundation in legend or chronicle. The main thread of each is purely imaginary ; though a certain veri-similitude to recorded quasi-historical legend has been observed throughout the work.

The heroes of the Mâhâbârât, selected as representative champious in the following "Tales of the Pandans," are :—

(1) YUDISHTIRA—called also Dharm-raja, the "*Just*" King —he was Lord of Indra-prástha (ancient Delhi). His name is derived from the Sanskrit word Yúdhi, "*battle*," and sthira, "*firm*,"=unflinching in the fight. He was eldest and perhaps the most interesting character of the five heroic brethren.

(2) BHIM-SEN or BHIMA, the "*Strong*" one. He was commander-in-chief of the Pandau armies.

(3) ARJUNA, the "*Valiant*"—Lord of the Sounding Bow —a most interesting character. The friend and ally of Krishna.

(4) NAKOOLA, the "*Wise*" one; sometimes called NIZKOOLA.

(5) SAHADEVA or SEDIVA, the "*Handsome*" man.

The five brethren are sometimes represented as types of the abstract qualities for which they were respectively distinguished.

The five stories are reproduced in the order in which they were written : one of them only (Sediva) has previously appeared in print.

These stories do not aspire to serve any "moral purpose:" they were written simply to *amuse* fellow-travellers; mostly at the localities introduced in each story.

No. I. was mostly written in camp during one long summer's night in the forest of Kujjear in Chumba, which forms part of its theatre of action; Nos. II. and III. were also written whilst travelling in the mountain districts of the Himalayas they respectively represent, and where of course reference to classic authorities was impossible; hence certain slight inaccuracies, in allusions to classic subjects, may have crept in, and might be detected by an exact scholar; a few of such, however, have been corrected on revision. Nos. IV. and V., though also sketched whilst travelling in the localities mentioned, have slightly more claim to accuracy of reference, and —though solely imaginary—owe something to consultation of such works as the *Rámáyána*, the *Máhábárât*, the *Hárivansa*, *Hitopadésa*, &c., and other Sanskrit chronicles. The sequel also (No. VI. to the end)—"The Wars of the Pandaus, &c., &c., may from similar causes evince more of the "lamp" in their composition, as acknowledged further on in the work by the "Wandering Cimmerian."* The Author would, however, respectfully deprecate learned criticism of these trivial Tales, written, as they were, simply to *amuse*.

It will be observed, in the course of the work, that certain minor deities of the Hindú Pantheon have been pressed into the service as leading characters in several of the stories. Here again the Author would emphatically disclaim any or the slightest wish to cast ridicule on the Hindú religion, *in its purity*, as enunciated in the early vedas of the old monotheistic Aryan age; though he believes that in its more modern corrupt and idolatrous form, as vitiated by priestcraft, it may present legitimate objects of laughter. Such characters as "Krishna," "Hanumân," &c. — regarded by some Hindú

---

* See pages 136—137,

schools of theology as emanations of Deity—may surely serve as vehicles of jest and laughter; and the Author confesses that during a long association with representatives of these cults, he has at times felt his sense of ridicule, not to say disgust, excited at many of their modérn fantastic manifestations.

Nevertheless, and notwithstanding these hard words, the reader of such works as the early Vedas (Rig Veda, &c.), and their upanisháds or sacred hymns, cannot with justice withhold his admiration, or fail to acknowledge the noble poetry they contain; in which also a belief in an undivided and universal Creator is not only admitted but emphasized. The first article indeed of the Hindú creed expressly affirms this:—"There is "one living and true God; everlasting; without body, parts, "or passions; of infinite power, wisdom, and goodness; the "Maker and Preserver of all things." And again, the Isára-syâni, an upanishád (hymn) of the Yajur-Veda, declares: "By "one Supreme Ruler is this universe pervaded;—over every "world in the whole circle of Nature. Enjoy pure delight, O "man! by abandoning all thought of this perishable world, "and covet not the wealth of any creature existing!"

The sage of the Yajur-Veda, in his perplexity, pathetically exclaims: "I am in this world like a frog in a dry well. Thou "only, O Lord! art my refuge; Thou only art my refuge!" So that any ridicule cast upon the fantastic semi-deities of the Hindoo Pantheon, as fabled by weak and unworthy successors of the ancient monotheistic Aryans, must not be imputed to the Author. Far be it from him to disparage the sublime poetry and thought contained in the works quoted. The cosmogony of the Vedas, and the morality of the Rámá-yána, merit the respect of all scholars.

It will be observed that frequent allusion is made throughout this work to Maya or "beavenly illusion." On this subject, a great authority (Sir W. Jones) has written: "The "wisest among the ancients, and some of the most enlightened "among the moderns, believed that the whole creation was rather

"an *energy* than a *work*, by which the Infinite Being—who is
"present at all times and in all places—exhibits to the minds
"of his creatures a set of perceptions   *   *   *   which exist
"indeed to every wise and useful purpose, but exist only so far
"as they are perceived, a theory no less pious than sublime,
"and as different from any principle of atheism as the brightest
"sunshine differs from the blackest midnight.   This illusive
"operation of Deity the Hindoo philosophers called "*Maya*."

A few quotations have been made from the Vedas in the
following Tales, especially in No. IV. Story.

Passing bye, however, these ancient poems of early Aryan
monotheism, we arrive at the era of the *Rámáyána*.   Of this
noble epic the Author of the "Iliad of the East" has written :
"In spite of several defects arising from oriental types of
"thought and expression, the work is so rich in poetic beauty
"and genuine humour, revealing at the same time so high a
"moral standard, and a spirit of such large and tender hu-
"manity, that we must place it far above the Máhábárát, and
"pronounce it an honour to any literature."

Next, after some centuries, we come to the *Máhábárát*, a
work of some eighty thousand slôkas or verses, which fore-
shadows a new philosophy, and, in fact, inaugurates the
Vedantic school of Hindú thought;* but is (as I think) a debased
cult in that religion.   It contains within its overgrown bulk,
however, a quasi-historical element which forms the gist of the
chronicles whence the exploits of the heroic Pandaus are ex-
tracted.   It contains, besides, episodes innumerable, strung
together into a vast repertoire, from which modern Hindoos
of all sects and castes can draw inspiration as to cosmogony,
religion, and ethics in general ; but it is clouded by mythological obscurities and metaphysical subtleties, which detract
from its poetic merit, and the reader has to wade through a
vast mass of trivialities before he can arrive here and there at
noteworthy points of interest.

----

* See foot note, page 161,

The *Hárivansa*—as the name implies—purports to be the history of *Hári*, or Vishnoo the "Preserver;" and also contains the exploits of his earthly representative (avatar) *Krishna*, the friend and ally of the Pandaus. It contains also a cosmogony or genesis of Narryána—another name of Hári—who is in it made the chief exponent of creation, and the champion of the Wars of the Gods against the Assurs or Titans, hostile to Indra and the Gods of the Hindoo Pantheon.

Sections VII. and VIII. of this little work are chiefly founded on its legends (and those of the Prem-Ságur), and have been added to the original five "Tales of the Pandaus."

These, and a few other works such as the Méghadatta, &c., have formed the chief books of reference alluded to above. They were but imperfectly known to the Author whilst—during a busy life—sketching the original stories whilst travelling; and in his pseudonym of the "Wandering Cimmerian," he has acknowledged his obligation to them in the "Cave" (see pages 136 and 137). He has also acknowledged in the proper place such other excerpts as he has made from other sources and authors from time to time.

Finally—repeating his caution that these stories are written without any "moral purpose"—he would still hope that, whilst aspiring only to *amuse*, these little legends of India may, in a modest way, possess some interest for such English readers as may not have had opportunities of becoming conversant with Sanskrit literature, or with the ancient manners and habits of thought of a portion of our Aryan brethren in the East.

Hillside,
   8th August, 1884.

List ✝ of ✝ Contents.

E R RATA.

Page 35, line 9, for Dionysius read *Dionysos*.

Page 151, line 18, word incomplete in accented vowels, it should be *Outâdâtchêhsrâvas*.

⸰⸱⸰The Story of⸰⸱⸰
⸱⸰ Sedíva the Pandau.⸰⸱

A LEGEND OF ANCIENT INDIA.

I.

SHORTLY after the golden age, when men and women of pure race alone dwelt in the wild mountains of Himâleh, a youthful hunter of Cashmere, having wandered beyond the limits of his own lovely valley, lost his way amidst the vast pine forests of Chumba. Game was, however, plentiful, and the youthful Pandau—himself of the Khsátriya or warrior caste—managed to support life by the produce of his bow and arrows, wild honey, and the many wholesome and delicious fruits and berries familiar to him from childhood, which abound in those mountains.

After some days' wandering he arrived at the banks of the torrent Rávi, whose stream was just beginning to swell from the first downfalls of the summer rains and from the melted snows of Muni-Mahésh—the glacier or sacred peak from which issue the head waters of the Rávi, and other torrents which rush from the Barmáwur valley—through the rocky chasms of the Chumba gorge. This, however, was of no account in stopping his progress, which he now determined to continue southwards. Plunging in, and holding his bow above his head, he stood in five minutes' time on the opposite bank, and re-adjusted his dress for the ascent of the adjacent mountains. It was not, however, till near sunset that after a long climb he entered the belt of pine forest that encircled a lovely vale of green pasturage. He there paused to gaze around him. The slanting rays of crimson glinted through the lofty stems of the cedars, which here and there lifted their tufted heads above the forest, some festooned with roses, and even a few of their number feathering into the lovely plain at his feet,

B

in which herds of wild cattle were browsing. Across the valley, from tree to tree, woodland birds were darting, seeking their nests before nightfall.

The youth stood on a pine-clad knoll of mossy turf, which, jutting out from the surrounding forest towards the west, commanded a view of the vale beneath. He determined to bivouac on the spot, and—as game seemed abundant—to make it his resting place for some days, and explore every nook of the lovely vale. His simple couch was soon spread: his wallet contained the materials of a supper, and by the time the full summer moon rose over the eastern mountains, our young hunter was enjoying the sleep of youth and health.

* * * * * *

But not dreamless were the youth's slumbers! The spirits of the wilderness had not then left the earth, and various forms of supernatural being, now denominated creations of the Hindoo mind, still roamed the mighty forests of Himâleh.

Siva, the Destroyer, still howled along the glaciers of Himôdi—the Land of Snow—or thundered in the mighty torrents which pour from its eternal snows. "Rachshásas"— Dæmons of the Wilderness—still roamed the forests, and "voices without a form" darkly whispered in the gloomy solitudes and mountain tarns, causing the benighted traveller fearful solicitude. Nor were fairer forms of supernatural being wanting; the more gentle Yakshas, and that benign spirit of solitude, since named by the Greeks Alastor—friend of the musing mind—and his fair sisters, nymphs of the dells and fountains, tempered with their gentle spells the austere tyranny of the evil races; and to them, and to Vishnoo the Preserver, the youthful Pandau had committed himself on closing his eyes in slumber:—nor was his invocation vain.

As the moon began to silver the cedar tops and moss-covered branches of the forest trees, a form of rare beauty arose quietly from forth the herbage of the lovely vale beneath, either from slumber amidst the wild flowers, or—as it seemed —from the margin of a tiny spring or fountain which gushed forth from the mossy soil, white and silvery as the moonbeams which touched it with their sheen. Whether Nymph of the dell or Naïd of the stream, she seemed the Peri* or tutelary

---

* Fairy.

genius of the vale, and the queen of these summer realms. Raising a wand which shimmered in the moonlight, in a twinkling, myriads of similar beings, but far smaller, appeared on all sides, forming a vast circle around her, and adoring her as their queen. Some armed with wands or spears, the points of which shone as diamonds or glow worms; others hovered like fireflies over the mossy streamlets, which, gushing from the fountain, meandered down the ˙ vale and watered the flowers of the meadows. Over all, the summer moonlight fell in soft showers through the feathery branches of the cedars, whose stems also shone like pillars of silver.

And still the youth slumbered on the western heights which overlooked this fairy dell, these mossy fountains, and the fair inhabitants of their margin.

But not alone were these lovely creatures the inhabitants of the valley. In a gloomy recess of the woods stood a dark form—one of the Serpent race, adoring his idol. The worship of the "tree and serpent," that ancient and mystic form of superstition was then young on earth, and the Nâga or Serpent-god was a votary of that dark religion. Hanging from the branches of an enormous forest tree, a hideous form like unto a huge brazen serpent was suspended, and around, on surrounding boughs, imp-like forms were peering round the stems, to which they clung with talon-like claws; their eyes furtive and evil, alternately watching their leader and the young stranger slumbering beneath the moonlight. These seemed the creatures of night, and kept within the shadows of the trees and tufted knolls of the pine ridge, whose dark shadows fell across half the vale. Suddenly the night grew overcast, and a still, brooding darkness fell on the valley; dark clouds began to roll up from the low country, lightning to dart across the mountains, and thunder to mutter in the distance. Whether the natural signs of an approaching tempest, or proceeding from the wrath of dæmons, who can say? Suddenly a wail or unearthly shriek sounded through the dark forest, and the echoes of the vale reverberated the dismal sound—the heralds of Siva, the dread Destroyer, are approaching. In the gleams of the lightning the tall, horrid form of the Nâga is seen to stalk across the glade towards the hunter. * * * And still the youth slumbered on the western heights which overlooked this fairy dell, these mossy fountains, and the inhabitants of their margin.   B 2

Darkness deepens on the valley. A low moaning sound of the wind amidst the pines is heard. The Destroyer, the spirit of the tempest, is at hand. Suddenly a gleam of ruddy light eastwards illumes the night, and discloses a silver cloud, or it might be the spray of the fountain concealing the fairy queen and her followers, and a gauze-like mist of silver butterfly forms floats over the cedar tops; perchance the winged portion of her subjects, startled, had flitted through the star-spangled night to other recesses. But the dark spirit of the pines—the gloomy creature of the woods with his attendant imps, peering from tree to tree, gibbering, howling, uttering dismal cries—slowly descends into the vale, and surrounds with a black circle the fountain within whose margin still rested the lovely fairy of the flowers and her train. Once more, however, a silver cloud arises from the fountain, and gliding away over the hills becomes lost in the purple distance of night. At the same time a lovely form seemed to stand by the hunter, and touching him with her wand to say :—

"Arise, oh Sediva! leave this vale; other destinies await "thee in thine own much-loved country, and me thou shalt "meet on the margin of thy native streams, ready to help thee "to rule thy race with wisdom, and to fill thy heart with "beauty and goodness! For thee, oh Nâga! oh Kajji of the "serpent race! I consign thee to the dark depths of the morass "prepared for thee, and which shall be called by thy name for "all the years of the age of bronze! so farewell, oh lord of the "black Nâg! We meet no more."   *   *   *

A dire tempest raged through the pines and cedars, and dark mountains of the "black" forest of "Diarkhoond.

It was daylight, and the sun was streaming through the pine tops; and the festoons of white roses—which floated from many of them like tassels—caught the rising sun, when the young Pandau arose from slumber, and having sung his hymn to Vishnoo the Preserver looked around.

In the very centre of the lovely vale lay a deep black pool, surrounded with dank spongy herbage, on whose dark waters two solitary, sad-coloured water birds were sailing. The hunter had not on the preceding evening observed the pond; it had seemed to him that merely the winding thread of a silver streamlet meandered through the green mossy herbage. Whether he saw these things in a dream, or whether the spirits of the mountains and dells had held their colloquy before him, ever remained a mystery to his mind,—but the bright Fairy's word came true.

Sediva returned to his home in Cashmere after many wanderings, and the recollection of the lovely Spirit who had appeared to him in the wild forests of Chumba remained with him. When and how the fair creature next appeared to him must form the subject of another chapter.

* *
*

II.

IN order to obtain a second glimpse of the youthful Pandau we must transport our readers to the sultry plains of Hindosthán—to the city of Hustinapoora, and Máth'ra in the land of Bráj—whilst Ogregund ruled Cashmere, and Krishna roamed and led the dance on the banks of the Yamúna;* whilst yet the kingdom of Magadha flourished, and the age of iron had scarcely dawned on the dædal earth ; ere the gods of Greece — fugitive from the East—had earned immortality, or the Thessalian nightfires ceased to illume the fields of fair Parthenopé; or the groans of Polyphémus ceased to echo along the wild Trinácrian shore. Behold our hero, therefore, during his return journey from the southern Himáleh and the source of the holy Gunga (Ganges), bidden to the marriage of Járásind, the King of Máth'ra, the guest of the King.

The youth, however, whilst paying his respects at court, as in duty bound—though banished from Thanésur, where his cousins the Koraus reigned—spent much of his time in the wild jungles along the banks of the blue Yamúna, rendered classic to the Hindoo mind of all succeeding centuries by the freaks of Krishna at that very period ; the Gópies of the land of Bráj standing in the same relation to that semi-human hero as the Nymphs of ancient Greece or Rome to the heroes and demi-gods of classic story.

---

* The modern Jumna.

The young Pandau in one of these hunting excursions—whilst the lilac báchain, and sissoo trees gave forth their fragrance, and the scarlet dák and kurél (wild caper) dotted at intervals the landscape—roamed along the banks of Hánsoráva (lake of the wild geese), through the groves of Bindrabun, and fields of fair Math'ra, to Máur-hun (abode of peacocks) and Chand-sárávar (lake of the moon), and took up his abode for a time at a hermit's cell in the wilderness of Koomunt (Gwâlior). From this point of vantage he could survey the surrounding country, note the wandering lion or leopard retreating to his lair, the droves of wild pig "whiffling through the tulgy wood," or the fresh herds of antelope which at that period—as indeed they still do—roamed over the land of Bráj. Denied a career in arms, the vigorous heart of the young Pandau gloried in contests with the wild beasts of the jungle.

One day, on returning from his morning's hunt for refuge from the sultry noonday heat, he was surprised to see reclining in the shade of an adjacent chámpa (jessamine) tree a fair damsel, who, though clad in the homely garb of the gópi (milkmaid), evidently betrayed the princess in disguise. Starting up on the approach of Sediva, she modestly veiled her face from his gaze in accordance with oriental ideas of propriety, and commenced to move away. Our hero, however, being a bold mountaineer, advanced, and saluting the fair unknown, respectfully offered his services to conduct her to her friends.

"Oh, dea certe!" exclaimed he, as the unknown timidly peeping from beneath her doputtih, or veil, thanked him, half revealing beauties of rare excellence, and according with eastern ideas of beauty, eye of gazelle, nose of the parrot, gait or waddle of the goose, etc., etc.; beautiful as the full moon as it ariseth over the sands of Hurdwâr and lighteth the waters of the dark blue Gunga. Something, moreover, in her served to recall to his memory the remembrance of the lovely Fairy of the Fountain, albeit under the assumed garb of the humble gópi. At this moment, however, a stranger appeared on the scene, bounding across the sward in all the exuberance of youth. By the bright Indra, *Krishna!*

The youth saluted; but the hero, surprised apparently at seeing people in this solitary spot, abruptly stopped, and regarding the young Pandau with attention, suddenly burst into wild laughter, and exclaimed:—

"Aree! oh hunter; we are rivals it seems! This then, oh
"Sediva, oh son of Pand, is the hunter's life in the jungles!
"Shábásh! Well, make love to her, young man; the gópi
"breathes not who can resist the golden anklet and the silver*
"tongue; make merry whilst the chámpa flower scents the
"air, and the turtle dove is mating in the mangoe groves;
"but, oh son of a Khsátriya, forbear to cross too often the
"playfields of Krishna, for there is danger in the act."

"Great sir," answered Sediva, "to hear is to obey; but
"whilst thy friend the usurping Korau rules Thanésur, not to
"Krishna even will the son of Pand the King give place in
"the smiles of his fair love."

The frolicsome Krishna smiled. "Thou art bold to say so,
"youth. So thus I withdraw my license, and thus assume
"possession of the maid."

He advanced to make good his words, but at this moment
the fair unknown, throwing back her chunun (veil), revealed
the countenance of the charming Fairy of the Fountain, and
a celestial car descending on the instant, she was borne rapidly
away from sight, but not before she had bestowed a sweet
smile on Sediva, who fancied he caught the words "Why
"waste life? Remember my promise in the Valley of the
"Fountain," softly wafted to his ear as she vanished in the
blue ether.

"Oh, dea certe," quoth Krishna, as he pulled out his pipe
(or lute) and drew forth such ravishing sweet music that the
wild antelopes gathered round to listen, and the báchain
drooped its tufted head across the feathery forest.

This was the second appearance of the Fairy to Sediva,
and from that day there was friendship between Krishna and
Sediva, youngest of the Pandau race.

* *
*

---

* An allusion to the Pandaus who were Chandrabuns—of the lunar or *silver* race
of Rajpoots.

III.

EARS have passed, and lo! our history leads us to Anant-Nâg in Cashmere (since called Islamabad), and to Martund (Fountain of the Sun), and the sunny karéwah (plateau) of Martund, sacred to the Sun-god. The Fairy of the Fountain has appeared to Sediva, and bid him build there a city and an altar to the triune deity, and a temple to the Sun-god—author of life and happiness—and the Pandau has commenced his labour. How, or in what fashion the Fairy met Sediva, whether as erst Egeria met Numa in the mossy dells of Tibur, there is no record to tell. Who shall say when and how the guardian genius descends to the musing mortal, or the whisper of the unseen guide is wafted from the star one loves?

By degrees the cyclopean walls rose above the plain, and the vast caverns—fabled to have been cleft by Susrávas the Serpent-god—yielded stone to the quarriers of the Pandau, and the pools of Anant-Nâg were paved with huge slates triform, and the temple of "Pandau-lerrie" arose on the sunny karéwah of Martund. The prince looked upon his work and was glad.

Standing on this very spot had the divine Káshyápá—after his labour of draining the primæval lake which had submerged the valley during the ages of silver and bronze—"contemplated with ecstacy the glory of his kingdom snatched from the waters of desolation; he beheld the glittering peaks of Himâleh lit up by the splendour of the sun sinking behind Baramoola, the scene of his labours, whilst the waters of a thousand streams—leaping from the hills in cascades—caught the fleeting glory. He cast down the mundane egg, and from its luminous core gushed the Fountain of Martund, sacred to the Sun-god," and he had prophesied that "in after years, hard by this hallowed spot shall arise the noble Temple of the Sun, work worthy of his posterity—worthy of the great lunar race (Pandaus) by whom constructed."

So stood Sediva one summer's eve watching the orb of day dipping beyond the western mountains of Waramool; and

thus he stood till the rising moon began to clothe the grey
walls of Martund in silver, and the lamps of night began to
shine over the mountains of the "cloudy" Dúdiná and of
"Wuster-Wun," the forest-covered; and the distant peak of
Hára-mookh stood out clear like the sentinel of the northern
sky. Suddenly beside him stood the ethereal form of the
Fairy-queen, and a gentle sigh was wafted in his ear.

Sediva was beloved of many fair ones of Cashmere, the
land of his exile, and royal damsels filled the house of the
Pandau prince, but more dear to Sediva the sigh of the gentle
spirit of wisdom and warning, than the smiles even of Shireen
herself, sweetest of the sweet! But the prince seemed sad.
The melancholy wisdom of Súliemán, the Syrian philosopher,
then recently uttered,* had penetrated those remote lands.
"Isaun," the cousin of the royal sage, had conveyed his wisdom into the land of roses, and the sad philosophy of the
"Preacher" filled the heart of the Pandau prince as he turned
from the sunset and paced slowly down towards his palace,
distant about two koss (four miles) across the lonely karéwah.

His converse with the Fairy may not be revealed;—words
of warning and whispers of approaching dangers, to be followed
however, by success and greatness, were vouchsafed, and an
encouragement to be brave and self-reliant; then gradually, as
he paced slowly onwards, the form of the Fairy faded from his
sight and floated away like the mists of the morning. He
now walked more briskly, for the night was becoming overcast, and clouds began to gather towards the north; the
úlúlátus of night creatures began to be heard, and bats flitted
ominously across the lurid crepuscule, and the signs of a
tempest seemed to be gathering on the forest-clad hills of the
Duchin-párá. Suddenly the hair stood erect on the head of
the prince. He knew that the spirits of evil were abroad, and
that the heralds of the dread "Siva" were approaching. A
whirlwind burst over the karéwah, and soon the gloomy,
many-handed deity of destruction—riding on the tiger steed,
wielding the sword of vengeance streaming with the blood of
victims slain—stood in his path.

---

* An anachronism. Solomon lived about 1000 B.C. The chronology of India,
however, is uncertain, and the two events approximate. It may be mentioned
that the text is in accordance with Mahomedan legends as to Isaun visiting
Cashmere.

"Death!" exclaimed the spectre.

"To the enemies of my lord!" quickly answered the Prince.

"To a crested head!" retorted the gloomy deity.

"Of the great crested Kajji-Nâg!" cried Sediva.

"How? of my servant and worshipper. Rash prince, be-"ware! I say, of a crowned head."

"A peacock shall be sacrificed," quickly rejoined Sediva.

"Of a man," howled the destroyer.

"Who is still unborn," retorted Sediva.

"Thou hast said it," exclaimed the gloomy destroyer. "Thine unborn *son*, the hope of thy Shireen, shall perish, oh "Pandau. Pass on; thou hast prophesied the destruction of "thy house." So saying, the gloomy deity of destruction turned aside on his way into the dark forests and wild solitudes of the Pir-Pinjâl.

Relieved of his presence the sky grew clearer, and the stars began to peep out of the purple sky.

"Cheer up, Sediva!" cried a voice at his elbow, and the frolicsome Krishna—pulling his pipe from his mouth—stood and tapped the prince on the shoulder. "Cheer up, Sediva! "Don't let your spirits go down; for there's many a maid in "Yamúna's shade waiting for you and your crown."

"Potstausend! that is, I mean Shábásh!" cried Sediva, stumbling over his Hindi,—"A thousand welcomes to Anánt-"ghur, oh Krishna!" and they walked off hand in hand to-wards the king's palace. Descending from the karéwah, they passed across the zone of marshy flat around its base.

Now, in those remote days the wildfire burned fiercely in the bosom of the marsh, and the great architect—Nature—had scarcely compelled the wandering wildfires of the elemental powers into the stony heart of Káli,* the Earth-goddess.

Before them waved the luminous spirit of the fens, and that vast, gigantic apparition called by the inhabitants of Cashmere "Brám-Brám-chuk," here presented his figure towering above the rocks and flags of the marsh, his eyes of flame glaring on the two princes.

"Ha! by Wittabah! the Jabberwoch!" exclaimed Sediva.

"Who may you be, great sir?" cried out Krishna. "Stop

---

* Demeter of the Greeks.

"where you are, my lad, my pipe is out! You're just the
"fellow I want to light me up again!"

But the giant knew his master; waxed pale, and "evanished,
"not without stench and with a melodious twang," as has been
said or sung of some more modern ghost.*

"I tell you, Sediva," says Krishna, "these Cashmere ghosts
"are pukka (arrant) howlets; laugh at them and their
"menaces, and all will go well;" but a shade was on the face
of the Pandau as he thought of Siva and his denunciations.

Now there was a very old Rishee (or hermit) living at that
time in the caves of Susrávas. He dwelt at the extremity of
the winding cavern of Brâmejo, sacred to the planet Mars.
He was a servant of Susrávas the Nâga. He had subsisted
on fir-cones for fifty years, till his beard turned green, and
bristled with spines like the porcupig of Chini. He was very
wise. Sediva bethought him of this sage, and as his way lay
along the entrance of his cell he tapped three times on the
brazen bell which hung suspended at the cavern's mouth.

"Who seeks Cuckchand, the grass-eater?"

"The Prince, great sir."

"Oh, Pandau! I know thy need; go to the temple of Vishnoo
"the Preserver; offer this bételnut in clarified butter, perform
"the *saptopuddie* (triple walk round the sacred fire seven steps
"at a time), recite a mantra (invocation), and ask a boon."

So still on through the moonlit night proceeded the two
princes. Arrived at the shrine of Vishnoo the Preserver,
Sediva performed the sacred rites, related his case, and asked
a remedy. A voice from the great Idol within the temple
answered, "The remedy has already arrived; thy wife Shireen
"has, since thine absence from the palace, given birth to a
"*daughter!*"

So Siva the Destroyer was wrong for once in his long life
—six Brahminical days=432,000,000 years, I think—and
his prophecy of doom became a dead letter.

That night Krishna and Sediva crushed a chaurasi† (84)
shells of Dardú wine; and Krishna put himself outside

---

* The so-called "Cock-lane ghost," believed in by Samuel Johnson. The allusion
to that modern portent, the Jabberwock, would lead us to conclude that the
legend has been touched by a modern hand.
† The multiple of twelve months of the year by seven days of the week. 12×7=
84 = one chaurasi, a mystic number according to Hindoo ideas.

($3^3=$) 27 pipes of Ron'd'ho bháng, and sang (3 × 7 =)21 slôkas or verses—each slôka containing an attribute of grace or of good fortune—in token of the escape of the heiress of Anántghur.

* * *

IV.

R.Y. 2268]. Transport we our readers to the field of Korau-khét (or Kirkhet) near Thanésur, where the mighty deeds of heroes were enacted in the year 1367 B.C., when the exiled Pandaus, having collected their adherents, appeared in arms for the recovery of their capitol from the usurper Jirjoodeen the Korau.

Sediva, the youngest of the Pandaus, marches with a band from the Cashmere mountains with Ogregund the King. Passing through the Nargäon purgunnah by the fountain of Neela-Nâg, they try their fortunes by the casting of the walnut in the mystic waters. Such is the omen. On, past Abhisaras, Jumin —native seats of Ogregund the King— through Indra-Kote and Nâgra-Kote—cities of King Hôdé— across Jalindrä marish-lands and the rolling waters of the Hyphasis, and so to Kirkhet and Thanésur, to besiege Hustinapoora, the ancient heritage of King Bhârut, and of the great solar and lunar races (Koraus and Pandaus.)

In arms appear the "melancholy" Yûdishtír, eldest of the Pandaus; his brothers, Arjûna of the sounding bow, Bhimsén and Nizkool, and now the youngest of the Pandau brethren, Sediva, with his power from Cashmere; a host as valiant as Ráma, as active as Hânumân, as numerous as the ants or locusts of the air, appears in arms on the field of Korau-khét, for the recovery of their ancestral throne.

On the other side—from Thanésur—Jirjoodeen, eldest of the Koraus, and seventy of the sons of Ditrâshtura the King, his brothers, appear in arms to defend the city and uphold their claims to the throne of Chitra-Boorje. Krishna, the jocund friend of Sediva, has also come, his intentions doubtful.

Now for the clash of shields and deeds of heroes, of the

shock of the war chariots, and trampling of the earth-shaking beasts—even elephants; of flights of arrows darkening the air like the wild fowl of Mânásbul, or the flights of the hornets of the Nerbudda; and the noise of the kettle drums of the riders like the thunder of the avalanches on the distant Hímôdi. No tongue can describe the noise and shouting of the warriors, and the fury of the contending hosts.

For many days did the heroes contend for victory. On the seventh day fell King Ogregund of Cashmere, pierced by an arrow from the hand of Bálárámá, brother of Krishna,* who, though friendly to Sediva, fought for the Korau host, and his steeds galloped wildly over the plain dragging the lifeless body of the King. As he fell he had time to call to Sediva—who fought beside him—"Oh Sediva, the Nâga was true! Did "not the 'trial of the walnut' prophesy disaster? Farewell! "oh Pandau. Let the bards of the valley sing how Ogregund "fell in the van of battle on a distant land." On this day also Sediva himself was wounded by Jirjoodeen, the Korau King, his cousin, whose elephant he sought to surround and capture.

On the twelfth day met Krishna and Sediva. Krishna had joined the King of Thanésur with powers from the land of Brúj, with Bálárámá, his brother.

Bulhudda-Déo that day fought opposite Sediva, a monstrous man of might, his shield like the orb of the moon as it ariseth, on the festival of Dwarkanáth, his spear like the palm tree of Sri-Lankapoora in far Taprobane (Ceylon).

"Ho! ho! Ha! ha!" laughed Bulhudda-Déo. Raising his mace with both hands, and whirling it around his head, he was about to discharge it full on the head of Sediva, who had that day dismounted to fight on foot amidst his mountaineers, but the latter—anticipating modern science—delivered a point in tierce, which, passing through his short ribs, would then and there have terminated the career of anyone less than the brother of a demi-god. As it was, he fell prone on the sand and bellowed like the bull of Bhûmthâl.

---

* So related in the Raja Tarinigini—the great chronicle of Kasmir—but this is scarcely in accordance with the Mahabarat, in which Krishna is represented as siding with the *Pandaus*, who are there related to have been commanded in the field by Bhimsen or Bhima. Balarama also is represented as withdrawing in disgust at the internecine character of the war, and afterwards dwelling on the banks of the Surroosootie in strict seclusion. (See page 65 "Arjuna.")

"Ah, Sediva, wilt thou slay the kinsman of Krishna?" he gasped for breath.

Then Sediva stayed his hand. He remembered his former friendship for Krishna, and spared his fallen foe. He called aloud,—"Arise, oh Bulhudda-Déo, and seek other foes else-"where." He then resumed the fight.

The night approaching, on this seventeenth day of the battle, put a stop to the strife of heroes, and Sediva retired to his tent. This happened on the sixth chait K.Y. 2268 (1367 B.C.) The same night Sediva lay beneath his spear watching the moon arise over a grove of date trees, in order to sing his customary hymn to Vishnoo the Preserver, when suddenly he became aware of the approach of a strange warrior clad in silver armour, whose crest glittered in the moonlight. He started to his feet;—"Stand! oh Khsátriya, and show the "sign."

The stranger advanced, and stretching forth his hand, bare and open; displayed a ring well known to Sediva as his own gift to Krishna in days of friendship long since at Anántghur.

"Hail, oh Krishna!" cried Sediva. "Art thou 'still the "friend of Sediva? Hail! oh, bright one! oh, merciful one! "and forget not the friendly token."

It was exchanged—it may not be told—and Sediva was satisfied that Krishna was still his friend.

He spake:—"I come, oh Sediva, friend of my mirthful "days, to bring thee news of the war. Enough! The battle "is finished. The war is over. Thy great cousin, the Korau, "Jirjoodeen the King, is no more. Despairing of the victory "he has this night drank poison, and he lies in his tent in "robes of state. At the dawn of day the chiefs will seek the "tent of Yûdishtír, thy great brother, and hail him king; and "Thou, oh brave young Pandau, wilt share this glory of thy "brother's. Arjûna, of the sounding bow, has departed with "Nizkool, of the shield; and Bhimsén, the haughty one, de-"clines the victor's meed. Thou and the great Yûdishtír are "alone left of the mighty Pandau race. Go to thy brother's "tent, and be the first to announce the tidings of victory. "Who knows? it may be for thy benefit."

"And thou, oh Krishna," said Sediva, "be thou propitious "and a friend to Yûdishtír."

"Nay, oh Sediva. Not so; I see within thy brother's

"horoscope (lagan-puttrie or junum-puttrie) the melancholy
" Saturn crossing the main line of life. Not to him will the
"gay and laughter-loving Krishna join his fortunes. I go to
"my land of Braj, and the smiling banks of Yamúna, and the
"jocund friends of Krishna! but when Thou, oh son of the
"Pandau, shalt succeed thy melancholy brother, then expect
"to see Krishna at thy feast—till then, farewell!" So saying, Krishna laid his hand on the head of Sediva, and gradually
vanished, and the night received his receding form.

Sediva looked around, not without awe, but nothing met
his gaze save the moonlit camp, and the moonbeam glittering
on his spear-head ; and the rustling of the leaves of the date
trees was the only sound that broke the stillness of the night;
then he remembered the words of the Fairy of the Fountain,
who had warned him of dangers, and prophesied to him of
empire, and he desired earnestly to behold once more his
charming monitress; and she came to him as before, in the
silence and solitude of night, and led him into the rustling
grove of date trees, like the Egeria of old Roman times, and
poured the words of wisdom into the ears of the young Pandau prince. What other testimony of love she gave may not
be revealed, but such love as may be bestowed by the fair
spirits of the immortals on frail humanity was vouchsafed to
the young Pandau. At the dawn of day his countenance had
changed, and shone like the sun when he ariseth through the
mists of the morning and lights up the yellow sands. Having
armed, he entered the tent of the great Pandau, and stood
like the prophet of the sun and cried aloud :—"Hail! oh
"great Yûdishtír, King of Hustinapoora and Thanésur! thy
"rival is no more ; and Thou alone art monarch of Hindosthán
"and the lands of the holy Gunga!"

    *   *   *   *   *   *

So ends this brief legend of ancient India, and this is all
that the chronicles tell us of Sediva and the Fairy of the
Fountain ; but history adds that "the melancholy Yûdishtír
ruled the whole of India for thirty-six years ; when, becoming
weary of the world, he retired into the mountains, and there
ended his days in austerity and poverty."

Whether Sediva succeeded to the throne, and whether the
predictions of Krishna and the Fairy of the Fountain came
true, there is absolutely no record to tell, beyond a tradition

that in the wild mountains of Chumba, the *King* Sediva dedicated a temple to *Jullundrie*, goddess of the waters and rains of spring, and appointed services and festivities in her honor from the time of the blooming of the white roses and the swarming of the halcyon butterfly till the fall of the first summer rains in the cedar forests of Kajjéar.   But a doubt rests on the exact locality, and the name of Sediva has almost been forgotten in history, and the name of the Fairy of the Fountain is unknown to the sons of the Rajpoots who dwell in the forests of Chumba and Kúlú, who worship her simply as *Jullundrie*, the goddess of the rains of summer and of the flowers of the earth.

A descendant of the western barbarians who dwelt in the Cimmerian wastes of the land of Thor—"*extra anni solisque vias*"—beyond the genial sun of the Hindoo Pantheon, wandering in those wild mountains one summer time, pitched his camp for many days amidst the cedar slopes of Kajjéar, and composed this tale of ancient India.*

---

* The quasi-historical allusions in this legend are mostly in accordance with Hindoo tradition ; though having been written in the forests of Chumba, where reference was impossible, a few slight deviations from the Mahabarat may have crept in.   The imagery of Chapter 1. is—deducting the supernatural—referable to the natural phenomena attending the setting in of the summer rains.   The representative of the Naga still lives—a prosperous Jogi—aged 100 years, whom I have myself witnessed frantically dancing at midnight before his idol in the forest with his disciples—a weird sight.

*   *   *

Temple of Lully-Ha-Chundu,
(at Midnight).

The Wanderings—
—of—
Yudishtir, the Pandau
King of Hindosthan.

A FRAGMENT.

I.

HISTORY informs us in the Mâhâbârât—the great epic of the Hindoos—that about the end of the Dwâpâ yôg—the age of bronze—Hustinapoora was the capitol of King Bhârut (brother of Ráma), whose posterity ruled in India eight generations, until the ninth in succession named "*Kour*" arose; hence his descendants were called *Koraus*. The thirteenth in succession, called "Chitra-Boorje," had two sons, "Ditrâshtura" and "Pand." The former being blind was excluded from the succession,* and his younger brother *Pand* succeeded to the throne. He had five sons—Yûdishtír, Bhimsén (or Bhíma), Arjûna, Nizkool, and Sediva, named after him *Pandaus;* but his elder brother, Ditrâshtura, had 101 children. Jirjooden, being the eldest, became king on the death of Pand, his uncle; but disputes as to the rightful succession occurring, Jirjoodeen challenged his cousin Yûdishtir to decide the case by throw of dice, the losers to go into exile for twelve years. Whereupon—the dice being false—the latter lost the wager, and according to compact went into exile with his brethren.

---

* This is in accordance with Hindoo law; upon this the Pandau's claim to the throne rested.

C

It is narrated that during this period they dwelt in Cash-mere, and other parts of India, where traces of their names are to be found both in that country and throughout the Himalayan range of mountains and elsewhere.

After twelve years they demanded their restoration to the throne, and appeared in arms before Jirjoodeen's capitol—Hustinapoora. After a desperate battle on the plain of Kir-khet or Korau-Khét,* near Thanésur, in the north-west of India, which is said to have lasted eighteen days, the King Jirjoodeen was defeated, and drank poison on the field. Upon this Yûdishtir ascended the throne, and ruled the whole of India for 36 years, when becoming weary of the world he retired into the mountains, and there ended his days in auster-ity and self-imposed poverty.

*   *   *   *   *   *

Thus much we learn from history; but the details of the "melancholy" Yûdishtir's life seem to demand more notice than is contained in the curt narrative of the Mâhâbârât above quoted. The career of a hero, a philosopher, and a hermit-king such as Yûdishtir, is suggestive. We will attempt some sketch of his supposed adventures subsequent to the great battle of Korau-Khét, which restored him to the throne of India 1367 B.C.

*   *   *   *   *   *

Let us consider a little as to the epoch of which our history treats. Troy had not yet fallen;† and the melancholy Súlie-mán, King of Israel, had not as yet preached the words of wisdom to the sons of men; the philosophy of Zoröaster the Magian had, however, penetrated into the northern regions of the land of Yûdishtir; but elsewhere a system of religion

---

* Kuru-Kshetra—the plain of the Kuraus—lies between the rivers Jumna and Sursooti (*apud* Bhagava Gita.)

† Troy was taken on the 12th June 1184 B.C. Solomon married the daughter of Pharoah King of Egypt 1013 B.C.

akin to that of the Aramœan idolatry had been introduced into India. At the period of Yûdishtír, the institutes of Mánû —comparatively pure and moral—modified the religion of Hindosthân, which, however, before the epoch of Yûdishtír had been moulded by the mythic traditions of the Râmâyânâ. These, together with the Vedas, the great epic poems of Kâlidâsa, Vyâsa, and other poets, and the quasi-historical myths of the Mâhâbârât, with other fables, eked out by later interpretations of priestcraft, have since moulded the Hindoo religion into a subtle and metaphysical idolatry, such as the world has elsewhere never seen. Any jests at the expense of this idolatry to be found in this brief chronicle must be regarded as aimed not at the essential truths underlying this Vedic faith, but at the fantastic machinery in which it is clothed, and which present to us mythic characters such as Krishna etc., who methinks, will appear to us in this work fit objects of jest and mirth.

The ancient traditions of India, however, leave us in doubt as to the probability or otherwise of many semi-historical events, which from certain coincidences in chronology lead the historian to suppose may have happened in the Eastern world. It is difficult sometimes to assign date or locality to such. Thus the Abduction of Helen, and the Siege of Troy, may possibly be but an adumbration of the expedition of Ráma to Singhâla (Ceylon) or Lankapoora for the recovery of the lost Sita; or possibly the two events may be but diverse renderings of the same quasi-historical or mythic event adorned by the poetry of their respective "*Vates sacer*," the Greek Homer or Herodotus, or the Indian Valmiki or Vyâsa. We incline, however, to a positive rendering of the main facts, and on the whole believe the wars of the Râmâyânâ and of the Iliad to be founded on a substratum of historic fact! * * * The childhood or adolescence of the human mind is observable in both, and the doughty deeds of demi-gods and semi-human champions is common to the Greek and Indian Aryan.

The mythic expedition of Sesostris,* King of Egypt, is assignable to a date prior to that of this history. His galleys may have perhaps harried the coasts of Malabar, and invading armies may perhaps have entered Northern India through Bactria, whose king—Zoröaster the great Magian—had perchance been dead several hundred years before.

The mythic invasion of Semiramïs, the Queen of Assyria, may also (if indeed of the least historical validity) be assigned to a somewhat earlier period (2000 B.C.), and its tradition was in the minds of men.

Such, then, are a few of the great historic events which may be supposed to have influenced the career of Yûdishtïr the Pandau.

*   *   *   *   *   *

Let us, however, now take ourselves back to the great day of history, when, on the field of Korau-Khét (1367 B.C.)† the victorious Yûdishtïr had been hailed King of Hindosthán by his brothers Arjûna and Sediva, and the chiefs of the Pandau host. The character of the chief must be left to develop itself: —A dweller, during his long exile, in that Eastern Paradise, the Vale of Káshmír, the soul of King Yûdishtir had been nurtured in scenes of grandeur and sublimity, and his mind expatiated in visionary thought; a wanderer after the sublime and beautiful, and a poet, the great heart of the Pandau King refused content with empty grandeur.

Now in those patriarchal days, when families and small tribes were allowed to govern themselves, the duties of an Eastern monarch were limited to leading in war, or in peace enjoying the delights of luxury and repose.

After providing for the protection of his people, Yûdishtïr having reduced to order his newly acquired kingdom, found himself free to wander. It is narrated, that in the course of these travels the King met with many strange adventures.

---

* Sesostris reigned about 1475-60 B.C.
† 6 chait K.Y. 2268—14 March 1367 B.C.

Let us endeavour to rescue from oblivion a few of such!

*   *   *   *   *   *

From the days of Keiumurs — according to the Shah-Nâmeh of Firdoosi, first "king of men"—it would seem that the very existence of an ancient Eastern hero involved that of many genii or "potential sequences," as attendant spirits of good or evil. We find, whether we turn to Indian or Persic sources of information, swarms of supernatural beings involved in the mikrocosm of a great man as part of his very *raison-d'etre;* and in the case of the mighty Yûdishtír, King of Hindosthán, we find a chief malign influence crossing his line of life, as hinted at by the mirthful Krishna elsewhere. It is narrated that this malign influence was embodied in the form of a small Scarlet Sprite or Elf, who had first appeared to the *Prince* Yûdishtír near the Lall Nâg, or Scarlet Fountain, in the wild mountains of Káshmír, as he lay resting from the chase one summer's noon amidst the ferns and wild flowers which clothe the margin of the Mânásbul Lake. Tired with the chase, he had slept in the shade of the pine trees, and on awakening had perceived a small Scarlet Elf, clad in the garb of the Nâgas or aborigines of these mountains and forests. Gazing at him, the Autochthon had exclaimed :

"Oh, Pandau! behold thine evil genius ; expect to see me "when evil threatens the race of Pand! above all, when thy "*prosperity* shall evoke the envy of the base and wicked!"

No more was said, and on arising and rubbing his eyes, the Pandau prince could see nothing save the bright flowers of the mountain potentilla dotting the herbage with its scarlet asters.

"Ha, ha!" laughed Yûdishtír, "I grow fanciful. I am "called the 'melancholy' Yûdishtír. I fear I must be so in "good truth."

He would have dismissed the image from his mind, but still the form of the Scarlet Elf clung to the prince's memory, and

would often recur in slumber. On the whole, however, the
fortunes of the Pandau had prospered ; and, apart from the
general misfortune of exile, but little actual sorrow or misfortune had reached him : albeit the melancholy drop was ever
mingled in his cup of life, and ever and anon the sad wisdom
of "the Thinker" would cloud his happiest hour. At such
times, too, he would fancy sometimes he caught glimpses
more or less distinct of the outlines of the Scarlet Elf of
Mânásbul—like that of the skeleton at Egyptian feasts—
obtruding as a check on his mirthful moods.

It was not, however, till the night of the great victory of
Korau-Khét that the King was again actually visited and
addressed by the baleful little fury, a description of whose
appearance has been narrated by the chronicles in doubtful
guise. At first glance nothing appeared in the figure to
denote the sex; it was not till she spake and announced
herself that it became evident. Clad in scarlet mail armour,
over which a more intensely scarlet tunic descended to the
knees; one long black feather or "kalgi," with elfin locks
escaping from the casque, broke the general scarlet hue of
the figure; large black eyes, blazing with baleful light; a
vulture's beak, a long glittering spear, its point tipped with
dazzling, burning red! Enough! The chronicles are vague!

*   *   *   *   *   *

This brings us to the real commencement of this history—
the night of the 14th March, 1367 B.C.

*
* *

At midnight, after the day of the great battle of Korau-
Khét, King Yûdishtir sate alone in his royal tent, having
dismissed his courtiers and attendants. He sat absorbed in
thought : the achievement of his life had been accomplished ;
the victory had been won ; the labours of twelve years of
growing resolution had that day been crowned with glory

and success, and he had been hailed by the assembled chiefs of India not only King of his ancestral throne, but with the augmented splendour of the whole Empire of India—acknowledged by the assembled kings and warriors. Nevertheless, sadness crept over the spirit of the Pandau, and the sigh of the unsatisfied soul of man fell from his kingly heart. The excitement of the battle over, and the glory won, gloomy visions oppressed his spirit.

"Farewell," he murmured, "ye visions of my youth and "manhood! The *hope* of glory and success. Ye are no more. "Beyond the glittering pageants of earth, and the splendour "which will surround my throne, I see vanishing the dear "friends and well wishers of Yûdishtír the Pandau *Prince* in "exile; and in their stead the false, self-interested courtiers "of Yûdishtír the King. It is not granted to man to be at "once feared and loved!"

As thus he sadly communed with his inmost heart, a shrill, small laugh sounded in his ear, and turning towards the sound, he beheld, as distinct as when she first appeared to him amidst the ferns and wild flowers of the summer, the Scarlet Fury of Mânásbul. She spake:—

"At length, Oh King Yûdishtír, behold me completely thy "slave; the vassal of thy greatness; the creature of the *envy* "attendant on power! Hitherto thou hast seen me but sel-"dom, and then indistinctly. Now I am thy constant minister "or master, as thou treatest me. Beware, Oh mortal! Thou "art from this day haunted by a spirit potent as Siva the "Destroyer, cruel as Kâli the Earth-Goddess! though seem-"ing beautiful as Indra, or Vishnoo the Preserver, in his "cœrulian car, as he holds the lotus flower and slumbers on "the bosom of Sésh-Nâg, the hundred-headed. Mark me! "Yûdishtír can be loved no more; but I can make him *feared*. "Be wise, Oh King! and accept the alternative. There is no "going back for great ones such as Thee. Thou hast gained "thy desire, and can *hope* no more." * * *

The King gazed mournfully at the Spirit. "Alas, I know "it too well, Oh envious one! No more—ah, never more— "can Yûdishtir know the pure, disinterested love of man or "woman; but it still remains to him to be *just!* Enough; I "abide the choice, and will be called by the sons of men "'*Yûdishtir, the Just!*' Let this poor heart, destined to the "ants and serpents, be sad; perchance its vision sometimes "fail; but by the bright Indra and the host of heaven, I will "be just and merciful."

The Pandau arose, and reared his kingly form: he gazed on high, as he spake, at the starlit heavens spread before his open tent. One bright star shot from the zenith as though in answer to his prayer, and seemed to fall over the king's tent, leaving a mild effulgence in the night air.

As, slowly, he withdrew his gaze from the starry night, the figure of the Scarlet Fury seemed gradually to grow less and less distinct, until at length it quite disappeared—vanished like the gibbous moon as it dips lurid and red into the waves of Coromandeb before the rising blast of the monsoon, or as the gleam of the red meteor of the fens as it vanisheth into the forest glooms of the "land of the tortoise" (Kumaön).

The King remained immersed in deep thought until the stars began to pale before the rising dawn; he then sought the inner chamber of his pavilion to rest, till the rising sun and the trumpets of the camp should call the Pandau host to arms before dispersing to their homes, to receive the last words and thanks of the great King Yûdishtir.

* *
*

II.

E pass from the tented field of Korau-Khết to the dim solitudes of the Vindhya and Aravelli ranges of mountain, which guard the great north desert of India—the Marôst-háli (plains of death) of more recent times —and the wooded intricate ravines and rocky heights, habitations of the Vânapûtras (children of the forest), since called Nâgas, Bheels, Goonds, or Sánthâls, according to locality; but all doubtless the aborigines of the Indian peninsula, before driven by the Aryan invaders into the fastnesses and solitudes of the land. At perpetual strife with the Rajpoots—Soorujbuns, Chandrabuns, and other lofty-descended tribes—these wild nations regarded all strangers as enemies, till once assured of their friendly intentions, but once convinced of the loyalty of a stranger, faithful to the death. Amongst these wild people the great Pandau King Yûdishtír sought to win confidence, and wandered down through the mighty forests of Western India till he stood upon the wild mountains of the Sahyâdri, and salt sea shore of Karnâta, and of Coromandeh.

At that early period the southern races of India had scarcely grouped themselves into the many petty tribes or nations to be found at the present day, but the kingdoms of Sugrîva and Karnâta extended down the coast; and the great island of Taprobane (Tápú Ravána), the modern Ceylon, embraced much of the coast now called Malabar and the Carnatic. Legends relate that a vast island or continent, embracing the Maldive, Laccadive, the Châgos Archipelago, and other islands on the west of Travancore existed, where now the stormy seas roll from the Western Ocean; the whole forming one grand kingdom, having for its capitol *Sri*—or holy—*Lankapoora*, by the ancient Indians called Singhâla, by the Arabs Surrindip. The wild waves now roll over the greater part of this submerged kingdom.

At the time, however, of which we write, the conquest of Taprobane or Singhâla by Râma had, generations back, occurred. Thither had Sita been abducted by Râwun its giant king, and there had the scenes of the war waged by Râma and his ally Hânumân for her recovery been localized.* Doubtless Hânumân (the Monkey King), the ally of Râma, may be held to have been one of those indigenous chiefs who allied himself to the conquering Aryans, and who, at the head of his Vânapûtras—children of the forest,—performed the doughty deeds venerated in the Râmâyânâ, which have rendered his name as that of a deity to all succeeding generations of Hindoos.

Along the coast the galleys of the pirates of the north, since called Runchores—perhaps also of Sesostris—pursued their depredations; and here again we shall encounter traces of our old friend Krishna, the merry companion of Sediva, whose first "avatar"† is fabled to have occurred on the western coast of India, near the ancient Larice or Somâshtra—the modern Káthiawâr—where the world-renowned shrines of Somnauth, Dwarkanauth, and, above all, Suukernauth, commemorate the sacred event of the "avatar" of the demi-god—victorious over the "Dæmon of the Shell?"   *   *   *   *

On his way south, therefore, in the vast forests of Odaipûr near the Aboo mountain, then recently colonized by the conquering clan of Soorujbun Rajpoots—children of the sun—whilst the scarlet dúk tree flamed in the forest like the flamingo of the Indus, or the scarlet crane of the Rann of Kâch, and the spires of the giant bamboo shot into the yellow air like the minarets of the palace of King Indra—the wandering Pandau King paused one hot noonday, at the dark grove or shrine of the primæval earth-goddess, venerated by the Bheels, the northern section of the Vânapûtra tribes. The roar of lions and

---

* The conquest of Ceylon by Rama—if indeed of any historic validity—is fixed by Asiatic chronologists at about 1400 B.C., but in relation to the genealogy of the Mahabarat it must be assigned to rather an earlier epoch.
† As an incarnation of Vishnoo the Preserver.

the hiss of serpents resounded in the thicket; and the attendants of the King had proposed to resume the march onwards,
when a cowherd—who had accompanied the cortége as guide
for the last few miles of their march—suddenly sounded his
horn, or "sánk" (shell). Suddenly the dismal sounds of
noxious creatures ceased; and, instead, the low of herds and
song of birds began to be heard in the grove.

The King turned to observe the cowherd who had performed
such a prodigy. Lo! he had vanished; and in his place stood
the bright "Narrain Sánk,"—Krishna in his glorified form as
an "avatar" of Vishnoo the Preserver, sitting on his cœrulian
steed Garood. He smiled serenely, and raised his lotus hand.
Sudden máya (glamour or heavenly illusion) fell on Yûdishtír
and his train. They seemed to stand in blissful abodes; a
golden pavilion seemed to overshadow the King, whilst flowers
and scented waters diffused their fragrance overhead; birds
were heard to warble; and a table, on which delicious fruits
and a feast were placed, stood ready to hand.

The "Heaven-born" addressed the King:—"Oh, Pandau,
"behold thy resting-place till the sun dips beyond the distant
"Aboo—my present dwelling! Krishna presents this feast to
"the brother of his friend Sediva; not to Yûdishtír the King!
"Nevertheless, oh, wise one! oh, sad one! I bestow on thee
"the shell torn from the grasp of the Dæmon below the dark
"sea of Sunkernauth, in which lay the stolen Véda. Be it
"thy sacred horn! Sound it if in danger, and the 'Pre-
"server' will aid thee; for Vishnoo loves thee and thy beneficent
"soul, though the earthly Krishna may laugh and deride; oh,
"friend and nourisher of the poor and humble; oh, brother of
"Sediva, farewell!"   *   *   *   *   *

He had spoken. The bright blue Vishnoo, seated on his
celestial steed Garood, vanished into the blue æther from the
King's sight.

"Hail! and thanks, oh bright one! and be still propitious
"to Yûdishtír!" cried the Pandau, as the parting deity

became as a speck in the purple heaven, like a glittering eagle
flying over the peaks of Aboo.   *   *   *   *

The King and his attendants performed the *saptopuddie*, a
sacred dance, and then fell to at the feast prepared. Golden
dishes contained the dainties of the world ; cups of crystal and
amethyst, and the agates and polished gems of Kâmbâgh and
the cornelian mountains of the west, sparkled on the board ;
the limpid wines of Bactria, and the aphim (opium) of Somâshtra* (Malwa) in crystal vessels.

"Aree!" cried the followers of the King, "the good Vishnoo
"knows how to entertain the friends of Krishna the Jocund!"
and without stint they all ate and drank of the heaven-bestowed
feast.   *   *   *   *   *   *   *

But lo! the day declined ; the setting sun began to blaze
red through the scarlet dâk trees of the forest, and the spires
of the bamboo shot into the yellow air like the spears of the
heavenly host of Indra against the purple sky.

Sleep began to oppress the followers of the King: one by
one they fell off into deep slumber—even the great Pandau
himself, tired, may be, with the long day's march, reposed on
his broidered carpet.   *   *   *   For how
long cannot be known. On awakening, all seemed as before
the appearance of Krishna ;—the silent forest, the deep shades
of the sacred grove surrounded them ; only no dismal sounds
of wild beasts were heard. Whether they in truth had seen
the god, and enjoyed his feast; or whether the effect of
heavenly illusion (máya); or whether the aphim (opium) of
Kámput† had been too strong—who can say! but what convinced Yûdishtír of the reality of the scene was that the
"sánk," or shell horn—whether of Krishna or the pretended
cowherd—was lying by his side ; but he found the rest of the

* Kambagh the ancient name of Cambay; formerly a district of the Hindoo
province of Somashtra or Malwa, which is still a great opium growing district of
Western India.

† The ancient name of Malwa according to the "Raja Taringini."

party deeply slumbering; and, as he arose in the early dawn of day, he observed that their beards and nails had at least a month's growth since they had slept. This also led Yûdishtír to suspect that, though friendly to the brother of Sediva, the once hostile and frolicsome Krishna had not refrained from playing off one of his tricks on his former rivals the Pandaus. No further evil results ensued: the noxious creatures were silent, and the King resumed his march, taking with him the sacred horn, which, in the future of Yûdishtír's life, will be found of considerable value and renown.   *   *.   *

So on through the western forests went the great King Yûdishtír; meeting on his way fragments of the great Vânaputra army returning from the wars of Ráma and Râwun to their homes in the Vindhya and Sahyádri mountains; uncouth "children of the forest," worthy of their leader, the Monkey King Hânumân. These men he feasted—partly out of policy, partly pity—for gaunt and worn appeared they after the long wars in Carnâta and the isles of Taprobane; and always did the King's philosophy embrace the opportunity of performing good deeds, and his charitable heart ever delighted in relieving the wants of the poor and helpless.

*   *   *   *   *   *

Many and various were the King's adventures during his long journey South, along the coast of Sugríva and Carnâta, till at length he stood on the salt sea shore of Coromandeb, and prepared to cross by Adam's Bridge into the isle of Singhála (Ceylon), the former Paradise of the pure races in the golden age of man; afterwards the abode of Nâga and Yakka savages, till rescued by Wijayo thirty generations after the age of Yûdishtír.

"This is the sea-beach; here was the victory;
"Here fought the heroes; struggled the brave;
"Mournfully sighs the wind in the loneliness,
"Mournfully breaks the desolate wave,"

III.

THE wars of Ráma and Ráwun had ceased, and Singhála (or Taprobane) had quieted down at the time when the great King Yûdishtír visited Sri-Lankapoora in search of knowledge and wisdom. The abduction of Sita had been avenged by his ancestor the great Ráma. The memory of the invasion of India by the great Assyrian Queen Semiramis had long gone bye : all was quiet in the land of Hânumân, except that the galleys of Sesostris, King of Egypt, vexed the coasts of Lerice (Malabar), and Sumâshtra.

From Asia Minor to the borders of India the kingdom of Bactria still flourished ; whence also the worship of the Sun—emblem of life and eternity, as enunciated by Zoröaster its great king—had superseded in these western shores the dark idolatry of the Indian aborigines; but on the other hand the subtle metaphysics of the Aryan conquerors of India had begun to vitiate the comparatively pure. moral code of Mánú; and the Sabœan worship of images and the host of heaven, so antagonistic to the teaching of the Magi, had penetrated the coasts of India.

The great Pandau's mind was full of *doubt*; priests, whether Brahmins, Aramœans, Chaldées, or Magi, were alike distrusted by the King of India. Not to such minds as those of Yûdishtír (nor of Gautáma the "Boodhist," his descendant), could priestcraft and its jugglery impart respect; and, notwithstanding Brahminical traditions, we may suspect that the mind of the Pandau King—finding no basis of truth on which to rest amidst the dreary metaphysics of his people—sought for the light of truth in foreign lands.

The royal wanderer determined to roam in the country of the Chaldees, and visit the seats of learning of the day. Accordingly we find the Pandau King wandering in search of wisdom and truth to "Tarshish and the isles,"—this very

Taprohane of which we write—perhaps even to Æthiopia and Egypt (?), and to the Court of royal Babylon, and the Assyrian monarch. It is difficult to determine the limits of his wanderings : his wise words and his knowledge of the starry wisdom of the Chaldees, and his love of the tenets of the Magians, lead us to conclude that at least he had visited Babylon and the plains of Shinâr, and the marches of Assyria; and that whilst a guest at the court of the great Queen Nitôcris in the city of Bélus, in the land of Assyria and the ancient Persia, the King met with the adventures to be narrated in the two following chapters of this chronicle.

*   *   *   *   *   *

The great King Yûdishtír had been feasted by Ráma-Sunker, King of Lankapoora, and had taken ship for the land of the Ichthyophagi—fish-eaters of the north,—and his stately ship rode at anchor on the blue waters of the Arabian Sea, in the port of Teredon, at the mouth of that great river the Euphrates, over against the Arabian shore. The King's ship anchored off the stately harbour on the eve of a bright day in the month of Kartik (March) K.Y. 2274 (B.C. 1361). The galleys of Sesostris, King of Egypt, also rode at anchor in the bay, and the argosies of Tarshish and the isles were landing rich goods at the seaport of Teredon. The ships of the "Queen of Assyria"—perhaps Nitôcris*—were decked with silken flags and gilded pennons. The "great queen," herself, had that day returned from war ; and the fleets of the allies, and the armies of Assyria were awaiting her in camp on that sultry eve when the Pandau King's ship arrived in port.

At moonrise the King sounded the " sánk," or horn, of Krishna. He sounded it loud and clear over the silver sea,

---

* Yudishtir must have arrived at that dark period in the history of Assyria which is absolutely unknown to history. Semiramis (wife of Ninus) had flourish-ed (if indeed she ever existed) about 1800 or 1900 B.C. Her mythic invasion of India is therefore assignable to about that age, if indeed of any historical import whatever; but until the death of Sardanapalus in 767 B.C., all is dark in the history of Assyria.

and the hymn of the Indians to Vishnoo the Preserver was
heard far across the waves of the harbour, and reached the ear
of the "great queen" Nitôcris, as she rested in her pavilion on
the sea shore, surrounded by her court.

"Who sounds the horn of the Chaldees to the starry host?"
enquired the great Queen, of Ménés the priest of Bélus, the
Aramœan, who stood before her chair of state. "Is it not
"forbidden, O! Ménés, to worship other than the great god
"Bäal within the coasts of Assyria and Babylon? Come, O!
"Ménés, we will ourselves examine this mystery."

The Queen, attended by the high priest and a few chosen
ladies of the court, stepped on to the moonlit beach, and
strolled towards the sea, on whose smooth strand the small
waves were breaking with a soft murmur. The tall spars of
the shipping in the bay glittered like silver spears in the
Eastern moonlight, and the sheen of stars quivered on the
waters of the Arabian sea.

"Oh, Ménés," saith the Queen, softened by the calm night
scene, "doth thy knowledge tell thee aught of these starry
"skies; of this unceasing restless throb of the salt sea?
"Whence this constant ebb and flow of the ocean's billows?
"this nightly rise and sinking of the starry hosts? O, great
"one! oh, wise one! Doth thy great god Bäal reveal to thee
"such knowledge? Why should not the horn of the stranger
"salute the silver moon as she ariseth to gladden the night
"and light the lovers, oh, son of an Assyrian! to their fair
"ones? Let not the judgment fall on the sounder of the
"shell, oh, Ménés!"

So spake the Queen* as she paced the solitary shore, and
gazed on the moonlit sea with softened heart.   *   *   *

But see, a skiff approaches: a tall chieftain, in whose helmet

---

* Nitocris was herself a Bactrian, who had married the King of Assyria, and
perhaps a Magian in religion, who were originally worshippers of the "Sun God,"
hut afterwards combined with the Sabœans to impose priestcraft on the Assyrian
nation,

glittered one large gem with the kálgi (heron's plume) of royalty, stepped on to a rocky ledge as the boat grounded. He advanced landwards, slowly pacing towards the camp; but paused on observing the Queen's tent and the royal party in front of the pavilion.

"Stand, oh stranger!" cried Ménés advancing. "Knowest "thou not the edict? To approach the great Queen's pavilion "is death? Who art thou?"

"A stranger and a pilgrim," answered the chieftain. "I "come from Taprobane and the blue ocean of the South; I "seek the knowledge of the Chaldees and of the wise Ara-"mœan race. I crave a peaceful welcome for the stranger "ignorant of your laws!"

"Dost thou worship the great god Bäal?" enquired Ménés, zealous for the religion of Bélus and his native Babylon.

"I worship the Powers of Heaven and the glorious Sun," replied the chief. "Ahûra-Mazda (Ormuzd), the symbol of "Light and Life; and the Moon, Goddess of the Night and "of the musing Heart of Man, and the placid Realms of "Thought!"

"Art thou then a Magian of the forbidden rites, and darest "to proclaim aloud thy religion in the very presence of the "royal Nitôcris? Rash stranger, thy life shall pay the for-"feit." He put a whistle to his mouth, and a shrill sound—such as may be heard betimes at eve from the lonely top of Bélus, Temple of Nimrod at Babylon or Nineveh—issued from his lips. In a few seconds a band of armed men—soldiers clad in jet black armour—appeared, and at a sign from the priest, surrounded the Pandau chief; their battle-axes glittering in the moonlight.

At this critical moment, however, the Queen herself stepped forward.

"Peace, oh Ménés! Let me confer with this stranger, who, "as I perceive, is of the Aryan race of India." She turned towards the King: "Oh, Khsátriya! who art thou? For

D

"the sake of thy great King Yûdishtír, I pardon thy pre-
"sumption in approaching our pavilion ; but say thy name."

"Alas! Lady," answered the chief, "I am that very Yû-
"dishtír thou hast named. I am the King of Hindosthán, in
"search of truth and wisdom for his people."

A dark flush deepened on the swarthy countenance of
Ménés as he heard these words. "Oh rash one," he exclaimed,
"then thus I avenge the defeat of great Semiramis ; and thus
"I seize the King of India! Advance, oh guards, and slay
"the stranger!"

But Yûdishtír—for it was he—stepped forward, and saluting the Queen, exclaimed : "Oh, Queen! oh, Priest! forbear,
"and listen to the words of Yûdishtír ; for I am he. In days
"to come I may serve thy kingdom as an ally, oh great Prin-
"cess! Behold the proof."   *   *   *   The King
sounded a long, loud blast upon the horn of Krishna, and,
behold! immediate máya (glamour) fell on the royal camp.
They seemed to be surrounded with a vast array of soldiers—
archers and-spearmen in bright blue armour, the garb of
Vishnoo the Preserver—whilst the bright Indra and the host
of heaven in their golden war-chariots seemed to hover around
in the yellow horizon. "Behold, oh Queen, the powers of the
"great Aryan Kingdom, and the mighty race of Pand ; the
"allies of Assyria if thou wilt, otherwise its foes."   *   *

The two bands confronted each other, apparently awaiting
the signal from their leaders to join in battle. The moonlight
streamed upon their armour. The glare of torches lighted up
the rocky shore.

"Enough, oh Queen! I know thy wish and royal heart,"
resumed the King. "Let not strife ensue between the two
"great races of India and Assyria—Aryans both—rather let
"peace and friendship prevail." He waved his hand. Suddenly the glamour ceased. The Queen saw simply standing
before her the tall chieftain who had landed on the moonlit
shore. At the same time, however, a whisper as from the
rocky harbour-ledge reached Yûdishtír's ear ;—

"Shábásh, oh Pandau! Thou art advancing in the art of
"pleasing the fair dames! Krishna will aid thee; away with
"thought! Be bold; be fortunate. Thou wilt find the great
"Queen Nitôcris much like the gópies of the land of Bráj!"

The King recognised the voice as that of the jocund Krishna;
and soon the wild demi-god appeared, leading the dance of
youths and maidens : and several of the ladies of the Queen's
retinue join in the jocund dance—whether seduced by the
merry strains of the Indian Dionysius, or impelled by native
mirth, who knoweth? The Queen's pavilion was lighted up,
and a scene of mirth and festivity succeeded the stormy commencement of the night.

* * * * * *

But the pale chieftain sate gravely with Queen Nitôcris, on
ivory chairs, by the calm sea, and joined not the revellers.

* * * * * *

From that hour there was friendship between the Indian
and Persian Aryans, and soon afterwards Yûdishtír and his
retinue accompanied the Queen in her progress up the great
river Euphrates to Babylon and the land of the Chaldees.

The King of Hindosthán became the friend and ally of the
Queen of Assyria; and the Aramœan Ménés—High-priest of
Bélus—no longer forbade the sounding of the sánk (or horn)
of Vishnoo, nor prayer and hymn to the Magian's Sun God;
nor invocation of the starry host at moonrise. * * *

So the King arrived at mighty Babylon, and a palace on the
inner walls of the city was assigned him for a residence, near
to the royal courts of Nitôcris, overlooking the waters of
Euphrates.

* * *

The chronicle is here obscure. Some have asserted that
Yûdishtír came to love Queen Nitôcris of Assyria, *par amour;*
and, indeed, it is written in the slokes of the shastrs of
Yûdishtír the Great, that máya or heavenly illusion gat hold

D 2

of the Aryan King; but at this especial point of his wanderings, we do not read of the loves of the Pandau and Nitôcris,
but instead, a weird story of glamour.   *   *   *

The "melancholy" Yûdishtír is still at times the victim of
metaphysical doubts and subtle thought. In the midst of
revels and festivities still would the sad soul of the Pandau
muse on the uncertainty of things, and plunge into eddies of
thought and self-abstraction, which sometimes led him to deny
all outward semblances of things—nay, at times, even his own
existence! Still he seeks in vain a standpoint of philosophic
verity! No truth consoles him! Unhappy Yûdishtír! Wise,
benevolent, and just—a heart of gold—but victim of a subtle
brain, whose Promethean wild-fire in the end led him—who
can wonder!—a hermit and a recluse to the snows of Himôdi!

*   *
*

One night we find Yûdishtír, about this period of his search
after the Sublime and True, brooding in his balcony in Babylon,
overlooking the waters of Euphrates. The dreamy books of
the Chaldees, and the slokes of the "souls of the planets," are
open before him : he raised his head ; there, on the margin of
the waters, appeared, after many moons, the figure of the
Scarlet Fury of Mânásbul—a baleful light in her eyes, which
are fixed upon the King.

"At length again, oh great Yûdishtír, behold thine evil
"genius! Shortly wilt thou know the cause."

No more was said ; but strange, it seemed to Yûdishtír
that by her side stood an indistinct reduplication of herself.

*   *   *   *   *   *

The chronicle is here again obscure. A story is related of
King Yûdishtír, weird and strange;—it is narrated that the
King himself often afterwards doubted the reality of his
visions ; and attributed them to the effect of máya or divine
illusion, which we find so often operating on his mind and
career. Be this as it may—though history telleth not what

and how great were the achievements of the King in the land of the Chaldees—one adventure, miraculous to the mind of the Aryan followers of the great Pandau pilgrim, is recorded, and must now be told.

* *
 *

IV.

AMIDST the rugged peaks of the "Black Mountains" of Irân, the Temple of the God Bélus or Bäal reared its dark turrets to the sky. The approach to it forbidden to all but the priests, except at stated times, when the people of Babylon and Nineveh, crossing the desert, would seek in pilgrimage the awful shrine of the great God Bäal.

Dark and mysterious were the rites of Moloch, performed at this temple amidst the gloom of those ironstone Plutonic peaks; and it was darkly whispered that the fire consumed the victims—both infants and those who had invaded the secrecy of the temple, or who had incurred the vengeance of the priests of that other great temple of Bélus or Nimrod at Babylon—where the high-priest Ménés usually officiated.

Nevertheless, the Pandau hero, who had during his residence in Babylou preserved friendly relations with Ménés, proposed to himself to surmount those dangers, and to solve for himself the secret of the mysteries of Bäal. Having clad himself, therefore, in the pilgrim's garb, concealing the light tunic of the Khsátriya warrior, the Pandau King selected one tried companion from his suite, and one sultry evening mounted the swift dromedary of Uɪr (of the Chaldees). All night he rode across the starlit desert, and arrived early in the dawn at the foot of the Black Mountain of Bélus. He there, with his follower, rested in a cavern during the day; but when again the evening star twinkled in the date tops, he commenced the ascent. The red sunset lit up the dark ravines of the mountain with lurid splendour; but jet black clouds pregnant with lightnings, brooded on its summit.

Before the King had advanced half the distance, a thunder-clap resounded down the mountain, followed by the crash of hail. Large crystal globes bounding from slope to slope, broke into thousands of keen jagged fragments, and went clattering down in the torrents which now began to fill the ravines of the mountain. The red lightning played above the peaks, and by its glittering light the King observed with horror that the torrents pouring around him were red, as with blood—who knows!—of victims slain. "Red came the river down, and loud the angry Spirit of the waters moaned;" and shrieks as of voices of the abyss, flew past them as they climbed; doubt-less signs of the fury of the offended Deity. Soon, however, the Pandau entered a grove of black cypresses, whose dark and melancholy shadows chilled the blood. An icy wind crept through the gloomy trees, on the gaunt branches of which obscene birds sate screaming; and weird, dismal forms flitted ominously through the gloom. The travellers were approach-ing the arcánum of Bäal-zébûb, "King of Flies," or Devils.

Onwards! The King had braced his heart to face all perils, human or divine; and the horn of Vishnoo "the Pre-server" hanging by his side assured him of supernatural aid if need should be. Onwards, therefore, he plunged through the glooms of the infernal thicket. They emerged into a long dark causeway, paved with huge slippery slabs of flint or slate, leading up close towards the summit of the mountain, whose thunder-riven peak could now be observed standing forth black and spectral in the lurid sky. Midnight was the hour it be-hoved Yûdishtír to reach the highest summit on which stood the frowning Tower of Bélus the Terrible, by distant nations yclept Bäal-zébûb, "King of Flies and Devils;" but beyond the frowning turrets the Pandau King beheld the smiling stars of the East, and he knew that there was safety to the true and valiant spirit.

*　　*　　*　　*　　*　　*

As they advanced, the mountain seemed to rock beneath them, and again the crystal globes began to thunder down the ravines, breaking into thousands of glittering hailstones, which clattered upon the rocky slabs on all sides; but, strange! none touched Yûdishtír; and his companion, cowering under an overhanging rock, sought shelter, and thus escaped the infernal deluge.

At length, resuming the ascent, the slippery pavement seemed to slide from under their feet, and in some cases vast rocks on which the King had stepped, broke off and went thundering down the mountain side into the darkness of the abyss! At length they turned the corner of a huge rock—itself a mountain—when a ghastly form—the skeleton of a Titan—suddenly stood at the King's side, and pointed down a chasm on the side of the mountain. The Pandau gazed below, and beheld there what would since be termed the "Witches' Sabbath." The monstrous forms of earth, and the embodiments of the moral deformities of the sinful mind of man; the grim chimæras of the abyss; and the monstrous larvæ conjured into apparent being by the erring perceptions of disease or excess, when the veil which hides the unseen spirit-world has been temporarily withdrawn under the influence of magic or of dæmons—more potent in those days than now. The King recognised the *simulacra* of several grim phantasms of the olden time; amongst them—enlarged to giant size—the dire Scarlet Fury of the Mânásbul—the Autochthon of the Lall-Nâg. He shuddered; but turned his eyes away, and calmly resumed his journey upwards; and soon, whilst the gibbous moon hung double-horned over the dark pinnacle of the temple, he reached the last ascent.

Behold! a monstrous form—black and terrible—Bäal-zébûb himself, the King of Flies (or Devils) stood—its outstretched wings across the path—huge and motionless! motionless, except that a tremulous shudder of the air alone told of life in the grim spectre, and a hum as of the "King of Flies" emanated from the dismal form! Astonishment seized the soul of the Pandau; and his follower fell prone on the rocks, insensible. The King's senses swam; his head began to fail; his feet to slip,—he would have lost his foothold and fallen headlong from the mountain—when suddenly remembering the horn of Vishnoo the Preserver, his heart was strengthened. He seized it, and sounded first with trembling, uncertain sound; but at length a blast such as had scared the dæmons of Himôdi and of Surrindip pealed amidst the rocky tops of Bélusthán.   *   *   *   *   *

"What, frightened at a Bluebottle!" A weird laugh as of the merry Krishna smote on the King's ear, as he gasped to summon breath and courage for the final trial.   *   *

The glamour ceased, and Yûdishtír soon found himself at the gates of the dark temple of the God Bélus of the Chaldees.

The door of the temple swung open, and Ménés, the Aramœan High-priest of Bäal, stood before the King.

"Welcome, oh great Pandau! he exclaimed. "Thou, who "hast bravely surmounted the trial of the senses, mayest ap-"proach the shrine of Bélus. We have no secrets from great "ones such as Thee! Now thou shalt be initiated into the "knowledge of the great Bäalim; but, oh Yûdishtír! dost "thou believe in the power of the primitive Titan? the Earth-"Kenner, who rulest this world?"

"Nay, I believe," answered Yûdishtír, "in this proper soul "do I know and feel his power; but I contemn and defy; "trusting to higher ones———"

"Not yet, oh Yûdishtír, mayest thou name such within "these halls," shrieked the Priest.

"I believe in Ahûra-Mazda,* the Sun-God; Author of "Light and Life," resumed the King; "who rules this lovely

---

* Yudishtir was evidently a Zoroastrian, and probably believed in Ahura-Mazda (since called Ormuzd) and Ahriman—the Good and Evil Principles—who were believed by the Magians, as also in later times, to divide the rule of the world.

"star, the Earth! Did not the Sheikh of Urr—Holy Ibrá-
"hím—fly from Bäal and from Moloch from the land of the
"Chaldees?"

   *   *   *   *   *   *

A sudden peal of thunder shook the mountain; and Ménés
stretched forth his hand towards the King: he held a small
pointed style, with which he touched the Pandau's breast; a
shock, and sudden darkness overtook Yûdishtír's senses.

   *   *   *   *   *   *

On awaking from his trance, the Pandau found himself
lying on a stone couch within the temple, Ménés gazing at
him in meditative aspect; and, strange to say—the first time
for many moons—Yûdishtír clearly beheld the Fury of Mânásbul, standing on a small tripod beside him. At the further
end of the hall was a gigantic idol of the God Bélus, around
which two huge serpents were entwined, their folds embracing
the limbs of the idol, their glowing eyes fixed on the Priest
Ménés. The latter observing Yûdishtír restored to his senses,
advanced to his side, and placing a hand on his heart muttered
to himself "Yes, it was too strong!" Then to the King,—

"Arise, oh great King! the danger has passed; but offend
"not again the mighty spirit of Bäal in this his proper temple;
"or, wise and strong as thou art, all my knowledge will scarce
"suffice to save thee. But now arise; let us resume our dis-
"course. Thou at least *believest!* so propitiate the God by
"prayer and the sacred rites."

"Oh, Ménés," said the King, "here I am in thy power,
"but cease these juggleries, oh Priest. Thou knowest I dis-
"cern their falsity; and even thou wilt shrink from sacrificing
"the life of the royal Pandau, the friend and ally of thy great
"Queen. I come to *learn:* be wise, and communicate.
"Priestcraft and deception are not for such as thee and me; ·
"thou knowest it in thy soul."   *   *   *

But deep silence fell on the lips of Ménés; no word did the
Aramœan Priest of Bélus utter: motioning to the King to

follow, he led him to the gates of the temple, where he pointed
to the star of the morning---Aldebaran—then just glimmering
above the northern horizon. He waved his salutations, and
withdrew within the cloisters of the temple, whose dark
shadow fell weird and gigantic across the mountain top. The
great gates swung back, and closed with a clang,. whose
echoes reverberated down the sides of the black mountain.
Yûdishtír took the hint, and lighted by the glimmer of the
dawn, slowly wended his way down by the path he had ascended. He found his follower on the exact spot where he
had fallen, just awaking from his trance. They descended to
the cave amidst the date thicket where they had remained
the preceding day, and there rested at the foot of the mountain. At midday they ate their frugal repast of dates and
conserve of tamarind and roses ; and when fair Hesperus—
Star of the Evening—began to twinkle over the high solitary
palm tree that overshadowed the entrance to the cave, and the
cool dews of night began to fall on the desert, they remounted
the swift dromedary of Urr, and skimming across the arid
plain of Shinâr, regained the King's palace residence in Babylon, before the dawn of day.

          *   *   *   *   *   *

Such was the King Yûdishtír's adventure at the temple of
Bélus ; and from that day there was enmity in the heart of
Ménés the Aramœan Priest towards the Pandau, and the
Scarlet Fury of Mâuásbul became a constant visitor to the
King ; but Vishnoo the Preserver had him in charge, and
no harm resulted to the possessor of Krishna's sánk—the
brother of Sediva, his friend : nay, the jocund demi-god even
condescended to play his pranks at Yûdishtír's expense, as
will be related in the next chapter.

───────────

[NOTE. I hope my readers will not be shocked' at the
introduction of "scriptural characters" into this chapter. I
am reminded of an anecdote—whether original or not I do

not know—introduced by the author of the "Eastern Hunters,"
in his excellent work on the wild sports of Western India,
which I am here tempted to repeat. "A Scottish widow who
had recently lost her husband, was accosted by the 'minister,'
who condoled with her on her loss. 'Aweel, minister,' said
she, 'nae doot the gudeman is now in Beelzebub's bosom!'
'*Beelzebub's* bosom, good woman!' exclaimed the minister
considerably shocked, 'ye maun mean *Abraham's* bosom!'
'Aweel, 'stir,' replied the gudewife, 'nae doubt ye may be recht,
ye ken best anent thae gentlefolks!'" Of course the machinery
employed by Ménés in the text must be held as material and
delusive.]

* * *

V.

BEHOLD our Hero, the Pandan King, established in a
palace on the walls of Babylon—those vast walls of
burnt brick described so minutely by old Herodotus
and by the Poet Isaiah, who, however, wrote several centuries
later than the period of our history.

The great Pandan's residence communicated with the open
country by a postern gate, and ofttimes did the King of India,
mounting his fleet horse or dromedary, pay swift visits to
spots in the surrounding plains of Shinâr and elsewhere, in
search chiefly of the wisdom of the Chaldees : one such has
been related. Disguised also—like the Caliph Haroun-al-
Raschid of a later age—he would visit the markets and streets
of the great cities, in order to learn the true condition of the
poorer subjects of the Aryan states, lest haply his just and
beneficent spirit should lose opportunities of helping those
"creatures of God"—those "poor cats," as they were contemptu-
ously called by the great satraps of Persia and Assyria.

Often, too, the King, wandering in the hanging gardens—built by this very Queen Nitôcris—of imperial Babylon, would chance to meet the Queen, and pay visits to his royal hostess. The Queen, also, with many of the great satraps of Assyria and Media, and of more remote provinces of the empire, and many Egyptians—men of learning and knowledge—would seek the residence of King Yûdishtîr, to hear his winged words, and all would return impressed by his wisdom and sublime knowledge. Nor were visits of the fair and gentle less frequent; nor was the wise and melancholy King averse to the society of the witty and poetic; or indifferent to the smiles of beauty, or to the gaiety of the young and fair. At times, indeed, guided by the advice of the merry Krishna, he seemed to court such recreation. Often, too, would the Queen Nitôcris—accompanied only by her dear friend Iönis, daughter of Arces, Satrap of Persepolis—pass long hours of the sultry eve by the waters of Euphrates in company of the wise Pandau prince, her hero and ally.

*   *   *   *   *   *

It was the birthday of Queen Nitôcris, and the royal Pandau had craved the honour to entertain her and her court at a great banquet at his palace amidst the hanging gardens on the walls of Babylon, along the great river Euphrates. The fête was a nocturnal one;—the coloured lamps of Cathay glimmered amidst the trees, and, swinging in the soft summer air, illumed the festive scene with softened light; coloured globes of crystal refracted the rays in divers colours, and a thousand torches fed with naphtha and balls of bitumen lighted up the walls and precincts of the palace, and glinted on the sweet bushes of rose and other flowering shrubs in the gardens around. The deep azure canopy of an Assyrian sky shed over all its purple.

Nitôcris' gay court of beauteous dames and damsels were seated on cloths of gold and colour, under an awning whose crimson and azure silk was embroidered with the flying Lion and Bull of Assyria. Vases of lemon, orange, jessamine, and other scent-bestowing flowers were ranged along the marble alcoves which overlooked the river. Nobles of the highest rank—nay, tributary kings—were there in gay apparel, in many-coloured gala-dresses dipt in the lovely pigments of the East. In a robe of Tyrian purple (spoil of the murex of the distant Mediterranean) even King Sesostris of Egypt accompanied the Queen to Yûdishtír's fête; for peace had been proclaimed between Egypt and Assyria, and the great Sesostris desired to do honour to the King of India—the friend and ally of Queen Nitôcris.

The sackbut, psaltery, dulcimer, and all kinds of music enlivened the ear of the royal company. The spray of fragrant waters, falling in soft murmuring showers, refreshed the evening air and lulled the senses, and the refulgent moon of the East shed over the marble domes and towers of Babylon the dreamy majesty of night.

After the congratulatory ode to Nitôcris the Court arose, and, dispersing, formed groups, who wandered along the terraces and bye paths of the gardens; especially Yûdishtír, conducting Nitôcris and her ever dear companion Iönis, into the inner garden, sought to surprise the Queen by the unveiling of a statue of herself, graved by cunning Indian artists of Indian wood, tinted to represent the visible and breathing effigies of the Queen. Descending some steps, they approached a small pavilion or kiosk, over which chains of roses and other sweet flowers shed perfume, or hung in graceful tassels from a dome of gold and lapis-lazuli. The Pandau, making a deep obeisance to the Queen, stepped forward to draw aside the silken curtain which veiled the statue, which occupied a pedestal in the centre of a small marble court within the kiosk. Around were set rose-coloured lamps burning in jewelled cressets, fed by perfumed oils from the rose-gardens of Atropatene (the modern Aderbijan), or from far Samarkand, and the fertile fields at that time existing at the embouchure of the Oxus and Jaxartes, then a blooming garden of sweets, now a melancholy wilderness of ravines and sand. *   *

The curtain was drawn aside by Yûdishtír, when lo! the statue of the Queen glowing as if in life: nay, it even seemed to breathe, as the draperies were made to appear to move and shimmer by a skilful arrangement of the lamps ; but not alone ! by the side of the statue appeared a refulgent figure in golden armour, with battle axe of war, and shield edged with great diamonds, which glittered intensely in the lamplight. The figure covered the Queen's statue, as it were defending it from the royal group approaching.

Astonishment fell on the royal group ; but after a moment's pause the Queen seemed to attribute this surprise to design on the part of Yûdishtír: she smiled, exclaiming,—

"I see, oh Prince, oh dear one! Thou hast added to thy "design a defender of Nitôcris! I presume the noble warrior "must be thyself! oh bold one! oh son of a Khsátriya! But "raise the helmet, and let us behold the face of our hero!"

But astonishment and anger had seized on the King Yu-dishtír. He stood gazing on the figure, whose eye gleaming from within the closed visor, assured him that the figure before him was a breathing mortal. "Nay! Queen," at length faltered the King, "I know not the stranger; and thus I "essay his proof." So saying, he swung round the light baldrick which hung across his shoulder, and drawing from the jewelled sheath which hung therefrom a keen blue sword-blade, he advanced towards the figure of the stranger warrior. The latter suddenly extended his shield towards Yûdishtír to the utmost length of his arm. Intolerable light evolved itself therefrom, and the King advancing, found his arm suddenly arrested as in a vice, and his steps, as it were, glued to the floor of the court; at the same time a merry laugh rang loudly from the mailed figure, and sudden máya (glamour) fell on the royal group. *   *   *   *   *

Yûdishtír fumbled for his trumpet—the magic horn of Krishna

—but alas! it hung not at his side; forgetful, he had left it
in his armoury when he had apparelled for the Queen's fête,
so the means to resist the supernatural impulse were wanting.
But Yûdishtír recited the "mantra of the rescued," and the
blue Narraian,* aider of the Pandaus, answered the invocation.
The glamour ceased; and behold, the statue of the stranger
had vanished from the scene. By this Yûdishtír knew that
the mirthful Krishna had again played on him one of his
tricks.

All stood serene within the marble dome, but Queen
Nitôcris frowned. "What is this, oh Pandau! Art thou
"magician as well as warrior! and darest thou to trifle with
"and make a jest of the Queen of Assyria and Babylon? I
"thought thee learned and discreet, but this is rude and rash,
"oh, Prince!"

The Queen in anger returned to her palace leaving Yûdishtír alone with his festive image.

From that day the friendship of the great Nitôcris for her
ally and guest declined; and the satraps and courtiers, following suit, began to look coldly on the Pandau King and his
followers:—all but Iönis; who secretly loved the stranger,
but, out of loyalty to her Queen and friend Nitôcris, had
"eaten her heart" in silence: she now sought the society of
Yûdishtír, attempting to console his darker moods, and to
persuade him to join more freely in the society of mankind;
she even offered to link her fate with his, and accompany him
back to his distant land, so as to soothe at all times, in the
years to come, his melancholy spirit. Nevertheless Yûdishtír
began to contemplate his return to his Aryan kingdom, by
way of India Alba and the great north river (Indus), and the
mountains of Caspira; but reasons for further delay and tarry-
ing in the land of Assyria shortly presented themselves.

   *   *   *   *   *   *

The Queen had departed for Nineveh—city of King Ninus

---

* A name of Vishnoo the Preserver.

and of the great Semiramis his spouse—but suddenly rumours of war arose throughout the land; and the chiefs of Babylon grew pale as they whispered of mighty hosts gathering on the frontiers, for the overthrow of the Assyrian Empire.

King Yûdishtír decided to remain, and aid his friend and ally the Queen Nitôcris.

*   *   *   *   *   *

The walls of Nineveh—those huge burnt-brick walls on which five horses can be driven abreast—appeared distinct in the hot air of the desert. Around, as far as the eye can reach, is encamped a vast array of the hostile host : a few pavilions of purple, azure, and gold, and the fluttering of pennons, tell of the Bactrian horse, each commander in centre of his troop, whose spears are fixed in the ground around. On one flank the black tents of the tribes of Media and Parthia, then, as now, nomads of the steppes and wild uplands—the Toorko-mans of the present age—Tartars of the Hindoo Caucasus and the black-capped Aryans of Emodus Mountain ; camped on the slopes of the Taurian mountains also, the Hyrcanian highlanders clad in tiger and leopard skins—all the tribu-taries of the Assyrian Empire, surround the City of Nineveh and besiege its Queen.

*   *   *   *   *   *

Clouds of hot dust announce the approach of each tribe of the vast array of warriors to the assault of Nineveh. With them they drag huge machines of war, destined to batter the walls, or to raise turrets, full of javelin men, to a level with the battlements and ramparts of the city.

Anon the trumpets sound ; and issuing from the various camps the rumbling of the chariots of the chiefs is heard to thunder over the plain like the car of far-resounding Bélus as he rides on the storms of the north. Soon bolts of red hot steel, and globes of naphtha, begin to hiss through the sultry air and fall into the city of the great Queen. Masses of half-molten bronze and other metal hurtle through the air ; even dead horses and dromedaries are hurled aloft by the balistæ —the mechanical invention of the great Sesostris of Egypt whilst the enemy of Assyria. Astonishment falls on the men of Nineveh and on the Assyrian soldiery of its garrison. Enervated by luxury and unchallenged dominion, now first assailed, they begin to fail before the sturdy Bactrian men-at-arms. The leaders fail to sustain their courage; no general issues orders; all seems lost; but not yet is Nineveh or Babylon destined to be overthrown—their cup is not yet quite full.* The arms and knowledge of the stranger supply that which native valour fails to furnish !

Already the walls are beginning to crumble under the fire and battering of the enemy, and the defenders are beginning to give way and forsake the walls, when a stranger chief, completely hid in blue armour, at the head of a chosen band of warriors—also in bright blue armour and vestments—is seen circulating round the ramparts, exhorting, encouraging, and arranging the defence. The men of Nineveh are seen to rally, and repulse the enemy on all sides; and, soon, even sallying forth to fall upon the rebel camps. The scene is changed; soon the hosts of Bactria, and the Medes, are seen to draw off discomfited, and their long standards begin to trail away across the desert and beyond the mountains.   *   *

Soon the Queen Nitôcris is seen advancing from the midst of Nineveh ; a vast crowd of chiefs and courtiers surrounding the golden chariot in which she rides. Silken banners, embroidered with the Lion of Assyria, wave overhead as she advances to the walls. Loud shouts summon the stranger warrior to her presence. He raises his helmet visor, lo ! the face of the Aryan King Yûdishtír, of late estranged ; now flushed with the light of battle ; his eye sparkling as on the day of the great victory of Korau-Khét.

---

* The reader need hardly be reminded that Nineveh fell in the reign of Labynit —the Belchazzar of Scripture—about the year 606 B.C., and Babylon fell nearly a century later, in the reign of Sardanapalus, about 538 B.C.

E

"Is it Thou, oh Prince, oh dear victorious friend!" exclaimed the Queen; "sit thou in my chariot, and be next to
"Nitôcris in Assyria. Nay," she added in a lower voice,
"share, if thou wilt, the throne of Babylon and Nineveh, oh
"saviour of Assyria!"   *   *   *   *   *

But Yûdishtír—for it was the Pandau King—gravely
saluted the Queen, simply saying, "Thus, oh Queen, I have
"repaid my debt to Assyria; farewell, and thanks, oh Queen!
"I go to my land of India, and the great races of my Aryan
"kingdom. Farewell!" He mounted a purple horse, and with
his followers, rode off across the desert towards Ctesiphon and
the mountains of Elymäis, and as the spear-heads of his party
caught the last glint of the setting sun, which sank in dusky
splendour behind the turrets of Nineveh—this was the last
that Queen Nitôcris saw of her guest, the great Pandau King
Yûdishtír.

*   *
*

VI.

"WHAT like of man the chieftain who slumbers 'neath
the shadows—the sad and silent shadows—of the
melancholy mujnoon (willow)? The waving of the
willows, and the whisper of the night-jar, winnows the gloomy
chief; and from the dark brown mountains, and the hoary
rocks of Khybur—the wild waste of the mountains that guard
the great north river—comes the desert-breathing air, crisp
with the salt bitumen and the flinty dust of hill tops, on
whose ancient wasted summits King Hôdi of the Punjanb
had erected gloomy beacons! Dreams he, the chief, of old
times, lost in the mist of ages where the feeble lamp of fable
scarce illuminates the darkness! when the old primæval races,
mid the gloom of superstition, and the worship of the Earth

Gods, kindled the fires of Moloch and raised the pyre to dæmons? Or, glancing down the rushing red river of times historic, doth he recognise the Aryans—the fair-haired sons of King Shem—driving the grim barbarians into the hills and forests? Or doth the Chief prophetic see the Macedonian phalanx glittering with iron war-gear? And the war ships of Nearchus? Or the swarming hordes of Asia, of Timoor, and of Ghengis? Or the thunder of the Saxons, and the rumbling trains of war-cars?" *   *   *   *

Such like was the dream of King Yûdishtir as he slept in the sultry midnight beneath the moon of India Alba, during his journey to his own kingdom. He had marched through Ctesiphon, Susa, Persepolis, across Caramania and the Arachôsian highlands, and so to India Alba and the lands of the Oxydracæ, the Malli, and the Sibs! At many points he had encountered—sometimes with arms—parties of the broken host which had besieged Nineveh, and were now making the best of their way to their own lands. It had seemed to him also at times that he was followed by a troop of the Persian cavalry—all clad in dazzling white—led by a son of the great Satrap Arces, father of Iönis ; and he supposed that his ally, the Queen of Assyria, had sent them for his protection ; but they avoided contact with the Indians. At Persepolis he had met the wise King of Bactria—father of Queen Nitôcris— himself perhaps a descendant from the great Zoröaster; a venerable sage who had put off the cares of state, and retired to a secluded valley, whence he gave laws to the Magi; but his subjects had usurped the power of the state, and against his wishes had invaded Babylonia—nevertheless he aided the Aryan King Yûdishtir. With him the Pandau much conversed on high questions of religion, and he it was who first contended that beyond the two antagonistic principles of good and evil—Oramasdes and Ahrimanius—was one Supreme Being, existent from all eternity. This doctrine, no doubt, had penetrated into Egypt and Assyria before the time of which we treat. He accompanied the Pandau King as far as Olan-Robât and the lands of the Affshineh—"children of lamentation."

On Yûdishtir's departure, the venerable white-haired prophet stood on the summit of the Bactrian hill, the rising sun lighting his snowy garments,—he exclaimed: "I bless "thee, oh my son, oh melancholy Pandau ; but I greatly fear "for thee! Avoid, oh Kheátriya, vain imaginings and pain- "ful thought. Trust to Ahûra-Mazda, and especially that "Great One I have told thee of, and leave the ordering of "Nature to their rule; obey thou the law, and love thy people, "and do good, and be blessed!" He raised his arms aloft and invoked the rising Sun—emblem of life and happiness. His image was impressed on the King's mind as he rode off that sultry dawn across the mountain, and the memory of his sacred figure as he stood in the sunbeam, remained with Yûdishtir for all the years of his sad and varied life.

At Andaca Yûdishtir met his brother, Arjûna "of the sounding bow," who had hastened even from the wilds of Kamroop and far Kathaya, to greet the royal pilgrim returned to his kingdom after long wanderings ; and at Torbela also his brother Sediva with the Prince of Káshmir presented themselves to their Sovereign the King of India.

* * * * * *

For many days did the Pandau brethren travel through the lakes and reedy marishes of the Cophes river to Taxila, Naulibe, and Nicæa,* cities of the Katti. Here they hunted the great river-horse, the hippopotamos of the northern Punjaub.† They skirted the mountains of Caspira and the Kaspatyri, until at length the camp of the Pandaus was pitched one summer day in a grove on the banks of Manásir

---

* The site of Alexander's battle with Porus on the Jhelum.

† Baber, writing early in the 16th century, mentions in his autobiography that as late as his time the hippopotamos existed in the rivers and marshes of the Upper Punjaub.

—that very lake where Yûdishtír had first encountered the Scarlet Fury, who had ever since dogged his errant life.

That night the royal Pandau sate in his tent alone. All had gone well with him; nevertheless, sad was his heart; the prey of melancholy and disappointment: how short of his high desire and hopes had been his pilgrimage after Truth and Wisdom!

Standing in a dark fir grove, before the symbol of the "Tree and Serpent," behold the Scarlet Fury—with her a companion elf.   *   *   Silently she crept along the margin of the crimson waters of the Lall-Nág: she entered the Pandau's tent. Pointing her flame-tipped spear at Yûdishtír's heart, she spake:—"Thus, after long absence, we meet, oh King, in thy "native hills! Hast thou thought to disarm *envy*, and her "companion *slander*, by absence? Nay, oh Pandau! the "fame of thy thoughts has reached the land of Himôdi; máya "and the evil of glamour has clutched thee! All thy high "resolves and virtues, thoughts, and winged words, exist but "in thine own imagination; the world regards thee as lost in "máya; rememberest thou not?" The flame of the Fury's spear touched the breast of King Yûdishtír. "Ha! an aspic's bite."

The ecstatic mind of the King was aroused to madness; he grasped his spear like Saul of distant Israel: no music to assuage the bitter fury of his soul: no mortal at that moment could have met his gaze and lived!

"Ha! is it indeed so," he murmured: "is this the doom of "the searcher of truth, to be the prey of idle mirth and insincerity, "or else of envy and malign hatred? Are moral tortures to "be added to the sad doubts of the thinker? Is all but vanity, "and Krishna right? His creed 'In evil, good; in mirth "great wisdom?' He is plausible, and oft in his subtle speech "puts sophistry like truth. Behold his many orations, such "as the Vedas and great Vayâsa sing of. His metaphysics "plausible. Ha! to live like the hog Sardanapalus, or die in "veiled sorrow like Philoctétes!"*

_____

* The above involves an anachronism, and seems added by a later hand.

*   *   *   *   *   *

But still further trials awaited the King: the mirthful
Krishna had never quite abandoned his old foe, the Pandau
Thinker, and ever and anon had renewed his tricks at his
expense, as in the palace at Babylon, and now again behold
Krishna, and his band of gópies, leading the dance beneath
the merry moonlight!

"Hail! Yûdishtír; thou art one of us.   Let mirth and
"pleasure banish the melancholy wisdom of thy soul!   Be-
"come thou as Krishna, beholding the mirthful side of things,
"and the laughter-moving aspects of humanity, and the world
"of máya!   A mad, merry world, oh, wise one! oh, sad one!
"Come, I bestow on thee escape from the dire scarlet ones;
"the malignant sprites of envy and slander, and vain know-
"ledge.   Be merry, and be wiser still!"   *   *

The wild demi-god led the dance beneath the moon with his
gópies from the land of Bráj,   *   *   but Yûdishtír
recited the "mantra of escape" (of the head from sin) and
blew a sounding blast upon the sánk of Vishnoo, and, behold!
the crew of Krishna vanished like a dream: and instead the
glorified form of Sank Narrain, the Preserver, stood before
him in place of the laughing Krishna,—

"Dear Prince, I venerate thy virtue; but what better dur-
"ing the interval of thy brief life on earth than to snatch at
"sunbeams and bright duty?   Come, let me show thee the
"true delights of earth, and the visions of the future."

He took Yûdishtír by the hand, and led him within the
inner pavilion, and seated him on a lion's skin.   The lamps
grew pale; a sense of weariness and of intense drowsiness
overshadowed the King's senses—he seemed to fall asleep—
and a vision of radiant beauty and of goodness, and celestial
divination—it may not be told—was revealed to him. *   *

The vision roused him from himself, and inspired him with
love for the lower creatures of his race, and of the children of
mankind, as commanded by Oramasdes.   Illusion had fallen

from his mind: he gazed around: Narrain had vanished. He raised the canopy of his tent, and looked forth at the silent night and its myriad stars. The deep shadows of the fir grove fell across the mountain, but soon the advancing moonlight began to creep higher and higher up the forest which clothed its side, and fairy music and the soothing plash of waters from the tufted dells of the fir forest, lulled the Pandau's soul. As he stood observing the fair night scene, the fireflies —like myriad sparks of fire—were hovering in the pellucid air of night. Every bush and leaf and tree lit with its fairy lamp; a few hovering o'er the dark waters of the lake, presented to his mind an image of his own bright spirit hovering o'er the dark waters of doubt and sorrow.—" It was a dream," quoth Yûdishtír, "or perhaps the poppy of Kâmput was too "powerful." So saying, the King raised the curtain of his tent and disappeared from view. *   *   *   *

But the soul of the great Pandau was kindled by the visions he had beheld; all next day he paced the grove before his tent in agonies of thought.

*   *   *   *   *   *

At the same hour the following night did King Yûdishtír again gaze forth from his tent on the silent night. A thunderstorm, succeeded by crimson sunset, had swept the heavens. In the cloudless East the full moon rose slowly; the air pellucid, the stars glittering in fresh glory; not a breath of wind; all still. The sigh of the summer woods only broken by the note of the distant bell-bird in the deep forest. Yûdishtír listened with softened heart to its melancholy cry—

"The viewless atoms of the air
"Around me palpitate and burn,
"All heaven dissolves in gold, and earth
"Quivers with new found joy.
"Floating on waves of harmony I hear
"A stir of kisses, and a sweep of wings;
"Mine eyelids close." What pageant nears?
'Tis Love that passes bye!

*   *   *   *   *   *

Yûdishtír's mournful heart was softened, and he felt an intense desire for sympathy and love. "Ah! for some dear "companion to cheer my solitary heart, and help me to rule "my people with love and wisdom! Is there none of all the "friends Yûdishtír has solaced and benefitted to cheer him "now?" A sigh was wafted on his ear; he raised his head: behold the figure of a warrior maiden clad in white—in pure white armour—met his gaze, who, raising her veil, disclosed the loving eyes of Iönis, filled with tender light and pity for the melancholy King.

"At last," she murmured, as holding out her fair arms towards him she fell upon his breast, and murmured on his bosom the happy sighs of love.

Yûdishtír soothed her agitation.

"Ah, dear one! did'st thou never suspect that it was Iönis "who led the troop of Persian horse which followed on thy "march, and escorted thee safely through the lands of the "Affshineh—children of lamentation? Nay, dear Prince! "the Persian men and women both are taught to be brave "and speak the truth, and desert not those they love. I obey "the request of my noble father, Arces, and of Zoröaster, the "great King of Bactria, who blessed thee at Persepolis; and "come to aid thee to rule thy kingdom with Truth and "wisdom!"

So Yûdishtír was comforted; and his kingly heart found rest and solace, and gained augmented strength from love!

*   *   *   *   *   *

[So ends this fragment of the travels of Yûdishtír.]

The following sequel has been added by a more recent hand.

King Yûdishtír had returned from the land of Assyria and Bactria, and had married the Princess Iönis, daughter of

Arces, Satrap of Persepolis. He mostly took council with his Queen and with his Pandau brethren—Arjûna "of the sounding bow," Sediva, from the land of Caspira, and Bhim-Sén, the aged war-chief. The King had cast many dark illusions from his mind, and his kingly heart impelled him to consider the welfare of his people, and of the busy world of men. Interest in his kingdom's welfare, and superintendence of the ruling mind, again occupied his attention; and plans for the good of his people predominated with the King, whose far-reaching mind foresaw and provided for the wants of all. The kingdom was at rest; the allies and tributaries faithful; and the foes afraid of the King of India. Soon afterwards he journeyed towards his capitol, Ajoodya (Oude).

*   *   *   *   *   *

Yûdishtír's return home may thus be paraphrased in the words of the Mâhâbârât :*—

" Thence fair Ayoodya's town he gained,
"And o'er his father's kingdom reigned ;
" Disease or famine ne'er oppress'd
" His happy people, richly blest
" With all the joys of ample wealth,
" Of sweet content, and perfect health.
" No widow mourned her well-loved mate,
" No sire his son's untimely fate:
" They feared not storm or robber's hand ;
" No fire or flood laid waste the land:
" The golden age seemed come again
" To bless the great Yûdishtír's reign."

Thus far we have traced the wanderings of the royal pil-grim, and have conducted him to his home at fair Ajoodya; but at last the melancholy inherent in the King's mikrocosm gained the mastery. Brave, beneficent, and wise, he had

---

* Translated by Ralph Griffiths, Esq., M.A., of Benares College.

reigned for the good of his people thirty years, for himself
and pleasure six.   Then the cry of the unsatisfied spirit arose
within his heart, "Oh virtue, art thou but a vain name?"
Having called his brethren and chiefs around him he resigned
the kingdom, and proceeding to the everlasting mountains of
Himôdi, there—amidst the evidence of glorified nature—took
up his abode.   Whether the light of Truth, that "inner sun" so
dwelt upon by the Indian mystics, arose to lighten his sad
and clouded mind, no man knoweth!   The King gave no
sign.   Let us hope, however, that some rays of comfort fell
on his kingly heart in his self-exiled solitude, and that the
hope of Nirvána—absorption into divinity—comforted his
noble spirit; else were human virtue fallacious, and justice,
generosity, and benevolence on earth a delusion and a snare.

Gautama the Bhooda, his descendant, discouraged at the
growing sin and errors of Brahminism, then declining from its
pristine virtue, had not yet arisen to preach the practice of
virtue for its own sake, and thus to purify men's hearts; yet
we seem to recognise in the character of Yûdishtir much of
the mystic self-communion and introspection which was more
fully developed in his great descendant Gautama—the " Light
of Asia"—for whose philosophy Brahminism was at the age
of Yûdishtir paving the way.   It had reached its epigee, and
was about to decline into priestcraft and superstition, and
absurd ceremonial, till a glorified materialism, such as indeed
is the Bhoodism of Gautama, the virtuous apostate, resulted
as a protest.

* *
*

One more scene in Yûdishtir's life, and we must leave him
to history :—

A multitude of mountain men and quarriers of stone were
carrying huge blocks of granite and stone, and slabs of slate,
hewn from the rocky top of Hattoo.   Cakes were broiling in

the giants' chulas (ovens) on the summit of the mountain amidst the pine trees. Already the distant walls of ancient "Pinjore" raised their turrets in the distant yellow haze, and its Cyclopian domes arose from the fragrant earth. The mighty torrent of the Hyphasis—river of Manasa-Râwa—from the snows of Kailâs roared through the dark glens of Keyonthâl and Kahloor.*

The Pandaus sat in council on Jâcâtâlâ,† and a great feast was appointed to conclude their meetings, and celebrate the completion of their work. Arjûna, Sediva, and Bhîma—great Krishna also, had condescended to attend the banquet. Two spare couches for the absent Pandaus—Bhimsén and Nizkool —were reserved on either side the royal table. Other tables were set for the courtiers, below the raised dais of the princes, in the hall of state. The jocund Krishna raised the shell. He spake: "A chaubisi‡ of libations to great Yûdishtír! Oh, "King, I know thy heart. The earthly Krishna has derided "and jested at thee; the heavenly Vishnoo has blessed thee, "and will still preserve! Be just; be merciful; and listen to "the sweet song of Vyâsa. Thus Vyâsa sang:—

"TRUE GLORY.

"To whom is glory justly due?
"To those who pride and hate subdue;
"Who, mid the joys that lure the sense
"Lead lives of holy abstinence;
"Who when reviled, their tongues restrain,
"And injured, injure not again;
"Who ask of none, but freely give,
"Most liberal to all that live;

---

* The chronicle seems vague hereabouts, but it is recorded that Pinjore was actually built by the Pandaus about this date. Bhimsen the second Pandau is specially named as being engaged in the work.

† The modern Simla.

‡ Chaubisi 12 × 7 = 84, the number of months in the year, multiplied by the number of days in the week, a mystic number.

"Who welcome to their homes the guest,
"And banish envy from their breast;
"With reverent study love to pore
"On precepts of our sacred lore;
"Who work not, speak not, think not sin,
"In body pure, and pure within;
"Whom avarice can ne'er mislead,
"To guilty thought or sinful deed;
"Whose fancy never seeks to roam
"From the dear wives who cheer their home;
"Whose hero souls cast fear away,
"When battling in a rightful fray;
"Who speak the truth with dying breath,
"Undaunted by approaching death;
"Their lives illumed with beacon light
"To guide their brother's steps aright;
"Who, loving all, to all endeared,
"Fearless of all, by none are feared;
"To whom the world, with all therein,
"Dear as themselves is more than kin;
"Who yield to others, wisely meek,
"The honours which they scorn to seek;
"Who toil that rage and hate may cease,
"And lure embittered foes to peace;
"Who serve their God, the laws obey,
"And earnest, faithful, work and pray;
"To these—the bounteous, pure, and true,
"Is highest glory justly due."*

Then Sediva took up the song. "Oh King, and dear
"brother, before I depart to my land of Kâshiapâ, hear the
"song which that Kokila—sweet bird of song—Valmiki sang
"to Ráma, our great ancestor—The Song of the Suppliant
"Dove." Again Vyâsa sang:—

From the Mahabarat (slightly altered); translated by Professor Ralph T. H.
Griffiths, M.A., Benares College.

"Chased by a hawk, there came a dove
"With worn and weary wing,
"And took her stand upon the hand
"Of Kasi's* noble king.

"The monarch smoothed her ruffled plumes,
"And laid her on his breast;
"And cried, 'No fear shall vex thee here,
"'Rest, pretty egg-born, rest!

"'Fair Kasi's realm is rich and wide,
"'With golden harvests gay;
"'But all that's mine will I resign
"'Ere I my guest betray!'

"But panting for his half-won spoil
"The hawk was close behind,
"And with wild eye, and eager cry,
"Came swooping down the wind.

"'This bird,' he cried, 'my destined prize,
"''Tis not for thee to shield,
"''Tis mine by right, and toilsome flight,
"'O'er hill and dale and field.

"'Hunger and thirst oppress me sore,
"'And I am faint with toil:
"'Thou should'st not stay a bird of prey
"'Who claims but rightful spoil.

"'They say thou art a glorious king,
"'And justice is thy care;
"'Then justly reign in thy domain,
"'Nor rob the birds of air!'

Then cried the king—
"'Mine oath forbids me to betray
"'My little twice-born guest;

* The modern Benares,

     "'See how she clings with trembling wings
     "'To her protector's breast!'
The hawk, replies—
     "'If such affection for the dove
     "'Thy pitying heart has stirred,
     "'Let thine own flesh my maw refresh.
     "'The falcon loves to feed on doves,
     "'And such is Heaven's decree.'
The King now offers himself for the Dove.
     " Hé carved the flesh from off his side,
     "And threw it in the scale;
     "And when alone was left the bone,
     " He threw himself therein.

      *   *   *   *

     "The blessed gods from every sphere,
     " By Indra led, came nigh;
     "While drum and flute, and shell and lute,
     "Made music in the sky.

     "They rained immortal chaplets down,
     " Which hands celestial twined,
     "And softly shed upon his head
     " Pure amrit, drink divine.

     "Then god and seraph, bard and nymph,
     " Their heavenly voices raised ;
     "And a glad throng, with dance and song,
     " The glorious monarch praised.

     " They set him on a golden car,
     "That blazed with many a gem ;
     " Then swiftly through the air they flew,
     "And bore him home with them.

     " Thus Kasi's lord by noble deed,
     " Won heaven and deathless fame.
     "And when the weak protection seek
     "From thee, do thou the same!"

*   *   *   *   *   *

But, behold! two monstrous forms—scarlet as fire—suddenly appear occupying the Pandaus' vacant seats. Astonishment and dismay fell on the royal circle ; but with a fearful shout the mighty Krishna—his figure changed into the glorified form of Sank Narrain, victorious over the "Dæmon of the Shell"—straight arose in his wrath visible to all. He spake: "Avaunt, oh, Furies of Mânásir : oh, envious ones ! Nar- "rain curses and will destroy the scarlet pests of earth—envy "and slander its attendant imp!"

He then delivered one of those moral and metaphysical dis-quisitions for which he is in history and poetry so remarkable.*

As he spake the Furies suddenly collapsed, and shrank to normal stature ; whereupon Krishna suddenly seized them in his grasp, and hurled them into the giants' chulas (ovens). A crimson glare illumined the forest. "Shabash! I score one "now, methinks, at last over these imps of Mânásir," re-marked the jocund Krishna. "Thus perish Envy and Slander "from the earth! Farewell, oh, Pandaus, and forget not "Vishnoo's parting blessing !"

A cloud enveloped him, and shrouded his radiant form as glorified from this his second "avatar," he rose above the mountain Hattoo on his eagle steed Garood ; and waving a last farewell to the Pandau brethren, floated far away across the mountain tops to the peaks of "Kailás"—the snowy Olympus of the Hindoos.

The Pandau company all arose: "Hail, oh bright one ; and farewell !" They performed the *saptopuddie*—the sacred dance—and sang the parting hymn to Vishnoo the Preserver, friend of the Pandau race.

---

* Vide the Mahabarat *passim* ; in which poem are interspersed—perhaps inter-polated by recent hands—strange metaphysical subtilties delivered by Krishna at the most incongruous times, even on the edge of battle. They form most remarkable episodes in the great Hindoo epic, and perhaps dstract from its unity and heroic character. The tricks of Krishna narrated in this story may perhaps be assigned to a certain jester or court buffoon of Yudishtir's suite,

*   *   *   *   *   *

The wandering Cimmerian who wrote of Sediva and the
"Fairy of the Fountain," roamed some moons later across
the waters of the swift-rolling Hyphasis, contemplated the
triform top of "Hattoo," and resting for refuge in a cavern,
whilst the hail rattled on the rocky summit of the mountain,
listened to the legends of the "Giants' Chulas" which loomed
across the valley before him, and weaved in outline this second
story of the ancient Pandaus—the weird Wanderings of
Yûdishtír, King of India.

[NOTE.—I would not be understood as wishing to scoff at
the Hindoo religion in its purity, but simply at a few of its
absurd interpretations by corrupt Brahmins of a later age,
whose priestcraft has obscured and brought into ridicule the
real moral excellence of many of its precepts. As regards
the enigmatical character of Krishna—the acknowledged exponent of Hindoo morality, and by many regarded as an
"avatar" or incarnation of Vishnoo the Preserver, and a
model hero—ample authority could be quoted for his merry
quips and pranks (e.g., the Prem Sagur passim). It will be
observed that, apart from a proclivity to the society of fair
milkmaids (gópies) — reprehensible no doubt — Krishna's
tricks are harmless in themselves, and generally conducive to
the benefit of their object. "Merry and wise" would seem to
have been the motto the hero adopted whilst in the flesh. He
is now supposed to be awaiting further avatar in "Kailas" or
"Swerga," an inferior heaven of Hindoo mythology, not
greatly differing from the Mahomedan Paradise. Happy may
he rest there till the crowing of the "Coq-Cigrues !"]

The Apotheosis of Krishna as Vishnoo.

(From a Native picture.)

⚜ The ✝ Regrets ✝ ⚜ of ⚜ Arjuna ∴ the ∴ Pandau ⚜

AN IDYL.

WE learn from the Mâhâbârât that the great battle of Korau-khét, between the Koraus and Pandaus for the throne of the kingdom whose capitol was at that period called "Hustinapoora," was fought on the great plain between the rivers Jumma and Sursootie near Thánesur, hence called Kúrûkshétra,—the plain of the Koraus. Chronologists have fixed the date at about March, 1367 B.C.

A few incidents of the great battle may be cursorily mentioned as a prelude to the following legend.

In the war between the kindred Koraus and Pandaus, the heroes on the side of the former were "Bhishtma," the aged general and commander-in-chief of the Korau host, and "Karma," "Kripa," "Ashwotlána," "Vikram," &c. On the other side "Bhîma" (the second Pandau) was commander-in-chief, and "Virta," Drapáda," "Purujit," and "Sharya," were heroes of the Pandaus in the great battle.

"Bhisthma" is represented as sounding the conch as challenge; then "Arjûna," the Pandau, answers, but on the eve of battle pauses and communes with "Krishna," who acts as his charioteer, upon which an extraordinary argument (as narrated in the Bhàgáva-Gita) ensues, and Bálárámá — brother of Krishna—is stated to have become so grief-stricken at this war of kindred as, soon after the commencement of the battle, to withdraw from the field and seek retirement from the world. The despondency of Arjûna, however, is overcome by the arguments of Krishna, and the battle commences.

F

The character of Arjûna is throughout represented in a very amiable light: he is mentioned as the friend and pupil of Krishna, by whose sister, Soobhádra, he had one son— Abimanya.

Arjúna's bow is named "Gandiva," and his conch or horn "Panchajanya"—being the tibia, or thigh-bone, of the giant Panchajána.

This preamble may perhaps serve to introduce us to the following legend or story of the hero Arjûna.

I.

AT eve, on the great day of Korau-Khét—6th Kartik K.Y. 2268—14th of March, 1367 B.C., being the seventeenth day of the great battle, "Arjûna of the sounding bow"—third of the Pandau brethren—having seen the battle won, rested on his spear at sunset. He summoned to his side three trusty chiefs:—"Oh, comrades of Arjûna," he exclaimed, "let us refrain from bowing before the King "Yûdishtír, my great brother, now victor of Hindosthán. "The battle is won! Let us depart hence, and swell not the "victor's triumph, achieved by us and the other valiant heroes. "We have saluted him victor, but the king will believe us "slain in the last great onset. Let us depart, and seek ad- "ventures in the sunny south; in that Kamroop—abode of "love—whose King fell by my hand in the battle of yesterday."

*   *   *   *   *   *

Ere the storms of the southwest had set in, or ere the rains of summer had began to deluge the fern-covered mountains of the South, the Pandau and his companions, journeying south-wards, had arrived at "Darjegling," that "bright spot" of the ancient Khâssia range which lies beneath the lofty wall of Thibet—the land of Bhóta under the giant peaks of Kanchan-jinga, of Gauri-Sankur, and of Deodunga. Thence they surveyed the glory of the Southern Himalayas. Range over

range of forest-covered mountain met their view; between
them green lovely valleys and mossy dells; trees of semi-
tropical character, tasselled with wavy orchids; gigantic tree
ferns and climbing arums; differing from the northern
mountains amidst which hitherto Arjûna had chiefly wandered.
Here were seen also lofty flowering trees, and shrubs and
wild flowers of varied hue, with orchids both dotting the herbage and hanging from the forest trees. Gay plumaged birds
and gorgeous butterflies—themselves like floating flowers—
flittering through the tufted groves, met their view on all sides.
The melody of falling waters fell on the ear with plashing
murmur, and the foam of rushing torrents glittered far below
them in the tufted valleys of the Teesta.

Et juxta scatet unda fugax de rupe supinâ.

"Here let us rest awhile," exclaimed Arjûna. "Here let
"us abide a space and learn the condition of mankind in this
"'bright spot;' whether haply in this paradise the Gods have
"granted to man content and happiness. Here let us rest our
"arms from the jarring clangor of war and the intrigues of the
"court and camp."

Burly indigenes approached, and pointed out the shrine of
the tutelary goddess—the Autochthon of these hills. So here
in the land of ferns and flowers, abode Arjûna and his companions for many moons.

*　　　*　　　*　　　*　　　*　　　*

Having hung his shield and sounding arms in the temple
of the goddess, Arjûna had adopted the garb of the simple
mountaineers: armed solely with the mountain staff and dirk,
he was wont to wander alone over these lovely hills, and thread
the mazes of the wild forests, and explore every nook of the
winding dells and flowery slopes which alternate with the fir
and cedar forests and pine-clad summits in these bright regions.
Soon, however, the summer rains set in, and the waters began
to pour down every rivulet, and cascades to gush from every
rocky ridge, and gleaming torrents to rush down the deep

glens between the mountain spurs which radiate from the
giant axis of Himâleh and Thibet.

The herbage and mosses of a humid climate rapidly clothed
the landscape, and ferns and lovely grasses waved their delicate
fronds across the margin of the waters. Fairyland, if any-
where on earth, is here! and the fervid soul of the Pandau
warrior soon caught inspiration from the spirits of the wilderness, and peopled the wild sylvan solitudes with fairy forms of ·
witchery and beauty.

Whether we are to accept his visions as realities, or as the
idyls of the imagination or of máya (heavenly illusion), we
must leave to the reader to determine ; are they not written in
the chronicles of the princes—the Sins and Penances of
Arjûna the Pandau !

Pass we on then through the preliminary steps of Arjûna's
life at the "bright spot," and proceed to narrate the first
adventure which led to the events recorded in the sequel of
this legend.

*   *   *   *   *   *

In a bright vista of the flowery woods dwelt an aged
hermit chief whose home was blessed with two fair children—
daughters of the varied type of the indigenes of these mountains. One, dark-eyed as the ebon-berries of the canthus, the
other fair and golden as the blooming spires of the clematis of
Kamroop. On a day in his lone wanderings, whilst the sun,
bursting through the mists, illumined the damp forest with
sudden glory, came Arjûna to the fern-clad flowery valley of
the chief—for chief of a wandering tribe was the hermit Olöaçhin. His fair daughters were wandering in the sunlight.
At first sight of Arjûna, like startled deer, bounded away
the damsels ; anon like deer, pausing to listen and gaze
from between the fern leaves, they began to consider that after
all the stranger was not so formidable as the fleet unicorn of
the steppes, or the mail-clad rhinoceros of the Bhâbur (Terai),
or the shaggy bear of the uplands which sometimes invaded

the forests. Soon the hermit appearing, welcomed the stranger, and appeased his daughters' fears. Fruits and the fermented millet were offered; and Arjûna related a fictitious tale of adventure and misfortune as his history. Tears fell from the soft brown eyes of Kalindra, the dark-eyed of the sisters, but smiles and sunny glances bestowed the sympathy and approval of the laughing eyes of Koreila, the younger of the fair sisters. Alas! which the lovelier? asked the eye of the Pandau of his heart! Meantime the sky gloomed over, and the rainful clouds of the south gathered over the mountain-tops. "Oh, courteous stranger!" cried Olöaçhin, "thread not the gloomy forest at this late hour; here rest "till the storm be passed, oh, wanderer from the north!"

So the Pandau stayed and brake bread and ate salt beneath the roof of Olöaçhin the hermit. Alas! for the broken vows; alas! for the hearts that love and break!   *   *   *
But the story of many moons must not be anticipated.

"Oh, son," cried Olöaçhin, "welcome art thou as the radi-
"ant arch which spans the valley of the Lachen when the
"stormy rains of the southwest recede, and the mists roll away
"from the snowy peaks of Donkria* and Nûbra,* and the
"bright face of Darjegling—heaven haunted—smiles amidst
"the clouds!"

But Arjûna departed ere nightfall, and slept not beneath the roof of Olöaçhin.

On the morrow, the subtle fairies who carry out the behests of Kâma (the Indian Cupid) planted the fiery seed of love in the heart of the Pandau warrior, and he loved Kalindra the soft-eyed and tender-hearted daughter of Olöaçhin the hermit; but Koreila, the fair-haired, loved the stranger who had sought her father's house ofttimes since the day when he first appeared to them in the forest amidst the fern-trees.

The rains still fell—the foliage still grew—and in flowery bowers hid the fairies of the dells. The trellised vines and

---

* Peaks of Kanchanjinga.

tasselled orchids hid the nymphs of the rushing streams, which
leapt in cascades over the rocks amid the wild flowers ; their
waters heard, but scarce seen amidst the foliage, were veiled
by lovely masses of ferns and grasses, and behind this leafy
ganzy screen the fair spirits of the summer waters sang, and
wove the songs of dreamland. "Art thou not one of us?"
they whispered, as Kalindra, the soft-eyed, passed along their
margin, and murmured love ; but to Koreila, the fair-haired,
the whispering näids of the waters sang not, only the spirits
who dance in the sunbeams and rainbows played in airy circles,
though invisible, around her sunny head.

*   *   *   *   *   *

So the birds sang, and the waters played, and the sunflies
flitted amidst the bowers of the land of ferns and flowers; and
Arjûna the Pandau loved, and was beloved by the fair
daughters of Olóachin the Hermit of the Lachen.

* * *

II.

IN these blooming pastures the simple people of the
mountain were wont to assemble on some pine-clad
summit to sing the songs of the forest and the mountain—the lives and loves of former times.   There the shepherds
and hunters would meet the fair ones of the valleys in some
moonlit grove or starry plateau, and dance and sing throughout the summer night.   To these gatherings would resort
Arjûna and his companions, and mix in the merry throng.
Thither also would repair Kalindra and her sister the bright,
laughter-loving Koreila—gems of the forest; and ofttimes
would Arjûna stroll beneath the stars, the love-warm breath
of the beautiful stirring his wavy locks, and the tresses of the
fair girls, caught by the soft summer wind, would float across
his face as he led them to the dance.   Then the fiery heart of
the Pandau kindled and he spake :—

"Oh, Kalindra! fair art thou, oh darling of the south!
" Wilt thou be the bride of the stranger, and live like the fairy
"forms we know of in the bowers of roses and scented braes of
" Kamroop? Be thou my love and spouse ! "

Kalindra answered not, but throwing back her head glanced
at him with love-lighted eyes. So those two became lovers,
and met in the dewy eve and starry night, and their souls became as one.

But soon Arjûna wandered in search of varied beauty by the
crystal waters of Rungeet and the verdant banks of the snow-
green Teesta. He had gazed on the roseate tints of the sun
setting over the peaks of Kanchanjinga; had viewed the
mossy forest glades and valleys of the Brahmaputra—God-
descended—even as far as Kamroop—abode of love—and the
moonlit caverns of Drâpâdârâ ; and the mystic city Alaka—
city of the blest—had glittered on the inner sun of the
Pandau's heart; but always he returned to the abodes of men,
and the loving Kalindra and the fair Koreila welcomed the
wandering hero to their home.

" When, oh rash one! wilt thou rest and enjoy sweet repose
"and the love of thy fair spouses?" And Arjûna soothed their
fair tresses, and whispered love, and for a space was silent, and
dwelt in love and the warmth of friendship whilst the snows
of the north rained on the "land of ferns and flowers," and
the "bright spot" was involved in cloud, and the wind howled
through the arches of the forest, and the withered orchids and
arums waved and flaunted in the wind like the rent flags and
streamers of the great day of battle of Korau-khét! Warm
in the beauty of youth abode the chief, and repented not of
his absent home.—Arjûna was content in the smiles of beauty.

Thus Arjûna sang:—

THE SONG OF ARJUNA.

" There by the mountain claspt in loving arms
"Alaka, city of the blessed, lies :
" Her bright feet bathed in Gunga's flood, she charms

" With marvellous beauty e'en immortal eyes.
" Thou too, free rover, shalt her beauty prize,
"And often wander to mine own dear town !
" Nor shall sweet Alaka thy love dispise,
" But proudly wear upon her domes a crown
" Of the pure drops of pearl thou pourest softly down.
"And she has charms which nought but thine excel ;
" High as thyself her airy turrets soar,

   *   *   *   *

"And for thy lightnings in the midnight air,
" Look in the maiden's eyes and own a rival there.

"Unmatched is she for lovely girls who learn
" To choose the flowers that suit them best, and bring
" The varied treasures of each month in turn
" To aid those charms which need no heightening:
" The amaranth, bright glory of the spring ;
" The lotus gathered from the summer flood ;
"Acacias, taught around their brows to cling ;
"And jasmine's fragrant white, their locks to stud ;
"And, bursting at the rain, the young kadumba bud.

   *   *   *   *

" The tell-tale sunbeam of the morning throws
" Upon the path each roving beauty chose,
" Falls on some faded flower, some loosened zone,
"A withered lotus or a dying rose ;
"A bracelet which her haste forgot to close,
" Here a dropt diadem of orient pearl,
" The fond impatience of its mistress shows ;
"And here the jasmine bud that deckt the curl,
" Lying upon the grass, betrays the amorous girl.

" O beauties, worthy of that beauteous place,
" That sweetest city which I know so well,
" Where mine own brethren of ethereal race,
" Blest with the love of those fair angels dwell,
" In homes too beautiful for tongue to tell !
" Those homes by night a starry radiance fills
" Shot from the jewelled flames where breathe the smell
" Of roses, and, while melting music thrills,
" They quaff the precious wine the heavenly tree distils.*

---

* From the "Messenger Cloud" of Kalidasa, translated by R. T. H. Griffiths, Esq.,
M.A., Principal of the Benares College.

Such was the song of Arjúna which he sang to the assembled
warriors and nymphs on the mountain-top, beneath the canopy
of cedar, in the starlit grove of Darjegling.

But alas for the errant heart of man! The soul of the
Pandau, after a time, began to chafe under the inaction of
soft delights. "Shall the warrior's spirit thus succumb, and
"be lost in sloth? Shall he who stood in arms for great
"Yûdishtír, beside the war-chief Bhîma, thus yield to silly
"damsels of the mountain? Mayhap Yûdishtír dies or wan-
"ders from his throne—he was ever sad and errant!—who,
"then, but Arjúna to rule the mighty kingdom of Hindosthán?
"The helmet, sword, and bow, rather than the flowery chaplets
"best become the brows of the Khsátriya chief!" Thus
would the Pandau sometimes murmur to his inner soul: but
Kalindra, enlightened by love, had art to penetrate the latent
sadness of his soul, and by soft caresses and endearing charms
still kept the hero to her side; yet ever and anon he chafed
his rosy chains, and his mood was such that any predominant
event might snap them. Ere the rains of the ensuing spring
had revived the blossoms of the flowery forests, this event was
suddenly supplied, through the arts of the evil races who dwell
in the wilderness of Himôdi, amidst the sounding avalanches
and glaciers of the regions of ice and snow which surround
the desolate lakes, whence issue the cold waters of the Lâchen
and Lâchoong, in the wilderness of Bhôt.

* *
*

III.

THE evil races who dwelt in the icy caverns amidst the
dark mountains and glaciers, which involve the sources
of the dark green Teesta, had seen the loves of the
Pandau and his mountain maids. Envy, the curse of the pro-
fane and evil races, sprouted in their hearts, and filled them

with rage and hatred : especially Lambrôn, who dwelt in the
path of the icy north wind, aroused his troubled spirit for
mischief. Calling around him his companions, he exclaimed :
"See ye, oh Nâga-born! this wanderer from the north hath
"gained the love of the fair mountain maids! Is the Lunar
"race of mortals (Pandaus) for ever thus to gain happiness
"on earth, whilst the great primæval serpent-race repines and
"languishes in gloomy forests and caverns of the icy wilder-
"ness? Shall not the ancestral hatred of our race to theirs
"be still predominant? Say, shall this Pandau mortal be
"suffered to enjoy soft delights uninterrupted by our spells?
"Haste, oh Sprites! and having invoked Nârok and Sib, the
"great Autochthenes of these mountains, devise some spell
"whereby the accursed strangers may feel the power of our
"great primæval race—the vengeance of the Nâga demi-gods !"
    A council of the Evil Spirits and Ráchshásas of the wild
Bhût mountains is held : a dire resolve of vengeance is taken ;
and plans for the destruction of Arjûna and chiefs resolved on.
    Forthwith—like fiery blood-red serpents—the wicked sprites
or sorceresses issue forth from the icy wilderness of Chúmul-
hári. On their errand of mischief they wind down through
the icy chasms and gorges of the Lachen towards the Teesta.
They emerge from the Cachâr belt of dark forest which clothes
the lofty ranges below the peaks of Himôdi. Arrived at the
swollen waters of Teesta they plunge in. Lo, a herd of swine !—
like black informed imposthumes, on touching water, appear
the foul sorceresses of the Nâga-born! Arrived at the hither
bank they assume the forms of fair girls, and ascend to the
"bright spot," where they present themselves at the dances
of the mountaineers frequented by Arjûna and his comrades,
and mix in the mazy throng. They lavish their witcheries
on Arjûna and the other chiefs.
    "Ah! give us souls," they cried, "like Kalindra and Ko-
"reila," and turned their eager black eyes on the Pandau and
his friends. Guarded by love, great Arjûna resists their

blandishments; but the other chiefs, not so fortunate in love, gaze on the false fair forms of the Nâga sorceresses. The Indian Anteros pervades their souls. Circe-like the foul fair sprites assert their predominance, and the degradation of the Pandau's followers is achieved.   *   *   *   *

But the subtle fire which visits the brain of Arjûna—heaven-descended—detects the delusive aspects. "I am weak "in love; but say, oh Kâma," he cries, "doth not the immortal "spark inherited from my bright ancestors give me power to "distinguish good from evil—aye, often good *in* evil, and evil "in apparent good? The pure soul, though errant, detects "the star of truth! How else regard the gambols of my "cousin Krishna, else so wilful! To the uninitiated, sinful; to "the bright soul-bestower of happiness, virtue! But this is a "mystery! Enough! Tell me not my love of the fair Kal-"indra, which guards me from such as these is sinful in the "sight of Indra and the heavenly choir!"

Thus mused the hero to his inner spirit, but earthly passion for the beautiful had dimmed his ken, and máya, or heavenly-illusion, fell on him too, and obscured his radiant soul!

  *   *   *   *   *   *

One day Koreila came to him in tears. "Alas, my brother!" she said, "thy dear Kalindra hath departed for the north; for "the cold waters of Llama-zeroo, where indeed is the home of "my father Olöaçhin. Thither hath he taken thy spouse to "wed her to the chief of Undes." She spake in guile: Kalindra was simply ill, fevered with the changing seasons; but Koreila loved the stranger, and wished to lure him for herself. "Shall we not also love, oh dear one of my heart?" sighed the sunny-haired maiden; "when my melancholy sister leaves "thee for another?"

The Pandau stood astonished. He had been some time

---

* Arjuna was a pupil of Krishna, and evidently imbued with the peculiar philosophy of the demi-god, whose metaphysics are before the world in the Mahabarat, where they may be consulted in the original.

absent on a journey, and had not seen Kalindra, nor heard of her illness. "Doth she willingly consent to wed the chief?" asked he of Koreila.

"Alas! yes," sighed the false maiden. "Oh, dear prince, "forget her. My affection shall console thee. My love shall "make thee forget her fickle heart. Let us, too, love in the "sweet spring season and be happy."

Arjûna sighed, and turned aside towards the yellow sunset. Alone, he stood in the silent shadow of the pines beneath the tearful clouds, whose misty shadows dimmed the mountain. "Inconstant like the moon, which lasts but for a month, and "then veils her lovely face behind the canopy of heaven. Alas! "Kalindra; I thought Thou at least wert constant, and the "light Koreila heartless. How different the truth!" He sought his couch as the moon rose dim and tearful over the cedar tops.

*   *   *   *   *   *

From that sad eve Arjûna sought Koreila alone; and the fair maiden—false to sister and friends—at length fled with the Pandau from her native mountains towards the seaboard of Ophir and the isles—land of merchandise and wealth.

* *
*

IV.

𝕿HE Pandau and his false enchantress had wandered to Kamroop and far Cathay—even to Taprobane and the islands—thence to the north-west; had met the great Yûdishtír on his return from the land of Assyria; and had journeyed with him to Ajoodya and Kumäon—land of the tortoise. Here he parted from the regal court, and left the king engaged in the active ruling of his kingdom, having recovered from the delusions and máya of his earlier years. Just, beneficent, and wise, the reign of the great Yûdishtír promised to be long and happy.

What else remained for Arjûna and his spouse but to return
to the sunny home of Koreila, amidst the ferns and flowers of
the fair south mountains? Moreover the heart of the Pandau
was moved by words of war, and danger to his friends and
people. The Nâgas—evil races of the snows—had descended
in force upon the hills of Darjegling—the bright spot—and
had proved too strong for the simple mountaineers of those
regions; though aided by their Pandau allies—the followers
of Arjûna. Urgent appeals for aid had reached the chief.
Arjûna spake:—"With Krishna's aid how easy to defeat
"them! but, alas! the merry champion hath sought Kailas!
"(the Olympus of Hindoos). Ah! mayhap the great Yû-
"dishtír will trust me with his sánk or horn to summon the
"warlike host of Vishnoo to our aid!" He sought the King
of India, and Yûdishtír accorded the boon of his desire. So
Arjûna journeyed with his fair false spouse Koreila toward
the southern mountains. Arrived there, he joined his powers
in arms. United with the friendly indigenes, they marched
into the land of Maimona and Tendong, and there found the
Nâga host drawn up grim and defiant along the banks of
Teesta,—Rachshásas and Yakkas, their allies, swarming on
the surrounding mountains beneath the snow. As the
Pandaus approached, these last hurled down rocks and vast
fragments of ice, which, splintering on the rocks, went thundering down the sides of the mountain, overthrowing many in
their course. A war of the Titan races seemed at hand!

The night fell dark, and the damp mists filled the forest.
The gibbous moon, whose sickly beams hung o'er the dark
and melancholy waves of Teesta, and the watchfires of the
contending hosts gleamed red and lurid on the snow-fringed
forests and haunted shades around.

In a hollow of the mountains, amidst the pine trees,
Olöaçhin the hermit-chief and his tribe, were camped, as allies
of the Pandaus. The Prince Arjûna, on the eve of battle,
sought the chieftain's camp. "I come, oh Olöaçhin, to de-

"mand the sign of peace. Wherefore, oh deceitful one, hast
"thou rent from me my Kaliudra, and wedded her to the chief
"of Chûmbi, our great foe?"

Olöaçhin started. "Alas! what sayest thou? oh Prince
"Arjûna, for at length I know thy rank and name, hast thou
"not forsaken my fair child Kalindra, and fled with her false
"sister, oh wicked one, oh inconstant one? Nay, thou shalt
"see Kalindra at dawn of day, and learn from her the truth."

Astonishment fell on the Pandau's heart. He paused, and
deeply meditating, sat beneath a giant pine tree awaiting dawn.
At length the yellow sun struggled through the mountain
mists, and revealed the armies of the Pandaus and the Nâgas
joining battle. Arjûna started to his feet. "The prince must
"not be late in battle; to *lead* his warriors is Arjûna's high
"behest. On sons of Khsatriyas!" he shouted, "on to the
"attack! Be brave, oh followers of the Pandau!" He
plunged into the rolling tide of Teesta, and attacked the foe.

*   *   *   *   *   *

Who shall tell of the fury of the battle between the warlike
Chandrabuns and the Dæmons and Nâgas of the snow?
Rocks, aud pine trees torn from the mountain side were hurled
adown the banks of Teesta, and deeds of fury and of magic,
not to be believed in days like these, were enacted in the dark
gorges of Bhôta. The battle fluctuated: the victory rolled
this way and that: at times the Pandaus forced back to
the river: anon a rally, and the stormy fight rolled upwards.
At midday the combat slackened; by mutual consent the tired
champions drew off a space to breathe.

Arjûna rested on his spear beneath a cedar; the flame of
battle waned a little in his soul. He recalled the words of
Olöaçhin, and thoughts of his beloved Kalindra stole into
his heart.

Suddenly she stood on the tufted slope beside him. "Ah,
"dear prince, I was faithful!" she exclaimed. "Behold the
"proof. The oracle hath said thou canst not win the fight.

"except a maiden sacrifice herself : I die for thee! Farewell!"

The maiden flung her arms aloft, and from a towering rock, whose dark cliff impended o'er the flood, like a wounded, stricken dove, fell fluttering into the abyss!

Motionless the Pandau stood, his arms extended towards the maiden of his love. Too late!

Koreila, in the shades of the forest, had been jealously watching the interview of her lover and sister; but now, suddenly struck with sorrow and remorse, she also—shrieking wildly—rushed from the shelter of the pine trees to the cliff whence Kalindra had fallen, and threw herself headlong into the waters of the rushing Teesta.

* * * * * *

Two streams now join the flood of Teesta at the point where the sisters fell. One, placid and murmuring over mossy beds, through scented, thickets, scarcely showing rare gleams of gently flowing water through the ferns and grasses of its marge; the other, turbulently rushing down its rocky bed within its storm-rent glen, its torrent broken by passionate, leaps over dark rocks and boulders; and finally, by one grand plunge, joining its sister stream at the deep green flood of Teesta. These streams are called respectively "Kalindra" and "Koreila," in memory of the sisters.

* * * * * *

Years afterwards a pious Jôgi was seen at the great temple of Kâma-káya in Kamroop, celebrated for his austerities and the severity of his penance. In form a noble-looking warrior, his face betrayed the melancholy of a great mind saddened by some sinister event, and the pilgrims who resorted to the shrine gazed on him with respect and pity.

At length, after many years, rumours came that the great King Yûdishtír had abdicated the throne and sought a hermit's cell in Himâlâya. Bhîma, the great war chief, was dead, and the nobles of the kingdom had sought in vain for Arjûna, the third Pandau, now heir to the throne of India.

Proclamation throughout the land was made, and the chiefs of the tributary kingdoms made search for the missing prince. At length the high-priest of Kâma-káya stood forth and summoned the people to the great temple. Advancing from the shrine he stood before the silent Jôgi and saluted. "Great "sir," he said, "behold thy people!" and to the crowd, "Oh "twice-born, behold your King, the long-lost Arjûna! Oh, "son," he resumed; "it is enough: thy penance hath redeemed "the errors of thy youth; and restored thy sad lost ones to "Nirvána (absorption), or at least to Swerga* (heaven): be- "hold the proof." He led the Pandau—for it was indeed Arjûna—within the temple, and there drawing aside a veil, Arjûna beheld the charming sisters reclining as in life in the Hindoo Paradise; and even as he gazed, immortal glory shone around them, and they gradually melted into rosy mist, and floated away to Kailas, the Olympus of Hindus.

So the heart of Arjûna was comforted, and he resumed his regal garb. Escorted by the chiefs, and followed by the acclamations of the people, he journeyed to Ajoodya—the royal city—and there ascended the throne of his ancestors.

*   *   *   *   *   *

The wandering Cimmerian who wrote the history of Sediva, and of Yûdishtír the Pandau, roamed down the valley of the dark rolling Teesta, and pacing on the sandy shore beside the whirlpool where the flashing clear waters of the Rungeet join the dark green flood of Teesta, wove this strain of the loves and fate of Arjûna and his two fair spouses, sisters of Kamroop.

---

* Swerga—the inferior heaven of Hindoos—a qualified paradise corresponding in some degree to the Mahomedan paradise.

*   *
*

Incremation of an Indian Raja

NOTE.—This scene actually represents the incremation of Thakoor Sing; last Raja of Kûlû, as witnessed by the Author at the Confluence of the two Rivers Beas and Parbuttie, on the 9th July, 1852.

✠ Bhima, ✝ "The ✝ War-chief." ✠

A RHAPSODY.

I.

WHAT, and how great, were the deeds of Bhîma the War-chief, the leader of the Pandau host on the field of Korau-Khét, in the Land of Brâj, previous to the great battle—are they not written in the Bhágavád-Gita and in the chronicles of the Mâbâbârât?

Here we will relate the adventures of the hero in Mâhârâshtrâ and the land of Hanumân, whilst in exile with his brethren, before he came to Kumäon—land of the tortoise—and to Mahendra in the mountains of Himôdi—abode of snow.

In rank second only to the great Yûdishtír, the soul of Bhîma had ever gloried in deeds of arms: he sought the society of heroes and champions such as Arjûna his great brother, and other warlike chiefs. Driven into exile by the adverse verdict of the dice,* he had collected a band of warlike Pandaus, sworn to the expulsion of the Koraus, and to the conquest of Giants (Dévs) and Ráchshasas (evil spirits) who at that time harried the Land of Snow, and had even descended as far as Káli-Kumäon and the lowlands of Brahmadeo in the plains of Hindosthán. They constituted themselves also champions and custodians of the sacred places in the lands of the Holy Gunga (Ganges); of Ootéra-khoond, and Kailás, the makrocosm of Hindoos; and of Mahendra, the axis of Himôdi in the land of snow.

But first Bhîma dwelt in Mâhârâshtrâ, in the wild Sahyâdri Mountains which bound the vale of Waee, where the hill of Pandoghur still bears the name of the errant chiefs, and where the heroes are still worshipped as ancestors in its temples.

---

* See page 17 "Yudishtir.'   G

In the land where, ages after, great Sivajee the "Mountain Rat," led his brave Mahrattas to regain their freedom, where black basalt and red laterite cliffs crop out amidst the forests of Sahyâdri and Mâhârâshtrâ like giant pyramids athwart the deep blue sky, the Pandau brethren dwelt, and brooded on the coming day which should restore their broken fortunes.

From Máhábuléshwár—great mountain of strength and power—Bhîma looked forth over the black waters of the western ocean, then just beginning to darken under the blast of the approaching monsoon, and pondered many things; and his soul kindled as he recalled to mind that the time approached in which it behoved the five Pandau brethren to return from exile and assert their rights in face of the usurping Koraus.

On his return to his castle-home one eve, the chief found awaiting him a messenger from the great Yûdishtîr, his elder brother, exhorting him to repair to the hills of Kumäon, there to levy war to meet the foe after eighteen moons had sped. Whereupon he called his Pandau brethren, who dwelt with him, and consulted also the chiefs who had followed his fortunes in exile, and they had said—"First let us consult the "champion Krishna, who haunts the banks of his loved "Yamúna, but visits also the valleys of the Godáveri and "Kishtna, which rush forth from the western mountains of "Inyádri and Sáhyádri hereabouts."   *   *   *

At the Pussurni defile Krishna led the dance, in the beauti- ful vale of Waee, his temporary abode, and soon the hero Bhîma found the merry champion. He spake—"I say not "brave Bhîma, that I will assist Yûdishtîr, thy melancholy "brother, for Krishna loves not sorrow and needless gloom. " Seek thou first my friend and pupil, thy brother, the valiant "Arjûna, and Sediva his friend. Who knows? he may per- " suade me to join thy host in arms.   But first go thou forth "through the forests of Nerbudda and of Omerkántuk.   To " the south thou wilt find great Hanumân and the Vânapûtras "—children of the forest.   Seek thou the advice and the " alliance of great Hanumân, the friend of Ráma!"

II.

IN the wild forests which clothe the banks of the sacred Godáveri—holiest of rivers*—southward of Goondwâna, in the densest shades, dwelt the Vânapûtras—children of the woods—Bheels, Goonds, or Sánthâls. Of these wild tribes great Hanumân was King. Whether *He*, the ally of Râma—since worshipped as the Monkey-Deity—or his descendant the legend telleth not ; though a demi-god may well be credited with longevity, and have lived the ten generations since great Râma lived on earth. Be it so : what then? An aged warrior chief, whose age exceeded that of man, and who had fought in the wars of Lankapoora and Singhála, centuries before the epoch of Yûdishtír, still lived on earth. Therefore the war-chief Bhîma sought his aged kinsman in the deep forest solitudes, where he dwelt, to consult him as to the forthcoming war against the Koraus. The aged chieftain's country extended from the wild west mountains of Súgriva and Carnâtâ, even to Omerkântuk and the eastern mountains of Vindhya, of Seöni and of Goomeh. Originally Commander-in-chief of the armies of the Toombûdrâ and of Carnâtâ, since the war great Hanumân had seized the kingdom, and, establishing a sylvan monarchy, now ruled the wild tribes of the south from sea to sea.

In a remote tangle of hills his stronghold reared its turrets above the forest ; the approaches, unknown save to the sons of the wilderness who served the chief, were guarded by fierce Vânapûtras—called like their chief also Hanumâns—monkeys of the wilderness ; such as they doubtless seemed to their more civilized allies, the proud and high-born Rajpoots of the north, descended from the Sun and Moon : but ever unsubdued, these children of the forest, and a terror both to friend and foe!

---

* See foot note page 100.

Arrived at Omerkântuk, great Bhîma paused, set up his tent, and sought an oracle from the shrine of the Dúrga on its summit. The goddess spake—"O Pandau! advance on the "meridian of Oojein 45 koss s.w., till Canopus gleams at sun- "set over the lofty sandal tree which impends over the sacred "stream of Mahanuddie: thence turn west, and take thy bow; "discharge three arrows successively over the lofty tree with "thine utmost strength, oh Vrikódâm,* and on the spot where "the furthest falls, seek further guidance to the presence of "great Hanumân."

The chief advanced according to the oracle, and on the third day at even found the omens good. Arrived, he drew the bow, and the arrows whistled through the leaves of the sacred neem-tree. Lost to sight in air the arrows sped, and each fell ten furlongs beyond the last, two koss within the forest shades. To this day the Pandau's bow-shot is shewn to the sons of the stranger who visit those deep shades. As the last arrow fell a wild and sudden yell broke the stillness of the forest, and presently three fierce men of the woods (called also Hanumâns) bounded into the glade where Bhîma stood. Prostrate they fell before him, their heads on Bhîma's feet. "Great sir, behold thy slaves; the servants of great Hanumân, "who sends thee greeting. Oh, Pandau, deign to follow! "follow!! follow!!!" They waited not for reply, but bounding into the thicket, presently returned with several hundred other apes—the sons of Vânapûtras—who, escorting Bhîma and his chiefs, and the ten picked followers who accompanied him, they bore him through the forest several koss till night fell dark on the earth. The moon had risen, and just showed the path beneath the gloomy arches of the forest: a flare of fire suddenly lighted up the dark background of trees, and showed the sylvan camp of the Vânapûtra King. Hanumân himself, arrayed in armour, stood alone in the crimson torchlight.

The Pandau advanced, and would have performed the genu-

---

* A name of Bhîma, signifying "great eater."

flexion due to ancestors—for Hanumân had been allied in war,
and even by a maiden given in marriage, to great Râma—but
the jungle chief embraced the Pandau and sate him by his
side on ebon chairs before the fire, and called for food and for
the juice of forest fruit, and soon made merry with his guest,
and called his wives and children and kinsfolk of the clan to
the feast, and spake no word of war or of wisdom till the morrow's sun lighted up the forest glades and meres.

As the sun arose next morn, great Bhîma sang the hymn
to Súrya (the Sun)—the "mystic orb triform"—to Lakshmi,
to Bhavâni the terrible, and to great Dúrga. Thus he sang:*—
To Súrya—
      " Fountain of living light
      " That o'er all nature streams
      " Of this vast mikrocosm, nerve and soul,
      " Whose swift and subtle beams
      " Eluding mortal sight,
      " Pervade, attend, sustain th' effulgent whole.
      " Unite, impel, dilate, calcine.
      " Oh Sun, thy power I sing.   *   *   *"
To Lakshmi—
      " Daughter of ocean and primæval night,
      " Who fed with moonbeams dropping silver dew,
      " And cradled in a wild wave's dancing light,
      " Saw'st with a smile new spheres and creatures new!
      " Thee, Goddess, I salute.   *   *   *"
To Bhavâni—
      " When time was drowned in sacred sleep
      " And raven darkness brooded o'er the deep.
      " The darter of the swift blue bolt I sing,
      " Till vanquished Assurs felt avenging pains."
To Dúrga—
      " O Dúrga! thou has deigned to shield
      " Man's feeble virtue with celestial night;
      " Sliding from your jasper field,
      " And on a lion borne hast braved the fight;
      " For when the dæmon Vice thy realms defied,

---

* These verses are from various Vedas, and form part of the Upanishads or Sacred
Hymns of the Hindoos. They have been partly translated into verse by Sir William
Jones and other oriental scholars.

"And, armed with death and arched bow,
"Thy golden lance, O goddess mountain-born,
"Touched but the Pest—he roared and died."

To Kartikáya—great god of war—Bhîma sacrificed a ram,
and to his followers gave of the sacred flesh.

But see! King Hanumân in state approaches from the deep
forest glade, where he had rested, and salutes great Bhîma.

"Hail, Vrikódâm! Now, O Pandau! Thou shalt view an
"exemplar of war, such as thou camest to learn, O war chief!
"Note it well, for the wise have said; the salutary counsels
"of Vishnu-Sárman* have declared 'Let the lion smell blood
"and he will know its taste;' 'Take the camel to the brook and
"'he will quaff enough for seven days.' And again hath Sár-
"'man said: 'Six faults ought to be avoided by the man seeking
"'success in this world—sleep, sloth, fear, anger, laziness, pro-
"'lixity.' And again: 'As frogs to the pool, as birds to the full
"'lake, so wealth and wisdom cometh to the active man!' and
"O Bhîma, I, Hanumân, have said. In knowledge of war, take
"lessons from the beasts of earth and birds of. air and creatures
"of the forest. Behold my servants advance to the review
"and to salute the morn. Observe around the forest edge an
"army of great apes—the sons of Hanumâns of the great
"Vânapûtra host who fought at Lanka; and in the mere and
"fens observe a vast array of cranes, with swans their allies,
"are marshalled under their King Hiranya-Gerbha. Oh Pan-
"dau, behold the attack and defence of the warlike tribes of
"Carnâtâ, and from them take lessons."

The old King shouted to the apes : "Advance, oh Sons of
"the Forest, and storm the fens!" and to the cranes, "Oh,
"nephews of a flamingo, defend the islands of the lake, and
"show the stranger prince the stratagems of war!"

He waved his hand, and in a second the army of apes
bounded into the forest and vanished in the shades.

---

* The Author of The Hitopadesa.

Bhîma beheld them not, and thought them dispersed. "Oh, "King," he cried, "the Royal Koraus and Pandaus fight not "thus. With pomp and sounding arms, amidst the clash of "shields, the sons of Khsátriyas meet the foe; and chariots of "war and earth-shaking beasts, as elephants and horses, bear "the champions to the shock of war!"

"I know it well," replied the King. "Did I not see great "Râma, and his brother, brave Lutchman, lead his warlike "Chandrabuns in arms to Serindip? but not thus do Vâna- "pûtras fight. Behold!"

Bhîma gazed towards the lake, and presently beheld dark forms like serpents gliding through the sedges, concealed by bush and sedge and tufted marish-grasses, but ever creeping toward the foe, themselves unseen.

"Behold the attack!" cried Hanumân, as suddenly a flight of keen arrows sped silently across the waters of the jheel (lake-marsh) over the heads of the flamingoes and cranes, and quivered in the forest trees opposite, for it was but mimic war. These latter no sooner saw the apes approach the margin of the lake than—concentrated in the very centre almost beyond the reach of arrows—they suddenly rose in one vast flock, and spreading out in form of the letter V—Hiranya-Gerbha at the apex of the wedge—flew past in mid air, filling the heaven with their warlike cries.

"Now," cried Hanumân, "oh Pandau, note well their flight; "and take thy second lesson in warfare. Observe the wedge- "like flight of the army, its wings contracted or expanded as "desired by skilful Hiranya-Gerbha their leader. Remember "Thou thus to form and bend thy cohort either way in battle! "Those cranes know well the secret of advancing and retreat. "Behold Hiranya-Gerbha in the van; he bends his flight to "north, his flank augments to left to face the foe, his right "thrown back. Again he whirls to east; see, without confusion "he supports his centre, himself the pivot: again he wheels to "south and back upon his centre, and lengthens or shortens

"the flanks at his desire. Suddenly descending, he drops into
"the further mere, beyond the apes. Enough! let the conch
"sound the peace! My apes shall join the feast, and brave
"Hiranya-Gerbha and his flamingoes, swans, and cranes shall
"also taste of Hanumân's *largesse*."

Such was the review of the apes and cranes; and such the
lesson of war given by King Hanumân to his guest in the
forest of Goondwâna.

For three days did King Hanumân feast his warlike
guests, and much did the aged chief impart of wisdom, acquired by long experience. Full of wise words and proverbs
was the monkey-king; and weird wisdom distilled from his
lips as honey from the calix of the full cadumba flower.
Scarlet was his hue like the dhâk;* azure the colour of his
garments in honour of great Vishnoo! his arms a mace, a
sword, a shield, with greaves and head gear of iron-bronze.

"Oh, Vrikódâm!" said he in course of talk, "avoid thou
"flatterers; especially on the march. Remember the fate of
"the elephant Karpúra-Tilaka, and be wary on thy march
"against the foe!"

"How was that?" asked Bhîma.

"Thus," replied the King. "Karpúra-Tilaka was wander-
"ing near a lake; Dirgha-Ráva (long yell), a jackal, accosted
"him,—'O king, mighty art thou! let me be thy slave, and
"'guide thee, oh monarch of the forest, to the sweetest flowery
"'trees and cane.' The elephant felt flattered, and turned
"aside from his well known browsing track to follow the
"treacherous crafty one, and presently fell into a deep marsh
"from which he could not extricate himself. The jackal
"laughed 'Ah, fool!' cried he, seeing his victim was helplessly
"engulphed, 'now get out if you can. Perhaps you would like
"'to take hold of my tail with your trunk and rise up!' So
"saying, he left Karpúra-Tilaka in the mud, and ran off to
"call his comrades, who feasted on the body of the unfortunate

---

* Erythrina fulgens.

"elephant. The hunter, Bhavâni (terrible), however, avenged "the king of beasts, and slew twenty jackals with his arrows, "amongst them Dirgha-Ráva."

Bhîma asked : " Is it right to study warfare in the field or "in books, as the wise have commanded? "

The King replied—"Vishnu-Sárman hath said : 'Knowledge "'of arms and books conduce to reputation. The first is liable "'to ridicule in old age; the second is respected always:' "Again : 'As a young woman loves not to embrace the old "'husband, so Lakshmi (good fortune—success) loves not to "'embrace the inactive, the lazy, the fatalist, the coward.'"

" But, come, tell me, O Hanumân! thou who hast seen the "wars of great Râma and of Lutchman, what should the "leader do who wishes obedience?"

" Conquer himself!" replied the King, "and all will cheer-"fully obey him."

" Should he be bold or prudent?" enquired Bhîma.

The King replied : " He ought to fear danger only so long "as it is distant ; but when we see danger near we ought to "fight like ten thousand Ráchshasas (devils). He who re-"joices on a design that has not come to pass, will incur dis-"grace like Dirgha-Mukha (long bill) the crane."

" How was that? " enquired Bhîma.

"A wary goose whilst seeking for the new shoots of the "water lily at night, was for a moment deceived in a pool "which reflected the image of the stars in great number. "Again, in the daytime he would not bite the white water-lily "fearing it to be a star. Thus a person once afraid of decep-"tion and imaginary dangers, looks for evil in truth itself. "Hence I say anticipate not evils."

" Oh, Bhîma, fear not things unknown. Be not like Pinja-"láka, the lion, afraid of the lowing of an ox."

" How was that?" asked Bhîma.

"Listen," said Hanumân. "Sánjivaka, a bull, having be-"come lame, was abandoned by his master in passing through

"a forest. He there grew fat. In the same forest Pinja-lúka
"(the tawny one), a lion, was enjoying the sweets of authority
"acquired by his own arm. One day, tormented with thirst,
"he went to the bank of the Yamúna to drink. He there
"heard the lowing of the bull, a sound hitherto unheard by
"the lion. As soon as he heard it he retreated from the water
"without drinking, and stood musing in silence what it could
"be. In this position he was discovered by two jackals, Kera-
"taka and Damanaka, sons of his minister. 'See, our master
"'fears! let us leave his service. How much more should we
"'fear, who live by his prowess. The miseries of a dependant
"'are manifold :—for silence, he is reputed a fool ; if eloquent,
"'crazy or a prattler ; by patient submission, regarded as
"'timid ; if he cannot endure bad treatment he is considered
"'ill-bred ; sits he at your side, is called intrusive ; at a dis-
"'tance, diffident. Oh, brother, let us fly, and keep our yells
"'to ourselves.'" Hanumân added : "The jackal who fell
"into the indigo vat was worshipped for his blue colour till he
"yelled at night and was found out. And it has been said—
"an alligator, dangerous as he is, becomes powerless when he
"leaves the water : a lion that has left the forest will be the
"equal of jackals!"*

"Aree! wise art thou, oh King Hanumân! I thank thee
"for thy lessons of life and warfare. Now let me depart for
"the land of the tortoise (Kumäon), where the dæmons of the
"snow from distant Potyid (Tibet) are oppressing the lands
"of Mahendra and of Ootéra-khoond—heritage of Abimanya,
"son of great Arjûna, my brother, the sounder of the bow,
"and of his dear spouse Soobhâdra, sister of great Krishna.
"Who knows? maybe, the merry champion will bring powers
"from Dwâraka, his great city, as an ally. But, first, oh
"ancestor, bless my son, Ghâtotkatcha, that he may be pros-
"perous in the coming war."

The Monkey-Deity raised his war-club, and waved it three

---

* From the Hitopadesa, or "Counsels of the Wise" of Vishnu-Sarman.

times over the head of Bhîma and his son; "Be brave and
"prosper, oh sons of Pand! When I hear thou hast slain thine
"enemies the Ráchshasas I shall rejoice; but when I hear
"that great Douryodhána (Jirjoodeen) the Korau and his
"brethren have fallen by thy hand, I shall weep; for ye both
"are descended from great Râma, my ancient ally and chief.
"But such is the decree of fate, and of Bhôwáni. I have seen
"the omen. The gloomy visions of the future throw their dark
"shadows on my prophetic soul. I have seen amongst the
"dead the shadows of old Bhisthma and of Drôna, with Ac-
"thathána his son, and of Karna and Sahya;* and many more
"brave Koraus, and other chiefs must fall. Such is the omen
"of Parváti; and great Dúrga hath revealed it, and so it will
"be!—Enough! I have spoken! Hanumân hath said it!
"Now to the parting feast."

Seated around the watchfires, Hanumân, his wives, and
children, with their guests, drank cups of the red juice of the
hybiscus, and poured libations to the manes of ancestors and
other great ones. The dark forest glooms were lighted up
with crimson fires; torches of the aloe wood and the perfume
of sweet sandal wood scented the night air. The weird forms of
apes and of other sylvan creatures at times passed athwart the
glimpses of the firelight, and the leafy turrets of the dwelling
of King Hanumân nodded overhead. Long did Bhîma remember the parting feast of his friend the Monkey-Deity.
Merrily they quaffed the effervescent juices of the south; and
songs of war and mystery were chaunted to the night. Strange
cries of the forest at times interrupted the conversation, and
still King Hanumân sate on his ebon chair nodding sagely,
and quaffing strong wine; and ever and anon conveying wise
words and sayings of mystic import to Bhîma. He spake:
"A decrepid old man cannot enjoy the pleasures of life, as a

---

* These five chiefs all commanded the Koraus in succession in the great battle
of Korau-Khet, according to the Mahabarat, and were successively killed, mostly
by Bhima and his son.

"toothless dog only licks a bone with his tongue!" He glanced
at the canopy of stars. "Enough! 'tis past the dark depth of
"midnight, and by the dawn thou hast, oh friend, to part on
"thy behest."

At length he called for bétel (the signal for ending a feast).
"Behold the bétel : it hath thirteen virtues, oh, Pandau!—is
"pungent, bitter, spicy, sweet, an alterative, astringent, a car-
"minative, a destroyer of phlegm, a vermifuge, a sweetener of
"the breath, a remover of impurities, a kindler of the flame
"of love. Oh, friend, these thirteen properties of bétel are
"hard to be met with even in paradise. Om, om! May
"Vishnoo, and great Kartikáya bless and prosper thee!
"Farewell!"

Having thus dismissed his guests, Hanumân, his wives, and
clan arose, and soon vanished into the leafy shades.

All rose and sang the hymn to Vishnoo—"Om, om, máni
"padmi hôm!" Hail to the dweller in the lotus! Amen!!"

*   *
*

III.

IN the morning an army of apes stood ready to accompany
Bhîma and the Pandaus on the march as far as the
mountain Chitrakúta, near to the plunging waves of
Nerbudda, in the dominions of Chitra-Varna—King of Peacocks, and to Jambu-dwipa in the Vindhyas, sacred to Kartikáya (or Skanda) God of war, Rider of the peacock steed.
Here also was Ráma's Mountain, so famed in after ages in the
poem of the "Cloud Messenger," the sweet song of Kálidâsa.
Here dwelt the Yaksha—spirit-servant of Kuvéra, god of
wealth—who mourned his sad lot or penance to wander for
twelve months apart from his beloved spouse.

He had been the friend of Nakoula (or Nizkoola) the Pandau,
brother of Bhîma ; and blessing him, thus he sang:*—

* From the "Cloud Messenger" of Kalidasa, translated by R. T. H. Griffiths, M.A.

"May favouring gales thy airy course impel,
"And tuneful rain-birds shall thy way attend;
"A pomp of wreathing cranes thy state shall swell,
"On silver pinions rustling round their friend.
"From many a stream shall lordly swans ascend,
"When the glad thunder of thy voice they hear;
"And wild with joy, their eager course shall bend,
"To Mana's mountain lake still following near,
"Till high Kailâsa's peak, thy journey's end appear.
"Now with one brief adieu, one last embrace,
"Turn from this steep away,
"Where Râma's blessed feet once left their trace,
"Though my hot tears will mourn thy shortened stay."
    *   *   *   *

"Here bend a little from thy straight career;
"And though thou speedest on to northern skies,
"Turn and behold a wondrous sight, for near
"Thy path Oojein's* imperial domes arise;
"Should'st thou not see her women's glorious eyes
"That flash to love or kindle to disdain
"In fire that with the lightning splendor vies,
"Those looks that bind the heart as with a chain—
"Thy birth has been for nought, thy life is all in vain."
    *   *   *   *

"Now from the level of thine airy road
"Glide gently down, and amorously sink
"Upon Nervindhya's breast, who long has glowed
"With love of thee.
"She with the wild swans clamorous on thy brink,
"And their white wings around her for a zone,
"From thy soft pressure will not coyly shrink;
"Her trembling wavelets will her rapture own,
"And testify her love by every gesture shown.

"Sail on refresht, dear envoy, nor forget
"To look with pity upon Sindu. * * *"
    *   *   *   *

"By Wittabah! desist, O Assur! or tell thy tale to soft
"Nizkoola. Nay, gentle Yaksha ; tempt not with promises of

---

* The Awanti of the Mahabarat, whose King, Drapada, became an ally of the Pandaus, and was afterwards slain by Drona the Korau at the great battle.

"soft delight. My vows are paid to great Kartikáya (god of
"war). I haste to free Kailás from the grip of dæmons.
"When soft Nizkoola—youth of wavy hair—shall seek thy
"cavern, then counsel him to visit Oojein, and comfort those
"fair ones thou hast named. Besides, King Drapâda may
"accord his alliance to my brother.   Farewell to thee, O
"Assur, and to the sounding waters of Nerbudda! I go to
"seek the great peacock shrine of Kartikáya in the sacred
"groves of Maurbun. Farewell, O bright Ones! and forget
"not Bhîma the Pandau." He had said.

He mounted his steel-clamped ráth (or war car), and with
his son Ghâtotkatcha—called "Ráchshas of the terrible aspect,"
by Ditrâshtura—and followed by his chiefs on purple horses,
the warlike Pandau was driven by his charioteer, Gâvalgáni,
into dusty space across Seöni forest to the East.   *   *   *

"Thence to the temple of the mighty lord
"Whom Chandi loves, and all the world reveres;
"There for a moment shalt thou be adored
"By those who serve him when thy hues appear
"Like Siva's neck,* as though their god were near.
"Then through the garden pleasant gales shall stray
"From Gandhavâti's fountain, crystal clear,
"Bearing the scent of lotus-blooms away,
"Shaken by lovely girls who in the water play."

        *   *   *   *

"There gleams the temple loved and honoured most
"By Skanda, Lord of war, who at the head
"Of the bright legions of the heavenly host,
"Embattled gods to arms and conquest led.
"Send forth thy thunder till the glorious voice
"By rocky dale and cascades multiplied,
"Bidding the peacock in the shade rejoice—
"Calls him to dance upon the mountain-side:
"Majestic bird, whom Skanda loves to ride,†
"Whom Skanda's mother holds so wondrous dear,

---

* Siva—azure-necked.
† Skanda, or Kartikaya, the War God, is represented as riding on a peacock.

"That when his moulted plumes in all their pride
"Of starry radiance, fall and glitter near,
"She lifts them from the ground to grace her royal ear.
"Thy homage rendered to the Warrior-God—
"Whose infant steps amid the thickets strayed
"Where the reeds wave over the holy sod,
"Speed on, but let thy course awhile be stayed,
"And through the lands her author's glory bore,
"Enshrined within her waves to spread for evermore.
"Then speeding on to Brahmavartha's land,
"Hover above the Kúrú's fatal field,
"Rich with the blood of many a slaughtered band—
"Where the proud banner waved, the war-cry pealed—
"Where the sword smote upon the helm and shield—
"When god-like Arjûna with arrowy hail
"Laid low the heads of kings who scorned to yield."

This last couplet of the Yaksha is prophetic. Bhîma in the sacred grove of Skanda listened. "Ha! prophesiest thou "to me of victory? O great Kartikáya! I thank thee." To Thauésur's fair plains he sped triumphant. Near there, on the solitary field of Korau-Khét, he stood and mused. The waves of Sárasvâti gently murmured o'er their pebbly bed: in the marshes fed the cranes and flamingoes of the south ; and flocks of wild geese and "koolen" of the North filled the air—their screams predominant. "Ha! this second lesson of the swans!" He watched their flight, and stood long apart profoundly thinking. "Yes, Hanumân was right : here shall be the battle-field. I "go to great Yûdishtír to consult the omens : but first to "help the warriors in the land of the tortoise." He turned to mount his car, but it had gone on past Thanésur, driven by Gâvalgúni—such had been the chieftain's order, for it behoved him to escape the notice of the ruling Koraus. So Bhîma alone stood on the wide plain of Kúrú-Kshétra.

The yellow sun had sank in dusky purple ; over the Eastern mountains the silver orb of the moon, veiled in mist, rose calmly. The heart of Bhîma was softened. "Alas, my brethren, and "my kindred, must ye perish that the Pandau's fate may be "accomplished? Doth great Arjûna pronounce it just? I "pause to consult him, and great Krishna his ally." He sighed as he sadly turned aside. Seldom had the strong heart of Bhîma softened; but now he lifted up his voice and wept. The clouds of the rising monsoon drove across the heavens, and the quick gleams of moonlight flickered over the wasted field and waters, and a vision of the future rose on the moon of Bhîma's inner spirit. He beheld the ghosts of the dead that *were to be*, the spectres of the dread harvest of Siva the destroyer, rider of the tiger-steed. The shades of the coming dead fled quickly over the plain, flitting before him across the moon's path, and Bhîma caught here and there the pale visages as they vanished in the night-mists. Fitfully the scream of owls and yells of distant jackals were wafted down the night-breeze; and the cruel moan of the ghoul-i-biabân (the dæmon of the desert) sounded in the darkness.

Presently he beheld a vision of the field strewn with slain, the Shades of Bhisthma, of Drôna, of Karma, and of Sharya, his kinsmen—all Koraus—with Takouni, King of Gándâra, and of the great archer Derichti-Kêba, Prince of Potyid (Tibet), and of Virta, King of Sirmoor and Keyonthál, slain by Sediva his nephew, and of Drapáda, King of Oojein.

The shades of night which veiled the ghosts of the Korau heroes, fell dark and sombre o'er the plain. The moon sent forth a baleful gleam over the sad waves of Sárasvâti; and at length its light was veiled in an eclipse; then darkness, profound and terrible, sank upon the plain, as Siva—rider of the tiger steed—and Bhôwáni the Avenger passed swiftly across the darkened land with raven wing.

＊   ＊   ＊   ＊   ＊   ＊

This was the vision of Bhîma, which he saw in the month of A'swina, in the year K.Y. 2266—1869 B.C.—when the moon was at the full in the 13th cycle of the Sosos or Brihis-pati cháka (cycle of Jupiter).

＊
＊ ＊

IV.

NEXT year in spring great Bhîma arrived in the lake country of Kumäon, whose Autochthenes—Naini-Devi and Richóba, goddesses of the waters of the Gangetic watershed—favoured him with their aid against the Ráchshasas and Assurs of the north who had assailed Kailás — the Olympus of Hindoos. The laughter-loving Krishna also—the sounder of the shell—had come from far Dwâraka to aid the Pandaus in the war. He loved the company of heroes ; especially of Arjûna, and of Sediva his young brother, and they had persuaded the demi-god to join his power to aid brave Bhîma in his war against the Assurs of the north and east. He had vouchsafed his aid against the dæmon-born. To the Pandau company also may be added the seven sages (Sáth Rikhi) who dwelt upon the border of the lake beloved of Bhîma — the Bheem-Tal of present times :

"The seven great saints who star the northern sky."

They supplied counsels of wisdom and sage advice, especially the sage Markhandaya—author of the "Vânapurána," Book of the Forest—had exhorted the heroes to arms. He it was who inspired King Hanumân with the words of wisdom which fell from the lips of the sylvan demi-god. At Jósimut, on Alaknanda stream, the Monkey-Deity arrived to view the children of his ancient friend advance to meet the foe. But Bhîma recollected the words of Hanumân, and whilst listening to all, formed his own plans for victory alone in his secret mind.

Arjûna had destroyed the giant Panchajanya, whose tibia or thigh-bone formed his war-horn. The giant's brood had vowed vengeance on the Pandau brethren, and were banded in arms along Mahendra crest of Himôdi, which overlooks the land of mountain and chasm, now called "Gurhwâl"—land of fortresses or steep-places—and of Káli-Kumäon—land of the

H

tortoise—at whose capitol, Champávat, Bhíma had assembled
one division of his army for the war.

On the eve of the advance brave Bhíma spake :—" O Chiefs,
" few words suffice in War! I, Bhíma, lead the van up Alak-
" nanda's stream; great Arjûna, chief of the sounding bow,
" my valiant brother, aligned on Bhágiráthi's stream, protects
" the flank; Nizkoola, with brave Purujit to aid him, will
" advance by Surjoo's flashing wave and form our right reserve.
" Enough! advance to victory, O Sons of Pand, and smite
" the serpent race!"

Let us follow Bhíma into the snowy solitudes of Kailás, and
the caverns of Alaknanda, where dwelt the spirits of the
wilderness; dæmons both good and evil, whose struggles for
ascendency in man's mikrocosm form the burden of many a
Hindoo Veda and Shastr.

On the banks of the river Káli-Gunduk or Surjoo, which
flashes through the green forests of those regions in silver and
in foam, had the Pandau's great ancestor Ráma (himself an
exile) dwelt and wandered with Sita his beloved spouse,
ravished from him by the giant Râwun of Singhâla, as has
been related in the Rámáyâná, and elsewhere in the slokes of
the bards. Bhíma was inspired by the memory of his misfortunes; and in his speech to the assembled warriors narrated
the idyl of the fair Sita and of the hero Ráma.

Bivouacked in the forest of Tupôbun (Tupásiabán)—grove
of lamentation—where the sad Ráma had bemoaned his melancholy loss with his dear loved brother Lutchman, the soul
of brave Bhimsén (Bhíma) glowed with pity, and inspired the
hero to noble deeds of arms against the giant posterity of
the cruel ravisher, Râwun. Arjûna, too, wept bitter tears as
he recalled the story, and vowed revenge. His penance, is it
not written in the chronicles of the land of Bráj!

Krishna, leaving his fair shepherdesses (gópies), in the land
of Bráj, arrived to greet his friend Arjûna, and joined great
Bhíma in arms at Gopie-éshur on Alaknanda stream.

Bálárámá, brother of Krishna—he who after, disgusted at the war of kindred, retired from the field of Korau-Khét, and dwelt on the banks of Sárasváti river—was also there; and, though the Pandaus were preparing instant war against the Koraus, now he stood in arms beside great Krishna, and did the mighty deeds the chronicles and bards narrate.

At the teerut or shrine of the meeting of the waters, Bhíma sacrificed to Kartikáya, the war-god, five hundred horses.[*]

On all the sacred river heads and *teeruts* did the Pandau host do *Snán* (religious bathing) and penance—"*dhoop dheep navéd*" of modern Brahminism. Need the march of the host be detailed? Shall the warrior pen tell of ceremonial such as priestly craft has in all ages sought to impose upon the lordly Khsátriyas?

As the Pandau invasion of Gurhwál is legendary—though somewhat mythical as to its *warlike* character—shall we be tempted to record the details? The pen of the stranger can supply the chronicles scarcely known to the sons of the Raj-poots themselves who live along those marches; but it were long to narrate them all: suffice to say they indicate the Pandau's march against the foe.

———

[From Haridwár—Siva's door or mouth—along the sacred streams, as many as fifty places of *snán* or bathing invite the modern pilgrim to his religious duties. I give those of the pilgrimage to Búdrinauth as an example:—

(1), The pilgrimage begins at Khún-khúl where was the palace of King *Khun*, an ally of the Pandaus in this invasion. (2), At Haridwár the mighty Gunga issues from between the mountains *Nil* and *Bhil*, on to the plain, where the footstep of Hári is seen near to Tupôbun. (3), At Rúdra-prayág—the meeting place of the eleven deities of the Hindoo Swerga—the pilgrims fast and bathe; and after worshipping the cow, gird

———

[*] Probably by the Aswamedha, which has been supposed to be an emblematic sacrifice or *dedication* of horses to Kartikaya.

up their loins and adjust their dress for the mountain journey.
(4), Again they bathe at Dêva-prayâg—the junction of the
Bhágiráthi* and Alaknanda waters.   (5), "Goopta-Gunga,"
the hidden or cavernous river, where the gods themselves come
and perform snán.   (6), On through the mountains of Bheek
(aconite), where the poison plant—sacred emblem of Siva, the
destroyer—grows freely.   The pilgrims, their heads muffled in
their cloaks, rush onwards over the hills to (7), Kédar-nauth,
where a temple, and flaming springs and holy rocks abound.
Here the pilgrims cast rings and bangles and necklaces and
flowers to Siva.   (8), Gopie-éshur—sacred to Krishna, who
here arrived—leaving his gópies in the land of Bráj—on to
the head waters of the Alaknanda, to (9), Peepulkoss, and
(10), Garoodgunga—the stream where sacred stones, charms
proof against serpents, are found (hence the exclamation
"Garoor, garoor," made by the Hindoos on seeing snakes).
(11), Jósimut (the cooking place); sacred to Hanumân, the
Monkey-Deity.   (12), Vishnûgunga;   (13), Kalliankote;
(14), Wâkimut;   (15), Bûdrinauth (where six minor places of
snán are found); to (16), Bussoodâra, on the Alaknanda
stream, where the pilgrimage terminates.   The whole may
perhaps represent the course of the Pandau's march in their
invasion of Gurhwâl, 1368 B.C., and I shall so assume it.]

The Pandau army marched from Kédar-Khûnd—now called
Déhra-Dûn—to Gunga's sacred stream.   Crossing the Sewâ-
liks, great Yûdishtír camped at Nâgsidh on the holy hill, there
to meet the foe should the Koraus haply attack the rear of
brave Bhíma's army.   Afterwards, when Bhíma had destroyed
the foe, he ascended the Alaknanda's mystic stream to Bûdrinauth and Kédarnauth, in the holy land of Ootéra-khoond, even

---

* The pre-eminently sacred rivers of India are : (1), the Godavery ; (2), the
Ganges ; (3), the Bhagirathi ; (4), the Sarasvati. The Alaknanda means the "river
from afar on high," but is not included amongst the pre-eminently sacred streams.
The reverence of Hindoos for the streams or waters tributary to the Ganges does
not extend further north than the spring-head of the Jumna, nor further south
than one *teerut* on the Gunduk in Nepal, where the sacred stones called Salik-Ram,
and grains of gold are found.

to the sacred peaks of Gungootri, Jumnootri, and to Bhágir-átha's sacred spring-head.

Here had Bhágiráthi (so the Vedas tell) performed auster-ities, till at last the holy Gunga (Ganges)—emerging from the cleft of heaven—had descended for the use of mortals on the dark blue head of Vishnoo, and thence to earth. The gushing waters of the mighty torrent mingled with the stream of Alak-nanda. Here the Pandau army pitched their camp on the margin of the rushing waters, hard by the fountain of Brahma-vartha's lake, where Arjûna, the friend of Krishna, had dwelt and pondered wisdom, as well as learnt to "lay low with arrowy hail the heads of kings who scorn to yield."

"On to the place where infant Gunga leaps
"From the dark woods that belt the Mountain-King;—
"Hurling her torrent down the rugged steeps;
"Those holy waters, as the sages sing
"To Sagars' children bliss and heaven could bring.
"Fresh from her native sky, a sportive maid,
"On Siva's awful head she dared to cling;
"And with the laughter of her foam repaid
"His consort's jealous frown as with his hair she played.

"Drink, for the flood is living crystal; drink—
    *   *   *   *

"Should Gryphon hosts, by mad presumption led,
"Vex't by thy thunder, mount the realms of air
"To ride thee down beneath their impious tread,
"Laugh with thy rain to see them baffled there,
"And with the dashing of thy hailstones scare
"Thy scattered foes.   •   •   •
"Skirting the mansion of eternal snows
."Compress thy form, and winding round explore
"Where Krauncha's parted rocks a pass disclose
"Traversed by swans—those rocks that burst before
"The might of Ráma and the axe he bore."

_____

NOTE.—These extracts are from the "Messenger Cloud" of Kalidasa (translated by R. T. H. Griffiths, M.A., of Benares). The plot of which is the supposed invo-cation of a Yaksha, or exiled spirit, servant of Kuvera—the Hindoo god of wealth —to carry his sorrow to his spouse at Alaka, mystic city of Kailas. The imagery

But the destiny of great Bhîma was war! Let soft Nizkoola sigh for mountain maids; brave Bhîma dares the fight with roving Assurs, and with Ráchshasas and Nâga dæmons of the waste and snows!

"*B'hùm, b'hùm, Mahadeo! B'hùm, b'hùm, Mahadeo !*"*

The battle is arrayed: swarming on the banks of Holy Gunga behold the Nâga-born, the foes of Krishna and of Pand.

" On, sons of Pand, and smite the serpent race!"

The battle closed. The roaring waters of Alaknanda rolled many a corpse to earth at Rudra-prayág or Tupôbun—forest of tears. The sorrow of great Râma is avenged. The cavernous dark cliffs reverberate the shouts of heaven-born chiefs and champions. The startled tiger slinks into the grassy lowlands, and the mailed rhinoceros of the Bhábur plunges madly into the marshes of Brahmadeo : and the wild elephant of the great Saul forests of the Gôgra escaping, hides himself in the deepest shades of the land of the black tortoise and of the Sewáliks, dread Shiva's rugged haunt.

The battle rolled upwards to Bûdrinauth.†

The corpses of Nâgas slain rolled down the torrents of the Alaknanda, the Douli, the Gauri, and the Vishu, as far as Lall Nágri and the plains of Káli-Kumäon ; and the watersheds of the Kôsila and Râmgunga became as *mirghats* or places of the dead : and the hot springs of Seetabhûmi, and of Chitrasellar, at the meeting of the lower waters, were choked with Nâgas slain.

The Pandaus advanced and planted their standards on the crest of Himalaya, and on "Mahendra" the axis of Kailás.

"*B'hùm, b'hùm, Mahadeo! B'hùm, b'hùm, Mahadeo!*"

---

of the whole poem is singularly true in its descriptive rendering of the natural features of its supposed path : and in fact forms the most romantic and graphic description of the route of the Pandaus towards Kailas supposed in the text. The reader is confidently refered to this beautiful little poem for the details.

*A military cry equivalent to the British *Hurrah!* or the *Ahoi* of the Anglo-Dane.

† Here the temple of Pandau-Keshwar, the most ancient in Gurhwal, was in after ages founded in the Pandau's honour by the sage Shunkur-Achaj.

Kailás is won! and its snows resound with shouts of victory!
The horn of Bhíma and of Arjúna, and the sounding shell
(sánk) of Krishna, sound the pæans and the pealing blast of
victory. The dæmons and the serpent race have fled into
black night and Tartarus! The cœrulian Vishnoo, on Garood
his sacred steed, has appeared as the Deity propitious to the
victorious Pandau host ; and even Siva—friend of the Koraus
—has veiled his head in Gunga's stream, in which a hecatomb
of dead has rolled from the crimsoned snows! Enough! the
vengeance of the Destroyer has been appeased and satisfied.

"*B'hùm, b'hùm, Mahadeo! B'hum, b'hum, Mahadeo!*"

*   *   *   *   *   *

But Bhíma remembered that still further trials awaited him,
and he returned with his host towards the plains of India.
He concentrated the Pandau Army in the Dûn of Déhra previous to advancing to the field of Korau-Khét, with the allies
collected from afar. Sediva the Pandau, with Ogregund the
King, had arrived with his mountaineers from distant Káshmír. Flushed with recent victory, with one consent they hail
brave Bhíma Chief of the Pandau host. Even his brother,
the great Yûdishtír, consents to serve under his command and
guidance during the approaching war.

After sacrifice to Kartikáya—God of War—Bhíma, with
the Pandau army, advanced towards Hustinapoora, and soon
found the Korau host drawn up in order of battle in front of
Thanésur.   *   *   *   *   *

The chronicles of the Mâhâbâràt tell us the rest ; of how
the noble field was won, and great Yûdishtír re-instated on his
father's throne. Are they not also recorded in the legends of
Yûdishtír and of Arjúna, and of Sediva, the Pandaus!*

---

* See page 12 "Sediva," and 65 "Arjuna," where however a very incomplete
account of the great battle is given, owing to causes mentioned at the end of the
"Story of Sediva," page 16 ; and in the rescript of the Mahabharat afterwards consulted by me (Burnouf's French translation) the names of the heroes on both sides
differ from those in other translations by English scholars. In the version above
alluded to, Ditrashtura occupies a conspicuous place, and his prophetic address
ending each sloka "O Sandjaya !" narrates in advance the eventualities of the

After the great battle, the lamentations of the women who beheld their fathers, brothers, sons, and kindred slain on the fatal field are recorded in the Mâhâbârât, where they are compared to a flock of screaming sea-fowl settling on the dead. The victorious Pandaus stand around. ,The reproaches of Gandhâri—mother of Jirjoodeen and the Koraūs—are answered by Bhíma. Gandbâri also apostrophises Krishna, showing him the dead, and praising them. Bhíma answers her reproaches; whereupon the blind Ditrâshtura—the aged father of the Koraus—seized with sudden fury, hurls a spear at Bhíma, and transfixes an image of the hero which, at the advice of Krishna, his charioteer (Gâvalgâni) had set up on his war-car. Bhíma thus escapes; and shortly he withdrew his people into the outer valleys of Kumäon, where he dwelt apart ; marrying thereafter a daughter of Sirmoor. He afterwards journeyed into Keyonthâl and the valley of the Sutlej. He assisted his brother, the great Yûdishtír, in building Pinjore, and setting his kingdom in order, as has been related in the " Wanderings of King Yûdishtír."

Such are some of the deeds of Bhíma the War-Chief.

The wandering Cimmerian who wrote of Sediva, of Yûdishtír, and of Arjûna, stood on the wild bluff of Mahâbuleshwâr (mountain of strength) and gazed at the fiery disc of the sun sinking into the western waves. Afterwards he threaded the forests of Mâhârâshtrâ and Sëoni plateau: years later, wandering amidst the woods and mountains of Kâli-Kumäon along the flashing waters of Surjoo and Bheem-Tal, and down the sacred streams of Ootéra-khoond, he realised the facts of Bhíma's and the Pandaus' valiant deeds in the "land of the tortoise," and composed this history.

---

great war, wherein it may be stated generally that Bhishtma commanded the Koraus six days, Drona three days, Karma two days, Sharya half-a-day. Bhishtma is slain by Bhima; Drona attempts a night attack, which is partly successful, but is finally killed by Bhima and his son Ghatotkatcha, or by the arrows of Arjuna; and the other Koraue slain as enumerated in the text at page 96.

Temple of Bhima,
Valley of the Sutlej.

" Nakoola," the Pandau.

A FAIRY TALE.

I.

AT the time when brave Bhîma was preparing war against the tribes of Nâgas and serpent-born Assurs, who had vexed Mahendra and the marches of Gurhwâl and Kumäon, Nakoola, the fourth Pandau, dwelt at Brahma-deo, in the great saul forests of the Gôgra, at the foot of the mountains of Káli-Kumäon. Here the united waters of the flashing Surjoo* and Ramgunga meet, and here had great Râma, his ancestor, wandered with the faithful Sita and his brother Lakshman. Here, in the flowery woods along the silver stream, the youthful Pandau—twin brother of Sediva—was wont to wander in pursuit of the wild deer of the forest and of the fairy forms of Nâga damsels. This was accounted a sin unto the youthful Kshatriya, and the champions did not cease to reproach him ; all save the merry Krishna, who would exclaim in jest — "Oh, Pandaus! in the chase all "game is lawful! Let not the sin fall on the head of Na- "koola, the wise† youth, for loving the fair shepherdesses of " Kumäon and of Kailás. Love is of no race or special progeny; "'Tis the gift of Kâma, and the joy of Swerga!" Neverthe-less it was inexpedient for the Pandau exile, whose behest

---

* The Surjoo is here called Kaliguuga, but the name Surjoo reappears at Ajoodhya in Oude, lower down, as the name of the sacred river. On this stream from its spring-head (at Surbamool) under the peaks of Panch-chooli to Ajoodhya —there are twelve places of snan, or religious ablution, the details of which need scarcely be entered on, though they bear in part on the mythic history of the Pandaus.

† *Nakoola* means wise. He is sometimes called *Nizkoola*, and it will appear fur-ther on that he so denominates himself.   I

it plainly was to aid brave Bhíma and his brethren to recover
the throne of their ancestors, thus to lose himself in soft
delight; so whether the magic spell about to be related fell
on the youthful Prince by design of Krishna or other great
ones to dispel illusion, or whether máya (heavenly illusion)
gat hold of him, who can say?

Hard by the oasis in the forest, where Nakoola dwelt, was
the evil wood of Dandaka, where roam multiform types of
dæmons such as cannibal giants (Ráchshasas) "that assume
forms at pleasure," on whom had fallen the curse of Yáma
(hell). Let us curse (with water in the palm of the hand)
such sons of perdition and their imps,— Bhutas, Pisachas,
Paimágas, Danávas, Daityas, Yéch, and all evil serpents!
Garroor! garroor!!!

"In the evil forest Dandaka, eternal silence seemed to reign :
the large trees towered till they reached the light branchless,
then they spread forth in massive boughs, and crushed them
down so as to exclude the sunshine.   If any attenuated beam
forced its way through the upper foliage it was strangled by
the creeping plants that twisted round the naked trunks and
swung their fibrous arms from tree to tree.   There were few
sounds and less movement; yet one was conscious that the
forest teemed with life—the intense stillness itself revealed
this.   It was not the calm of solitude, but the suspended
breath which betrays the lurking-place.   The large-bladed
grass grew to a monstrous height : it was of a bright metallic
green that showed the dank mephitic slime which nourished
it.   Fungi of all sizes and shapes and colours sprung up
amidst it; but there were no flowers—none save spotted
orchids, the impure daughters of mortality, who thrive upon the
fetid air, and draw their poisonous brilliancy from corruption.
It was the home of such as loathe the day; but for all the
dæmons and evil that it sheltered, and the silent menace of
the faint musky air, it was not without a dangerous fasci-
nation and a sinister beauty of its own.

"Reader! deceive not thyself! the ugliness of sin is not always apparent. No! the Beautiful the Ideal (for they are one) includes all the opposite principles of life: here, too, all that is involves the existence of its contrary. The Angel of Light infers the Prince of Darkness; the music of the spheres the sombrous harmony of Gehenna; the radiance of the empyrean the magnificent gloom of the abyss!"*

The glamour of the dangerous forest had fallen on Nakoola; the obscurity weighed on him heavily, yet had it a mysterious charm for him. Involved in lurid thought he paced the silent arches of the forest—his bow in hand, lest haply he be assailed by ghostly terror of magic, such as great Râma—wandering with the Hermit Agastya in the gloom—had encountered; Khidimba or Vaka, or "Kirmira of the brilliant eyes." Prone on the spongy soil he saw, still mouldering after the long ages, the giant skeleton of Dunboodhi, slain by Balin in the mythic ages. The crows dance on the slain giant. And other mossy skeletons of giants slain, were there; under the gloomy arches of the forest, they sometimes rose and walked in silence, their tall forms reaching to the topmost branches of the forest, the gleam of decay glittering in the cavernous sockets of their skulls where eyes had been.

*   *   *   *   *   *

Nakoola had one day wandered in the direction of this haunted forest, and had approached the sacred grove of Raméshwar and Trizoog-narrain, "temple of the three ages," when he chanced to arouse a stag—silver white—whose antlers branched like the fronds of the sissoo tree, a prodigy of beauty! He pushed on, bow in hand, and soon sighted the quarry amidst the cedars of Bhimesur, and pressed it even as far as Gauri-Goophar—the cave of stalactytes, sacred to Mahadeo—into which the stag rushed headlong, Nakoola in hot pursuit.

---

* This passage—paraphrased from the Ramayana—seems to point to the Assyrian creed of Ormuzd and Ahriman alluded to in page 40 of "Yudishtir." I am indebted to a work by Fredericka Robertson—"the Iliad of the East"—for this suggestive passage.   I 2

He found himself in a sylvan park, unknown to him but, as
he afterwards discovered, a place of evil omen to the Pandaus,
for here his great descendant, Raja Kuttool, was defeated,
and his progeny destroyed, by the invader Anook Pal, who
came by way of Sëul and Bhâgésir, and planted his standards
at Bûdrinauth, where also he set up a stone of victory.

The silver stag, now glancing amidst the pine trees, anon
plunging into the feathery brakes along the banks of Surjoo,
misled the ardent Pandau further and further into the snowy
solitudes towards Kailás; his branching antlers swaying in
the wind like the tufted báchain of the forest of Maurbun—
abode of peacocks—its rustling fronds, like unto the palm tree of
Lanka, swaying in the blast of the monsoon of the southwest:
a portent! and Nakoola eagerly pursued, as the stag rushed
into the cavern of the silver fern, into the mossy grotto, where
the gleaming stalactytes hung in festoons like roses from the
lofty dome of Swerga!

Soon the deepening shadows warned him he had left day-light far behind: at length he paused, and gazed around him. A soft green valley met his view, on which a softened light, as though of fairy stars, was shed from the canopy of heaven; but the rocks seemed to have closed around him, and his exit seemed barred behind. At the same moment the silvern stag appeared to vanish in the glooms of the cavern, and in its place Nakoola saw a venerable sage, with flowing silver tresses sur-mounted by the kalgi of royalty, and by his side a venerable fairy queen, in garments of light green tissue.

The hermit spake:—"Oh, Prince, I know thy quest; the "fairy forms of earth are thy desire. Thou art beguiled. "Here have I led thee that thou mayest behold the varied "forms of Fairyland and the faces of the Apsáras, and the "celestial nymphs of Swerga (paradise); only thou must obey "one condition I will tell thee of on the morrow. Enough! "Rest here to-night; behold thy couch. Eat freely of the "feast prepared by fairy hands. Sleep well, and awake in "'Swerga' of the immortals: not to many of earth is such "boon vouchsafed."

Nakoola paused irresolute. "Oh, elephant amongst sages, "can I afterwards return to earth? Sufficient for Nizkoola "the fairy forms of earth—the fair daughters of men—the "mortal maidens of Aryavarta!"*

"Fear not," replied the Fairy Sage; "after due time thou "shalt return and aid thy brethren to battle for their rights: "but first thou must purge thy soul of weakness: such is the "command of great Krishna, thy friend and mine, for I am "Rishyasringa, the Sage, "Son of the Doe," giver of the rains "of summer; who married the Fairy Queen of Swerga, and "reigns in Fairyland; King Indra also, ruler of the host of "heaven, hath commended thee to my care."

Nakoola was thereby somewhat reassured, and after singing his customary hymn to the "Preserver"—Dweller in the Lotus—he partook of the Fairy's feast; and, tired with his

---

* The land of genuine Hindoos.

long day's chase, soon fell fast asleep on the verdant couch of
ferns and wild flowers, lulled by the plashing waters of the
fairy grotto which soothed him with their murmur. * * *,
    The Pandau slept, and awoke in "Swerga," the Fairyland
of Hindoos.   *   *   *

O Sakantala! who shall describe the fairy forms of Apsáras,
and of Gandaras, celestial nymphs, beautiful as the morn!
Narrate, O bard! the names of some of the angelic throng
that people the rosy realms of Swerga and the heaven of great
Indra!—Menáka, fairest of the nymphs, Swirna-Rékha, Ratna,
Rámbha, Kandápa, Karpúri-Manjári, Kalindra, and Koreila,
a thousand of the daughters of Káma and of Yákshas,—

> "The bards that chaunt celestial lays
> And Nymphs of heavenly birth!"

Only one mortal, Lilavâti, was amongst them;—the Fairy
Queen of the silver locks was there as queen of the celestial
revels. She spake :—"Oh, mortal! behold the Beauties of
"Swerga. Thou hast doubtless heard of the *swayambara*
"[the choice of a husband by a young princess]. Now thou
"shalt choose from amongst this bevy of fair angels thy bride,
"to whom thou must be faithful henceforth, and love no other,
"else thou canst not escape from Nára (hell)." She turned
towards the fair flock of nymphs: "Essay your various graces,
"oh, daughters, for the sake of the Pandau Prince, whose
"choice is free!"   *   *   *   *

Not to the pen of the wandering Cimmerian is it vouchsafed
—or even lawful—to recount the graces and beauties of that
fair host. Let the picture rest behind a rosy veil! The
Pandau youth was lost in máya; but at length, last of all the
beauties, came fair Lilavâti, daughter of Oojein, alone of that
fair group a mortal.

"Enough, oh Queen," cried Nakoola. "Enough for Niz-
"koola the fair maids of earth. I seek no further; but choose
"fair Lilavâti as my spouse."

As he spake, a violet shadow passed across the rose pavilion of the nymphs, and fair Lilavâti advancing, bent her head before the Prince, and by the Queen's command took him by the hand and raised him from the mossy fountain on the brink of which he had reclined. No sooner had she done so than the Sage Rishyasringa and his Queen threw a silver broidered mantle over their heads, recited an unknown mantra or charm, and waved above their heads, as they stood before her, three times, her fairy wand; and in an instant they found themselves on the flowery banks of Sipra in fair Oojein, queen of the Vindhyas, Lilavâti's native city, where, in the sweet gardens and pastures on the banks of Sipra, on the slopes of the forest glades, King Drapâda had constructed fair alcoves and marble fountains, and terraces planted with scented shrubs and glittering flowers.

*   *
*

II.

HIMALAYA, King of Mountains, and the steep and lofty Vindhya, stand scowling on each other, and exchanging looks of defiance. "I am the King of Mountains," exclaims proud Himalaya; "the clouds have "robed me in purple, and crowned my forehead with snow. "I tower up to heaven, rending the azure veil which conceals "the home of the immortals. The secrets of the three worlds "are mine; I overlook the whole earth, and from the sighing "ocean the dark-winged vapours ascend and whisper to me "their griefs. I am in the confidence of the stars, and know "the story of their loves; I know, too, why some of them fell "from heaven."   *   *   *   The sullen Vindhya wraps his misty cloak around him. "I am weary of this giant," he cries; "he impedes my view, and robs me of the sunlight: "his ill-bred boastings offend me;" he adds, "but for this "shapeless monster I had been King of Mountains!"

Fair Gunga, daughter of old Himalaya, King of Mountains,

was beloved of Súrya (the Sun). She heard the sullen speech, and turned away her head. The young and dreamy Gunga trembled. Oh youthful maiden, whose dreams are haunted by wonder, whose heart is fluttered by whispers, awake! 'Tis Love awaits thee, O graceful daughter of Ména.

The friendly Yaksha who had sung to brave Bhima as he passed by Râma's mountain on his way to the land of the tortoise, saw the passing pageant: thus he sang:—

"The sweet cool smell of lakes and pleasant showers,
"The beauty and the perfume of the flowers,
"And all delights of sight and sound and smell,
"Dear youth, be thine!
"Oh, gentle youth, mark thou each place of rest,
"Where thou wilt fain with weary wings delay,
"To gather strength upon some mountain crest,
"Or drink, exhausted, from some river's breast,
"Of Love the draught divine."

Unlike stern Bhima, Nakoola lent an eager ear to the Seraph's glowing words. Much did the youth question the friendly Yaksha touching the fair ones of whom he sang.

"Ah, friend," replied the Seraph, "rest at Oojein -(or "Avanti) the city brought from Swerga.* There are the gar-"dens built by King Drapâda on the shores of Sipra's fairy-"haunted fountains. Listen!"

"Near there the bright imperial city stands,
"The blest Avanti* or Visala, glorious town
"Brought by the happy saints, unsatisfied
"With all that Paradise can offer, down
"To be their best reward, their virtue's worthiest crown.

"The sweet soft zephyr laden with the scent,
"Which every lotus opening to the air

---

* It appears that the exhausted pleasures of Swerga are insufficient recompense for certain acts of Hindoo austerity, hence some are permitted to revisit earth to work out the balance of merit for final absorption—Nirvana—or emancipation, with the fairest portion of Swerga. This portion is held to include the city of Avanti or Oojein, which is built on the river Sipra, alluded to by the Yaksha in the poem—*The Cloud Messenger*—quoted in former tales.

" Of morning from its rifled stores has lent,
" Plays wooingly around the loosened hair
" And fevered cheek of every lady there ;
" There as it blows o'er Sipra, fresh and strong,
" Bids all the swans upon her bank prepare
" To hail the sunrise with their sweetest song,
"And loves with its own voice the music to prolong.

" Rest on these flower-sweet terraces, and feel
" From open casements where the women braid
" Their long soft locks, delicious odour steal.
" Here hail thy lovers with a loving glance;
" O, rest in this sweet spot, nor lose this blessed chance.
" Whilst thy dear image in the crystal deep
" Blend with the fancies of her maiden dream,
" Then will she work to win thee with the glance
" Of finny darters for the love of eyes.
" Steel not thy heart against her love, nor deem
" Her lily's smile but to allure the prize ;
" O, yield thee to her prayer, O yield thee, and be wise.

"Ah, yes! I see thee in her loving arms,
"Those feathery branches of the tall bamboo;
"And spread beneath thee are her yielded charms,
"And her smooth sides uncovered to thy view;
" How could such loveliness unheeded woo!
" Who could resist her softly pleading smile,
" With heart all cold and dead, if e'er he knew
" What joy it is to kiss each breast like isle?
" Who, who would turn away, nor linger there awhile?

" Then will celestial maids with laugh and shout,
"Open their lovely arms thy form to seize."

Nizkoola listened to the Seraph's siren song, and dwelt
a space at Oojein ; and fair Lilavâti, finding herself amidst
the scenes of her youth, soon collected around her a troop of
companions as beautiful as herself.

In the gardens of King Drapâda, King of Oojein, along
the verdant banks of Sipra, the Pandau strayed with Lilavâti
and other fair ones in the cool of evening, beneath the refresh-
ing rain-clouds of the monsoon. There he roamed with his

beloved. The sweet smell of earth and of flowers, renovated
with the showers, pervaded the thickets, and the voices of the
woodland birds smote on the ear with pleasant sound. The
buds of roses and sweet jasmin, and the crimson of the pome-
granate glittered like stars amidst the green and revivified
foliage; whilst the glance of the peacock and other brilliant
birds in the setting sun, lighted up the terraces and bye-paths
of the mangoe groves ; and the plash of the fish, and scurrying
eddies of the water-fowl on the pleasant lake and streams of
Sipra, added to the charm of the scene.

Fair Lilaváti and her companions there appeared with the
tiláka (brow mark) of love on their fair foreheads.

Amidst playful laughter and conversation and songs the
fair nymphs there assembled, passed the happy hours. Some
swinging in the trees, others dabbling in the water-channels,
presenting a scene of oriental *abandon* such as poets of a later
age have sung of.

Seated at the feast—whilst a pause in the conversation
took place—Nakoola urged fair Lilaváti to sing a song of
dreamland, or at least a tale such as she had heard in the
fairy's palace. Thus she sang :—" O, Khsátriya champions,
"and dear companions, listen to the Story of the Hermit
"Rishyasringa, Son of the Doe, who became King of Fairy-
"land, and married our brilliant queen. Vibhandaka, the
"morose anchorite, dwelt with his son Rishyasringa in the
"deep forest. Blameless was the life of the young hermit,
"whose only companions were the innocent animals of the
"forest, and birds of the musky thickets. His fame had
"spread throughout the land, till at length King Somapadma
"grew jealous. Said he,—'How will it be when the youth
"'beholds for the first time the lovely face of woman?' He
"then commanded, 'fit me out a spacious vessel ; plant it
"'with trees and shrubs, with mosses, ferns, and flowers, so
"'that it may seem a blooming island : let the loveliest
"'maidens in the kingdom embark ! then let the wind and

"'floating river drift these blooming young messengers to the "'solitary hermitage of the youthful Rishyasringa.'

"It was the marvellous hour which closes the tropical day, "when light becomes an illusion, and ecstatic nature beholds "the vision of her expired lord. The greyness of twilight is "not there; mystery casts off the shade, and clothes itself in "radiance. Overhead the hushed twittering of birds nestled "close under the canopy of leaves; the narrow path through "the flowery wood stretching into the heart of the silent forest; "the long grass and feathery ferns kissed by the translucent "light. Jasmin and the glossy leaves of asoka and of champa, "magnolia, and of myrtle, rustled in the balmy wind. The "youth felt that they concealed a secret. What?

"As he stood, on the air came floating to him gradually, "slowly, as sail the swans adown the sacred river, a breath that "grew into a whisper—a whisper that broke into a song—a song "that woke the jealous birds up in their nests. The young "maidens—in guise of anchorites—approach; radiant as the "sun, their gems sparkling beneath their homely garments; "their silver núpurras ringing out the rhythm of their footsteps. "They salute Rishyasringa. 'Show us your hermitage, gentle "youth,' they cried.   *   *   *   *

"What more to say? Need the rest be added? After "much speech, and gentle conference, the damsels departed, "leaving the youthful hermit to his reflections,—the prey of "Love! He describes his longings to his father, the morose "Vibhandaka; but ultimately he escapes from the forest, and "traces the footsteps of the departed fair ones, and marries "the princess, daughter of King Somapadma, and at length "becomes King of Fairyland! Hence I say, oh youths and "maidens, woman is to be both loved and feared; great is the "power of woman's love!"

Again Nakoola enquired:—"Thou art learned, oh fair Lila-"vâti, in the wisdom of Bhuscara,* tell me then this question:

---

* The eminent Hindoo mathematician, Bhuscara, was author of a work on

"Of pure lotus flowers at a sacrifice, $\frac{1}{3}$ was offered to Siva

　　　　"　　　　　　　　"　　　　$\frac{1}{5}$　　　"　　　　to Vishnù

　　　　"　　　　　　　　"　　　　$\frac{1}{6}$　　　"　　　　to Súrya

　　　　"　　　　　　　　"　　　　$\frac{1}{4}$　　　"　　　　to Bhôwâni

"and six flowers remained for the venerable priest. Tell me "quickly the number of flowers."

Fair Lilavâti laughed and scarcely turned aside, and answered "120 flowers were there, oh youth."

Again did Nakoola ask—"The square root of half the "number of a swarm of bees is gone to a shrub of jasmin, and "so are 8-9th's of the whole swarm; a female is buzzing to "one remaining male that is humming within a lotus in which "she is confined, having been allured to it by its fragrance at "night. Say, lovely woman! the number of bees."*

Fair Lilavâti smiled, and turned away her face towards the flowers; then laughing, she said,—"Oh, learned youth,† the "answer is easy; the number of the bees is 72; and now, in "my turn, will I ask thee a question: 'If the earth is sup-"ported, as sages say, on an elephant which stands on a tortoise, "which again swims in a sea of milk; how many apples can "I, Lilavâti, pelt thee with before thou canst catch me?'" So saying, the fleet, laughing girl fled like the wind adown the shady grove, ever and anon turning to fling an apple at her lover who eagerly pursued her, like the classic Galatea.

"———— *lasciva puella,*
"*fugit ad salices, sed cupit ante videri.*"

algebra called *Lilavati.* His era is uncertain, but has been assigned to about 1150 A.D., so that an anachronism is involved in the text; but Sir W. Jones attributes the origin of Hindoo algebra and astronomy to as early a date as 2000 B.C., and Oojein was always considered its nidus or nursery, and in fact was a sort of Indian Greenwich, as the first parallel of longitude is drawn through that ancient city to Lanka. Tradition asserts that Varaha-Mihma, the father of arithmetic, lived in the era of Vikramaditya, about 56 B.C. The Surya Vidhanta is the celebrated work on astronomy of Bhuscara the great Hindoo astronomer. The tables of Tirvalore claim the epoch 3102 B.C., at which time a conjunction of all the planets is asserted—the beginning of the Kali-Yog or iron age of Hindoo my-thology. Gungadhar and Suryadhara were also eminent Hindoo mathematicians.

* From "Colebrooke's History of Algebra" (slightly altered); translated from the Sanskrit of the Bija Ganita or Viga Ganita. 　　　† Nakoola—wise.

But the swift-footed Nakoola presently overtook the flying
fair in the glen lit by the evening star, arresting her further
flight. He laughed, "Ah, fair one! answer, or I seize thy
"zone: oh beautiful and dear Lilavâti. 4 doves can be had
"for 3 drammas, 7 cranes for 5 drammas, 9 geese for 7 dram-
"mas, and 3 peacocks for 9 drammas. Let us take 100 of
"these birds for 100 drammas to the King,—say how?"

Lilavâti considered a little; then she laughed and said:—
"Find the pulverizer,* oh, Nakoola, and I will tell thee!"

Again she fled, and again fleet Nakoola overtook the nymph.

Panting, she said,—"Oh, wise one, tell me this: In an
"amorous struggle $\frac{1}{3}$ of a necklace of pearls fell to the ground,
"$\frac{1}{6}$ rested on the couch, $\frac{1}{6}$ was saved by the lady, and $\frac{1}{10}$ was
"stolen by her lover, and 6 pearls remained. Say, of how
"many pearls was the necklace composed?"

Nakoola plucked a stem of jasmin and wrote on the sand
$\frac{1}{3}$ $\frac{1}{6}$ $\frac{1}{6}$ $\frac{1}{10}$ 6 pearls=answer, 30.

"Right, oh wise one! Now tell me this one thing more,
"and I cease to tease thee. How many drônas are required
"to pluck a mangoe from that fruit tree, the lowest mangoe
"being 16 cubits from the ground?"†

Nakoola laughed in triumph. "Now I have caught thee,
"auspicious woman! 1 Bhíma equals 16 Drônas! Therefoie,
"auspicious nymph, Drôna the Kûrû is *pulverized*, and ex-
"cluded from the problem. Go, ask dear Mahru."

Nakoola caught fair Lilavâti, and led her to the jasmin
bower and rested till the long evening shadows crept across
the grass beneath the trees of the grove, and the cool breeze
of evening drew their fair companions also from their shady
retreats to wander in the scented gardens.

The company reassembled under a blooming champak tree.

---

* The common multiple of fractions is so termed in Hindoo arithmetic.

† A drona, a mystic number=one-16th of a cubit; hence the joke in the text.
Bhima the Pandau being the rival of Drona the Kuru, as will have been gathered
in former stories.

Again the maidens enqnired, "Tell us a story, dear Lilavâti."
Again Lilavâti related—"Vashist, or Vishvamitra (I for-
"get which), was, oh companions, truly said to be an elephant
"amongst anchorites. His austerities could call down Dévs
"and Gandaurs to his aid, and the bolts of Indrâ fell on many
"at his desire. Then the question arose, 'Who can stop this
"'saint, who threatens to conquer the gods? No one seems
"'capable of mastering this ascetic!' Then the Apsâra
"(fairy) Menáka laughed, and said, 'I am!'—A dream that
"Love had wrought into the form of woman, seemed this
"lovely Menáka: tenderness softened her eyes, and deepened
"the shade of their lashes; and laughter played around her
"mouth, and kissed her cheek with dimples; fancy unbound
"her hair, and twisted it into wavelets; grace moulded her
"form, and passion touched it with langour.   *   *   *
"Down amongst the rushes and sedges of the shores of Lake
"Pushkára, the nymph laid her in the still eventide, her lus-
"trous hair floated down to the water, and swam on the glisten-
"ing ripples. The timid reeds just touched her with their
"shadows, and the golden flags leant towards her and grew
"pale. Listening to the bubbling waters Menáka lay, gazing
"upwards through the sedges, watching the soft tints of evening.
"Thus the Hermit found her. 'Who art thou, star of
"'beauty? I love thee!' he exclaimed.
"She answered, 'Oh, Bull of Hermits! I am Menáka.' .
"Need I say more? oh, companions. Vashist was con-
"quered, and remained five years in the bonds of love.
"Therefore, again I say, oh youth, woman is strong!"
Nakoola said, "Bho! oh auspicious nymph; but you forgot
"to say that the Apsára Rámbha—whose eyes are like the lotus
"—tried her hand in vain to ensnare the saint when Menáka
"ceased to charm; and finally that elephant amongst hermits
"at length escaped, and obtained emancipation from the desire
"of love."*

---

* Partly paraphrased from the Ramayana.

The friendly Yaksha who had sang to Nákoola when he reached Nerbudha's sounding waters, now joined in the festivities. Being urged to prophecy, or sing a song of dreamland, he sighed, and called on Kúvera and Ganésh. The company all stood silent. The Yaksha sang:—

"To distant Alaka fly uncontrolled,
"Where dwell thy brethren in their stately halls;
"Mid gilded palaces and marble walls,
"On which the silver light of Siva's crescent* falls.

"Hence, as thou mountest up, each lovely maid,
"Passing her tresses from her brow in glee,
"Thy rapid course through realms of air shall see,
"And whisper blessings as she looks on thee!

"Quick from this garden, moist with verdure, rise,
"And turn thee northward; in thy lofty flight
"The nymphs of air, with eager upturned eyes,
"Shall look on thee with wonder and delight.

"Then turning east,' yon glorious gems that blend
"Their light and shade in Indra's heavenly bow,*
"To thy dark ground a softened light shall lend,
"And make thee glorious with a borrowed glow,
"As the gay splendors of the peacock throw
"New beauty round the youthful Krishna spread.

"Linger awhile, then launching lightly forth,
"Leave the dark glades which wood nymphs wander o'er,
"Pursue thine airy journey to the north;
"Soon over Vindhya's mountain wilt thou soar,
"And Sipra's rippling stream, whose waters glide
"Beneath their feet, without their rush and roar,
"In many a rock-barred channel, summer-dried.

"Each sylph shall watch thee with observant eyes,
"And mark the rain birds eager for the rain
"Flocking to meet thee from the distant skies,
"Will with her tender glance thy heart prevail,
"With too successful blandishments assail
"Thy yielding heart!

---

* The crest of Siva is the new moon, and the Himalaya mountains, amid which Alaka is situated, are his favourite haunt.   Indra's heavenly bow—the Rainbow·
Note by R. T. H. Griffiths, M.A., on the *Cloud Messenger* of Kalidasa.

"On, on my herald! as thou sailest nigh,
"A green of deeper glory will invest
"Visala's groves where the pale leaf is dry.
"There shall the swans awhile their pinions rest,
"There the rose-apple in full beauty drest
"Shall show her fruit, then shall the crane prepare,
"Warned of the evening rain, to build her nest,
"And many a tender spray shall rudely tear
"From the old village tree, the peasants' sacred care,

"The famous hill of Chitrakúta* woos
"Thy friendly presence!"

*   *
*

III.

NAKOOLA, thus urged by the Yuksha, proceeded to the forest of Yanda-Madána in the mountain Rishyamukha, where was the dwelling of King Hanumân—Son of the Wind. The Monkey-Deity was there, with all his Simians—Gaya and Gavótsha, Sarábha, Mánda, Dvirida, Nila, Nála, Téna, and Jambával, "most ancient of apes." The sage Markandhya also, the compiler of the Vâna-purâna, was there as guest of King Hanumân. He it was, indeed, who is said to have inspired the wise words and deep sayings of the Monkey-Deity, King of the Woods.

Surrounded by his apes and cranes, Hanumân stood and welcomed Nakoola by the eight rites of hospitality (Arghya), such as he had before extended to Bhîma.

"Wittabo! oh, brother of Bhîma. Goest thou also to the "war? or seekest thou the fairy forms of earth? for well I "know thy heart, O youth. I say not unto thee 'tis well, for "hath not, Vishnu-Sârman said, 'The beauty of the cuckoo is "'its song; the beauty of woman is constancy to her husband; "'the beauty of the ill-favoured is kindness; the beauty of "'the poor is patience; the beauty of princes is *valour!*' So

---

* Near Omerkantuk—see "Bhima," page 92.

"there are many kinds of merit, oh Pandau. Perhaps thou
"hast found a guide in Lilavâti. Listen:—In Sriparónti a
"rumour was prevalent that a goblin—by name Ghanta-Karna
"(bell-ear)—haunted the summit of a mountain. The case was
"this—a thief, who had stolen a bell, was killed by a tiger.
" Some monkeys picked up the bell, and kept ringing it. The
" people all fled from the continual ringing, believing that a
"fury was there. A certain woman of that place, however,
"had satisfied herself that monkeys were ringing it. She
" proceeded to the forest with fruits, and scattered them about.
" The monkeys therefore left the bell, which the woman seized
" and returned to the city, where she obtained great rewards
"from the king.* Hence I say, despise not woman's wit!
" Perhaps thou hast done wisely in trusting to a woman's
"guidance ; but remember Lakshmi (wealth, success) some-
"times favours the base ; Parvâti is found associated with the
"plebeian ; Kâma pays court to the unworthy ; the cloud
" rains on the mountain."

Nakoola replied,—" Nay, O ancestor! my dear Lilavâti
"hath left paradise and kindred to follow my destiny."

" 'Tis well, oh tiger amongst princes ; but in the sandal trees
" are serpents; in the water are lotuses, but alligators also; in our
"enjoyments are envious spies; no pleasures are unimpeded."

Nizkoola laughed. " By Wittabah! oh, King, who then
"can trust a woman? Canst thou truly say, oh ancestor,
"that a fair one e'er betrayed thee?"

Hanumân replied, — " Listen, Bull of Pandaus. In a
"pleasure-lake of the south—in times long past—I fell in
"love with Karpúra-Manjári, daughter of a flamingo named
"Karpúra-Keli; and at the same time the Princess Ratna-
" Manjári, daughter of King Kandápa-Keli, King of Vidyad-
"hára in Singhâla-dwipa (Ceylon), regarded me with favour.
" The two young ladies equally favored my suit ; but it hap-
"pened that Princess Ratna being jealous, sought the advice

---

* Paraphrased from the Hitopadesa.

"of the Fairy Swirna-Rékha, who presented her picture, only
"making it a condition that it should not be touched; where-
"upon the Princess Ratna-Manjári took an occasion, when I
"was conversing with her rival, Karpúra-Manjári, the beauti-
"ful flamingo, to invite us both to visit the niche where the
"fairy's picture stood.   We did so, and I—my curiosity being
"excited—touched Swirna-Rékha with my hand.   For so
"doing, I was spurned by her—though only a picture—with
"her foot, beautiful as a lotus, and found myself in my own
"country, a thousand koss distant, and I never saw my dear
"Karpúra-Manjári more; hence I say, fairy guidance is a
"doubtful thing."
        Again Nakoola laughed, "O, Lilavâti! hearest thou?"
        But fair Lilavâti, offended, turned aside her face—beautiful
as the moonbeam—and wept, and said: "There are to whom
"all kindness and just persuasions are thrown away; to whom
"one must ever speak in words of menace."
        Hanumân shook his head gravely.   "O, Pandau, a hundred
"kind acts are lost upon the wicked; a hundred wise words
"are lost upon the stupid; a hundred precepts are lost upon
"the obstinate; a hundred sensible hints are lost upon the
"fool.   Nevertheless, I say not, oh, fair Lilavâti, that *thou* art
"like Swirna-Rékha, that cruel fairy I have told thee of. Listen,
"oh, auspicious woman! and answer me this riddle— *Wisdom*
"and *Beauty* are twins; caust thou choose between them?"
        "No," said Lilavâti; "I choose both."*
        Nakoola enquired: "But say, oh Ancestor! what were the
"deeds of Great Râma and the faithful Lakshman when the
"heroes, with Thee and Súgriva and the Simian army, des-
"troyed Râwun in Lanka?   Be pleased to narrate the circum-
"stances, oh, Son of the Wind."

_____

        * A play upon the words Nakoola (wise) and Sahadeva (beautiful, handsome),
who were the twin sons of Madri, and so only half-brothers of the three elder
Pandaus.   I fear we have the authority of the Mahabarat for the existence of
polyandry as a recognised institution of ancient India,—even the possession of a
wife amongst a family of brothers seems to have been no uncommon practice.

Hanumân paused, and pondered apace; then he sighed and "said, "Oh, young tiger amongst heroes! Though the shades "of night involve the forest, and before the sun rise in the "morn I and my guard of Vânapûtras must part for the north, "I will recall the great war of my youth to tell thee, his de-"scendant, of great Râma's deeds in Lanka and the southern "lands; but first I must perform the agnihobra sacrifice to "the manes of great Râma and his noble brother Lakshman." He resumed,—"Mâla the 'magnanimous ape,' who built the "mole across the sea to Lanka said, 'Once in the hill country "'Vishnu-Kârman, the celestial architect, met my mother, "'the beautiful ape, on the mountains of Mahabun, I am their "'son.' Guided by Nâla, therefore, O Nakoola—when great "Râma and his brother Lakshman both lay sorely wounded by "the sea before Lanka—I, Hanumân, Son of the Wind, alone "went to the hill country of the Hû, Hû, and Hâ, Hâ princes "of the Gandaurs, to fetch thence the simples growing there "to cure their wounds; and missing them, I tore up by the "root this hill Yanda-Madâna, with all its simples growing "on it, and carried it to Lanka. Did I not also rescue the "Apsâra (fairy) Yandakâli from the slaughtered alligator? "Behold, she is my wife. Hence I say, oh, Pandau, thou "hast done wisely in asking me to relate the heroes' deeds."

He paused, and the surrounding apes applauded.

Again Hanumân spake:—"Thou knowest, oh, Pandau! "how the noble Râma, with the fair Sita and his faithful "brother Lakshman, went into voluntary exile, so that the "oath of his old father Dusarâtha, made to Kaikeyi, Bhârut's "mother, might be fulfilled. Thou hast heard how, on the "banks of the flashing Surjoo and elsewhere the hero wandered, "and how the lovely Sita—ravished from his forest home by "the cruel giant Râwun—was carried to Lanka. The faith-"ful and 'eminent' vulture, Jaytayu, fell in defence of his "friend's wife, fair Sita, and, dying, disclosed the route the "ravisher had fled. Thus much thou hast heard, and may be

K 2

"knowest that after deep sorrow and much adventure in the
"wilderness seeking further trace of his lost love, the noble
"Râma found King Súgriva, Chief of Apes, amidst the Vind-
"hya's wild domain.   Oh, Prince, I was great Súgriva's
"friend, and followed him in exile when, unjustly driven away
"from the pleasant forests by Bálin, his jealous brother, he
"remained an exile in the Vindhyas.   Great Râma lent his
"aid, and with our assistance slew great Bálin, and reinstated
"Súgriva on the throne of the Simian races;—but still no trace
"of Sita lost, and Râma languished in his sorrow!   *   *

"At length one day we ate our frugal meal beneath a lofty
"peak in Vindhya's solemn mountains.   Below us lay the
"gorges of Nerbudha, and the gleaming waters of its channel
"—then a chain of lakes—forest fringed, and haunted by the
"flamingoes, cranes, and birds of air.   On a terrace below us
"two eagles were conversing, and we Simians who know the
"voice of birds, heard them say how lonely Sita was in far
"Lanka's isle.   Enough! the word was told to noble Râma,
"who, aided by the Simian army, marched to Lanka.   Has
"not great Valmiki (and Kálidâsa in his sweet song of
"Sacantála) told of the great war of Lanka!   Súgriva led the
"host of which I, Hanumân, was also chief.   Oh, excellent
"youth! I recall the famous deeds of heroes such as Râma,
"and Súgriva with his apes.   The Simian host marched
"gaily through the pleasant forests of the south.   I laugh
"when I recall the active days and festive nights around
"the sylvan fires.   Oh, excellent asoka tree, under whose
"sacred shade fair Jánida gave me the parting kiss! oh, cave
"of bliss! oh, pleasant, wholesome times! may blessed Mark-
"andhya and fair Vyâsa note ye in the annals, so that all
"posterity may know the record!   At length we reached the
"sea.   Thus did noble Râma order the array of battle:—' Let
"Súgriva be in the midst of the army—a king is the centre
"round which his people gather.   Nila, with a chosen band,
"shall precede the host; at its head shall march the giant

"Simians Naya, Gaya, Gavaya, and Gavotsha, as in the
"prairie the large buffaloes lead on the herd. Let the noble
"Simiau Rishabha—because he is a bull amongst apes—com-
"mand the right wing. The left shall have for chief Gandh-
"ânâdava, whose impetuous valour is like that of an elephant
"in the season of rut. I, with Hanumân, Son of the Wind,
"will follow; and near me Lakshman, borne by illustrious
"Angada—like Siva, carried by the supernal bull! Jambâva l,
"Sushéra, and Véga Larsin, shall protect the rear. Thus, if
"it seem good to thee, O magnanimous lord of quadrumanous
"creatures! will we determine the order of your army.'
  "'Let the noble Râma be obeyed,' cried Súgriva.
  "But the heart of Râma was very sad; he whispered to his
"brother, faithful Lakshman—'So long! so many hours quite
"'lost! So much of beauty and of fervour missed! How shall
"'all be given back to me since life itself is short—too short
"'for love. Each moment spends it. Time drives him ever
"'on. At each step, weeping, he leaves a fragment of his soul.'
  "'Nay, brother,' answered Lakshman, 'surely the stars are
"'gentle. Râma, dear Lord! hold high thy heart; thou art
"'marching to conquer back the radiance of thy life!'
  *   *   *   *   *   *
  "The scene is changed.
  "Night. Râwun—scourge of the three worlds—stood
"alone on the ramparts of his celestial town of Lanka. He
"was not deceived; he knew his hour was come. Standing
"there with folded arms he watched the Simian army landing
"and ranging on the beach. Scorn—the master-passion of
"the fiend—pervaded him. The shore was too far off for
"any tramp of feet to reach the solitary watcher. At length
"his brother Kambukurna, at last aroused from apathy, ap-
"proaches him. 'Oh, brother, Râma is very noble. They call
"'him the friend of living creatures! It had been better to
"'dare this prince to combat than to carry off his wife. My
"'counsel, brother, is to send back Sita. A bad deed weakens

"'the arm, and spoils one for honest warfare.'   But Râwun's
"brow grew dark, and he gave the word to close in battle.

    *   *   *   *   *   *

  "The battle closed on the shores of Lanka.   Râma is
"wounded, as is also Lakshman, sorely, and Súgriva thus
"laments: 'O, Râma, King of Men! my Benefactor, King,
"'and Lord!   O, heavens, that I should see thee thus. * *
"'I will die with thee, my Lord.   Thy poor Súgriva will
"'stretch him by thy side.   Angada shall lead the Simians
"'back to the sweet, quiet forests ; I will return no more.   I
"'will not see again the pleasant cave of Rishkandya, nor
"'Tárá, gentlest of the apes.   Bear her my greetings, Simians;
"'and say I perished with the noble Râma.'   But wise Vib-
"hishama reproved the afflicted ape. * * * 'Twas then,
"Oh Prince, I flew to Mahabun, and brought back the
"mountain Yanda-Madána with all its simples, to cure the
"noble Râma and brave Lakshman.   Meantime the faithful,
"loving Sita was prisoner in Lanka's town.   The cruel
"Ráwun seeks her love, and urges unlawful arguments to
"move her.   Thus that noble lady answered:—'You speak
"'to me of passion, and fire of throbbing pulses, and longings
"'for more full delight.   Love has another sense to me: it is
"'a radiance, not a flame; and kindles rather light than heat.
"'Love! I have known its rapture, O King of Ráchshasas.
"'I, your captive, have known its rapture!   Think you to
"'waken unholy fire in the breast where reigns a star? to
"'drag down to lust a heart that has been given wings?'
"Holding out both her arms she called on Râma. * * *

  "Oh, Nakoola! I saw Naráda—messenger of the gods—
"descend from Swerga to comfort the dear, faithful lady; the
"while the noble Râma, recovered from his wound, and saw
"his lovely, faithful Sita in a trance.*

---

  * In this passage the quasi modern idea of "rapport" is clearly foreshadowed;
and throughout the mystic literature of India we meet with the *modernized* idea
of *odic* force in the mysterious force in nature called *akas* in Sanskrit occultism.

"Soon after this the assault is given, and Lanka and its "band of Ráchshasas destroyed.

"I stood and saw the reconciliation of noble Ráma and his "lovely Sita—faithful proved by the eight rites of Arghya "sacrifice—who then departed for Ajoodhya, his native city. "I stood and pondered all these great events. Again the "Simian army crossed the sea, and the brave Vânapûtras— "children of the forest—dispersed to their sweet leafy homes "amidst the woods.*

"Now, oh Prince, I must depart for Jôsimut—the cooking "place—there to make ready to welcome brave Bhíma and the "sons of Kûnti—the elder Pandaus—when they shall arrive "to storm Mahendra, axis of the Land of Snow. Be thou "also amongst them, oh tiger of princes, else posterity and "the bards will curse thy name. Go, seek thou thy brother "Sediva—beloved of the gods—who now has left Kashmír, and "now awaits thee near to Indra-Killa and Nâgrakôt, where "great Arjûna heard 'sweet voices from the sky.' Consult "with him and Ogregund the King, how best to aid brave "Bhíma in the war. Be brave and fortunate; and I, even I, "Hanumân—Son of the Wind—will bless thee."

The aged sylvan king waved his war-club thrice over the head of Nakoola, and disappeared into the silent shades; but as the sun rose next morn Nakoola heard the rush of the Simian army as they bounded through the forest trees on their way to distant Himalaya.

---

* The above may be considered, in few words, as the "argument" of the Ram-ayana of Valmiki, a work of 24,000 slokas or verses. It has been translated, and parts beautifully paraphrased in Fredericka Robertson's "The Iliad of the East,' to which work I am indebted for the speeches of Rama, Sugriva, Sita, and Ra-wun, given in the text in an abreviated form, as also for other excerpts in the story of "Nakoola."

*   *
*

IV.

NAKOOLA, aroused from soft delights, then journeyed towards Káshmír to meet King Ogregund, who, with the young Pandau Prince Sediva, was marching towards the south to join Yûdishtír in the Dehra Dûn.

He arrived at the forest of Rishyamukhi, and first sought the cell of Markandhya, the Hermit, but it happened that through this selfsame forest, great Hiranya-Káshipû, King of Daityas—giant aborigines—was passing on his way to war with Ananta, King of the Nâgas and Assurs, who inhabit Patála (hell).

Nakoola called aloud to Markandhya :—"Oh, elephant "amongst saints! Bho! I perceive adverse omens. What "means this vast array of evil powers?"

He turned and beheld the Hermit dancing the *saptopuddie* (mystic dance) in front of his cell in a glade of the forest. Entranced in ecstacy appeared the Hermit's countenance ; his white hair streaming in the wind. The birds of the forest were staring at the sage with astonished eyes.

Nakoola called aloud :—"Bho! bho! Vibhu! Why art "thou dancing in rapture?"

Markandhya stood in silence ; his arms extended. At length after long cogitation he recited the *gayâtri*,* and spake as follows :—"Who knoweth the old King Indra-dyumna, "eldest of anchorites? The old owl knew him not ; the old "crane Nádi-jangha knew him not ; but the ancient tortoise "Akupára was older still, and knew him. I have wrested the "omen. Hence I say, oh Prince, after meeting Ogregund and "thy twin brother, go to the Land of the Tortoise (Kumáon) "and join brave Bhîma in the war."

*   *   *   *   *   *

---

* The Gayatri is considered the holiest verse in all the Vedas. It is to be found in the Rig Veda—"We meditate on that excellent Light of the Divine Sun : may he illuminate our minds!"

Nakoola enquired again—"What means this array of hell, "O Vibha?"

Again the Hermit stood in silence, and deeply pondering, sought an omen. The sough of the evening wind sounded in the pine trees : the moan of evil spirits was heard in the gloom of the forest.

At this moment a chariot, drawn by two milk-white steeds, was seen approaching. Behold! the merry, merry Krishna! —Govinda the cowherd—drawn by the steeds Súgriva and Saivya, had entered the forest. Seeing the Hermit and the Pandau, he stayed his course, and alighted at the Hermit's cell.

Nakoola saluted. "Hail! oh, hairy one!* there be adverse "omens."

In answer Krishna recited a mantra (invocation) and in-voked the Sun. "Let us implore Light, oh son of Madri! in "this gloomy forest, then shall we plainly see with whom to "fight. Where is Vyâsa, my Sûta? (charioteer, bard, hench-"man), oh Indra! I call for Light! Rudra, "the weepers," "and the spirits of the winds are abroad, and moan in the "gloomy trees. Would that the friendly Hanumân—Son of "the Wind—were here to chase the evil races and malignant "spirits of Damáka from the forest. shades."

Markandhya now raised his voice and cried :—"Oh "Champions! this is máya (illusion). It is the sixth. lunar "day, when spirits fly abroad! Let us invoke Súrya (the "Sun), Lord of Light, under his 108 names, by the Agni-"hôbra sacrifice. Pull the mandára flowers, oh stag-eyed! "Bho!" He again recited the gayâtri, and lo! the evil crew of dæmon giants vanished, and the wood nymphs and spirits of the fountains began to peep forth from behind the leafy screen of foliage as the flush of sunset lighted up the arches

---

* A name of Krishna. It may be stated that in the Vedas—I think the Athar. vana Veda—a thousand synouyms of Siva are given, and each deity of the Hindoo Pantheou had numerous epithets or etymons.

of the forest, and the glow-worms lit up their tiny lanterns in the mossy dells as the "stars of the north arose and showed their heads of fire."

The Hermit invited the champions to his cell, and spread beneath the stars the frugal meal of sweet herbs and fruits, with crystal water from the holy stream. So Krishna, with Nakoola and Vyâsa the poet—reclining on the grass—entered into conversation on many things—wise, beautiful, and sublime—with the sage Markandhya, author of the Vânapurâna chronicle.

Nakoola enquired: "Oh, elephant amongst saints! he "pleased to narrate events since I, with Sâhâdeva, assisted "great Bhîma to slay Játasûra and Munimán the cannibals: "the surviving cannibal fled to the east. I also parted from "my brother, and journeyed to the south."

After a while Markandhya proceeded to relate as follows: "When the exiled Pandaus dwelt in the forest of Dwaila, and "lived by the produce of the chase, the surviving wild animals "of the wood came to great Yûdishtir and petitioned, 'Oh, "'just one, spare our remnant!' Whereupon the chiefs de- "parted to the Kamyáka wood near to Vindhu Lake. They "afterwards dispersed for sake of hunting,—Yûdishtir to the "east, Bhimsén to west, Arjûna to south, Sâhâdeva to the "north, oh Son of Mâdri! But first I saw Arjûna: he pro- "ceeded to Indrakilla, where he 'heard sweet voices from the "sky.' There he devoted himself to heaven, and performed "Yâpa. He fought with Náráyáma—Lucifer himself—and "obtained from Siva the Gandiva bow, as a gift to destroy "Karna, Bhisthma, Kripa, Drôna, and the Kuraus; also "Danávas, Ráchshasas, Bhûtas, Pisáchas, Gandharas, Paimá- "gas, and Daityas. May they be accursed! 'Om!

"Kuvéra and Varúna gave weapons and a divine car to "Arjûna, who resided in paradise five years, and consulted the "heavenly bards. Chitrasena taught him songs and music; "Partha taught him to hunt; and Urvâsi, best of Apsáras "gave him secret weapons, oh greatest of males! After this

"he bathed at Jambu-nugger and in Agastya Lake, and per-
"formed the Agnipatra sacrifice. 'Om!"
Turning to Krishna, he continued:—"Oh, hairy one! thy
"pupil Arjûna visited the island Tri-Kuta-Swétun.* He
"narrated to me his maritime adventures. He sounded the
"devadatta conch-shell, and Naráda, messenger of the gods,
"appeared at his behest.

"At the mountain Swéta-Mandara, the superior Yaksha
"Manivara—under Kuvéra, King of Yakshas—rules 88,000
"swift Gandharas, and four times that number of Kimpur-
"ashas and *Kinéras.*† To reach them the son of Kunti
"(Arjûna) performed Samádhi; and at Vadara he obtained
"the merit of the Vajapeya sacrifice. 'Om!

"Oh, tiger of Princes! listen to advice:—Kartikáya—God
"of War—delights in Sárasváti waters: its spring is in an
"ant-hill. Seek the teerut of the Aswinis, there one becomes
"handsome, oh Partha! At Vansa-Mutáka bathe and obtain
"the delivery of thy race! 'Om!

"I have seen at Manusha, on Papaga river, the antelopes
"changed to men by the power of austerity. I stood on holy
"ground at Brahmagôni. The omen hath declared the Pan-
"daus shall visit the leafy hermitage of Naka and of Narayána
"in Kailâsa; also the gardens and palaces of Maináka and
"Visâladâri, in paradise! but first they must endure war and
"hardships: such is the omen I have wrested. 'Om, 'om!"

Such were a few of the words of Markandhya the Hermit.
The poet Vyâsa, "the compiler"—then a youth—heard them as
they fell in slôkas from the Hermit's lips. Afterwards, in ex-
treme old age, when called on to narrate the events of the
great war, which he had witnessed in his youth, he wrote them
in the Vedas, and compiled the chronicles of the Mâhâbârât.

*   *   *   *   *   *

As the sun rose next morning, lo the army of King Ogregund of Káshmír, with Sediva the Pandau, his ally, is heard

---

* Believed by some to be Britain.
† Note the similitude to the classic "chimæra."

approaching with sound of trumpet, drum, and cymbal from the north; and soon the warlike pageant entered the deodára grove which overshadowed Markandhya's cell; Sâhâdeva (Sediva) the Pandau Prince, advancing in the van of the army, whilst Damoodâra—son of Ogregund—brought up the rear of the Káshmír army. On Sâhâdeva's banner appeared the Lotus of Káshmír; on Gonerda's standard—borne on a golden stick —was "an inhabitant of water, having an expanded mouth, destructive of all fishes, and conducive to fear;" on Prince Damoodâra's banner, the serpent Sésh appeared in warlike guise.

Nakoola hastened to the front, and fell on his' brother Sâhâdeva's neck and wept.

Afterwards Krishna mounted his car, drawn by the two white steeds Súgriva and Saivya, and drove the twin sons of Mâdri — Nakoola and Sâhâdeva — to the beautiful city of Súkhtimâti, the destined spouse of Nakoola. The lady started on first meeting him: she had beheld him in a dream, and loved him; and now the vision of her youth was realized. The day was spent in feasting and in courtly pastimes.

But now a portentous incident occurred : Hiranya-Káshipû, King of Giants, had been scared, not killed, by Markandhya's charm ; in the evening, roused by envy, he stole great Krishna's milk-white steeds, and drove away towards Nâra. Thus had Sála, son of Ayû—King of Frogs—stolen the horses of holy Vámâdéva, who cursed him, and his fate soon overtook him, being killed by Yátudánas; and his sister Súsobhána languished in silence, and would not approach water even at the command of the Raja, her husband. So did Markandhya's curse affect Hiranya-Káshipû. In the morning the dead body of the giant was found in a ravine. Like Phaeton, he had essayed to guide the fiery coursers o'er the mountains, but they had spurned the car, and hurled the giant from his seat; and lo! his body rolled down the cliffs of the Dhaola-Dhar, and lodged on a vast rock near Nâgra-killa. The vultures danced on the dead giant.

Fair Lilavâti had followed Nakoola to the city of the beautiful Sûkhtimâti, and had there met the Princess, also Sâhâdeva, "the handsome man." Love, the anteros of Kâma —the Indian Cupid—suddenly possessed her soul. Voiceless, the ready-tongued nymph gazed upon the "handsome one." On his part, Sâhâdeva was transfixed with admiration. On the other hand, Nakoola saw with rapture the lovely Princess who had dreamed of him in youth, and now for the first time beheld the image of her fancy. Amidst such fires of contrary destiny what could spring but the garood (phœnix) of desire!

In the warlike sports which followed on the meeting of the twin-born Pandau chiefs, the two fair ones' eyes were fixed, each on her new found champion, who on their part engaged in the warlike games in view to the admiration and applause of each his fairy mistress.

The words of Hauumân and his far-reaching riddle, "How to choose between *wisdom* and *beauty*" came to remembrance, and Lilavâti sighed and wept in secret as she recalled it; but Kâma was strong within her horoscope; and although the wise and auspicious lady remembered the warning of the Fairy Queen in the grotto of Rishyasringa, son of the doe, whilst she was an inhabitant of the fairy halls of Swerga, the impulse of the god was too mighty to resist.

In the soft evening twilight, as the stars came out and lighted with their glimmering radiance the grove where the camps of the warlike Pandaus lay, Lilavâti sought the pavilion of the Káshmír Prince and declared her love.

Alas! Shireen, the "Sweet one," had accompanied Sediva from far Anant-Ghur, with the gem of love, her blooming daughter, she who had escaped dread Siva's curse,* and Sediva turned away his face, and wept for the fair and false Lilavâti.

"Oh, auspicious woman! oh, best of Apsáras," whispered he, "be faithful to dear and wise Nakoola, and let us together

---

* See "Sediva," page 11.

"face the foe as becometh twin-brothers; besides, I love the
"beautiful Shireen; and even should a second spouse be law-
"ful to the youngest Pandau, be sure 'twould not be Thee."

Sediva spake in honour, and Lilaváti trembled. Covering
her burning face in her doputtuh (mantle), she went slowly
forth from the pavilion into the silent grove. Awhile she
stood beneath the sacred· peepul tree which shaded her pavilion,
and wept bitter tears of love and shame and sorrow; then she
hastily cast aside her diadem and the mystic charms she wore,
of silver and of burnished copper and of gold, and plucked a
champuk flower, which she placed on the coverlet of Nakoola's
couch, together with a fairy picture of herself, made by the
poet Chitrasena whilst she dwelt in Swerga; then covering
her face with her fair hands, she fled wildly into the night.

The Kshatriya guard who paced in front of the camp beheld,
as the moon rose, a white form flit across the darkened grove;
the peasants gathered at supper in the village hamlet on the
mountain slopes beheld a misty form glide amidst the shadows
of the pine trees and ascend the wooded upland; a hunter, as
he sate with bow and arrow watching the forest slopes under
the starry top of Maimona, beheld a fairy form rush past him
towards the snow; he trembled, for he remembered the story
of the yech, who beguiles and devours men, and had tempted
the hunter Bhairáva to the abyss which led to Nára (hell): he
turned toward the crescent moon — the crest of Siva—and
recited an invocation for the "escape of the head from sin."
The goorul-antelope of the cliff rose from his rocky lair upon
the wild hill-top, and gazed at the intruder, then bounded
into the moonlit glen beneath; and the ancient owl, who
had dwelt for ages past in the deep grove of cedars which
shaded the alpine Temple of Deodára, hooted wildly from his
gloomy eyry, as he blinked and saw the shadowy form of Lilaváti rush through the shadows of night; and the lion of the
uplands, as he stood on a moonlit top of Sveta-Parvat, and
gazed around to seek his nightly prey, trembled, and with tail

drooping on the ground, slunk gloomily away as he beheld the
wild dishevelled form of Lilavâti still ascending towards the
sacred hill Kailás. Lastly, the Hermit Markandhya, who had
ascended the mountains and was gazing on the midnight
heavens to observe the starry host and cast an horoscope and
wrest knowledge from the constellations, saw the fair nymph, ·
and raised a hymn of thanks to great Bhôwâni for the auspicious omen of the flying fair one.

And this was the last of mortals who beheld dear Lilavâti
on earth ; and no man knoweth further whither she went—
whether to Kailás, or whether she returned to Fairyland or
Swerga, and resumed her place amongst the Apsáras she had
left to follow Nakoola, who can say? But this one thing
Nakoola knew, that ever and anon at moonrise—and often in
his dreams—the fairy form of dear Lilavâti stood trembling
in the vague twilight, and stretched forth her lotus hand towards him as though invoking a blessing.

So Nakoola was comforted,' and wedded fair Sûkhtimáti,
and allied himself to Sediva his twin-brother. Accompanied
by Krishna, together they marched with Ogregund the King
adown the slopes and forests of Himâleh towards the camp of
brave Bhîma in the Dehra Dûn, where also great Yûdishtir
and the Pandau reserve were camped. Nakoola proceeded onwards to the Land of the Tortoise (Kumäon), and near his
old dwelling place in the oasis hard by Brahmadeo, he joined
the band of Kshatriyas and warlike Pandaus; afterwards,
guided by tall Purujit, his kinsman, he advanced with the
right reserve along the banks of flashing Surjoo, and aided
brave Bhîma in his victory over the Ráchshasas and Nâgas of
the snow.   *   *   *   *   *

Rishyasringa, "Son of the Doe"—-he who had become a
king in Indra's paradise—again met Nakoola as he returned
from the war. In the cedar grove where the youthful Pandau
had first sighted the silver stag, the Fairy King stood beneath
the canopy of the lofty deodara trees; thus he spake—"Young

"Chief! thou hast redeemed thy name, and so far hast done "well thy part to vindicate the Pandaus' destiny! More yet "remains; so draw not back thy hand. Be brave! be faith-"ful to thy fair spouse the Princess Sûkhtimâti! She who "was appointed as thy guide of life—dear Lilavâti—has her-"self fallen short of *wisdom:* she hath returned to paradise, "and thou mayest not meet her more; nevertheless, she and "the Apsáras of our lofty dome in Swerga will observe thy "fate with sympathy and love. Me thou shalt see no more on "earth; but on thee I bestow the Fairy blessing. Farewell, "oh child of wisdom!" Rishyasringa, "Son of the Doe—giver of the rains of summer"—waved his wand over Nakoola, and vanished from amidst the stems of the cedar trees into the glooms of the silent forest.   *   *   *   *

Nakoola then aroused his heart. He collected his adherents, and, followed by tall Purujit his nephew, again he joined brave Bhíma for the great final battle with the usurping Kuraus.

───────

The wandering Cimmerian now lays down his pen; much had he roamed over the fair face of earth, and traced the wanderings of the errant Pandaus. in the Land of 'Ind, especially the mountains where the heroes had dwelt. He threaded the leafy solitudes and mountain summits of Him-âleh, of Nilaghirrie, of Sahyádri, and of Aravelli, in search of knowledge, and found it not in the busy cities, nor yet on the lofty mountain tops or in the silent forests; but at length he found it in the "cave,"—in the wise words of sages who had pondered and written ages before he lived on earth; so he pondered their words of wisdom, and read the record of their thoughts, and seeing that they were wiser than himself he retired into solitude and dwelt a space apart, and wrote these histories of the errant Pandaus to beguile the tedious hours of travel, and raise the drooping spirits of his companions, and evoke their laughter.
     *   *
         *

Uma or Parbuttie (Lady of the Mountain),
Wife of Siva.
(From a native picture.)

⁓⟨Ꝥ̣e⟩·⸱ꟽar⟨ꝺ⟩⸱⸦

of the

⸱⸱ Kuraus·⸱·and·⸱·Pandaus. ·⸱⸱

[THE wandering Cimmerian having found in the Cave* many chronicles describing the wars of the Kuraus and Pandaus, including the great battle of Kúrú-Kshétra, resumes his pen and narrates as follows.]

I.

D URING the exile of the Five Pandaus, the Kuraus—under Karna and Sekûni—engaged in war with King Chitrasena and the Gandavas, but were defeated; whereupon King Duryodhana (Jirjoodeen) and his Princesses, Vinda and Anuvinda, with Dúhsásána, applied to their generous rivals, the exiled Pandaus, for aid against the common foe. They were reviled by Bhîma, but Yûdishtír in noble language reproved Bhîma, and consented to aid them.

The Pandaus then engaged in war with the Gandavas, and rescued Duryodhana and the Kuraus; but, jealousy of the former prevailing, Duryodhana contemplates suicide : he is, however, encouraged by Karna, who vows to kill Arjûna—who was greatly distinguished in the war—after three years.

Some of the Kuraus in this war were, Dúhsasána, Bhuresráva, Somadutta, Vahlika ; besides "the Gambler," who returned with Karna to Hustinapúra.

Some time after these events, the Pandaus—whilst dwelling in the forest of Dwaila—are themselves attacked by Yayad-

---

* An allusion to the Libraries of the "British Museum" and of the "India Office," to whose treasures the author owes much ; especially for the subject matter of the latter portion of this little work.

L

ratha, King of Sindhu; whose army, however, is defeated
with prodigious slaughter—"the crows dance upon the slain."
Yayadratha is taken prisoner, and "his hair parted"—prepar-
atory to being made a slave—but is pardoned by Yûdishtír,
who, in noble language, quotes the Kshatriya's oath "to spare
the fallen foe who says 'I yield me.'" Yayadratha is released,
and escapes by way of Gungadwâra.

Many are the adventures of the exiled Pandaus, as related
in the Varna-Parva, which contains an enormous mass of
legends and myths disconnected, but strung together so as to
form the great chronicle of the Mâhâbârât, which has been
asserted to contain—if all could be recovered—as many as
one hundred thousand slôkas or verses. Cosmogony, ethics,
duties of and toward Brahmins and holy men, social duties of
all classes and castes are detailed; and the reader has to wade
through an immense mass of trivialities to arrive at the few
points of interest to be found in this overgrown epic, so inferior (to my thinking) to that noble poem the Râmâyânâ.
There are, however, episodes of much beauty in both.

In the Mâhâbârât we meet with the legend of Satyavân and
Savitri,* wherein the duties of a wife and widow are suggested,
whose child is related to have been committed to the river
Ganges (in a basket, as Moses), and floated down the waters
of the holy stream Yamûna to Champa lake.

Again, the episode of the temporary deaths of the four
younger Pandaus—Bhîma, Arjûna, Nakoola, and Sâhâdeva—
strikes the reader as a strange myth, and seems to be emblematic of Strength, Valour, Wisdom, and Beauty, succumbing
to death, till rescued by heavenly virtue (Dhurma), represented
by Yûdisthír, who is often designated Dhurm-Raja in the
chronicles. The legend is something as follows:—The four
younger Pandaus successively approach to drink of sacred
water without the consent of a certain Yaksha, its custodian.
They successively fall dead. Lastly, Yûdishtír approaches

---

* Savitri was also the "mother of the gods."

and essays to drink the sacred stream, but is first questioned by the Yaksha on several philosophic points; all whose queries however he answers so satisfactorily, that he not only obtains the Yaksha's consent to drink, but obtains also the boon of his brothers' restoration to life; whereupon he cogitates whom first to restore. His sense of JUSTICE—the predominant feature in Yûdishtír's character, as represented throughout the Vedas—prompts him to select Nizkoola (or Nakoola) as first for resuscitation, who, as his half-brother only, might be considered less dear to him than his own brothers Bhíma and Arjûna; the former of whom indeed is throughout represented as his favourite brother; but he declares his father's two wives —Kûnti and Mâdri—to have been alike in his affection and respect; hence he selects Nakoola first for resuscitation, afterwards Sâhâdeva (Sediva), Arjûna, and Bhíma in succession, as granted by the Yaksha.

The following are a few of the questions propounded by the Yaksha, and of King Yûdishtír's answers:

Q.—What is swifter than the wind? and what is more plentiful than grass?

A.—The mind is swifter than the wind. Sorrow is more plentiful than grass.

Q.—What is born that does not move?

A.—An egg.

Q.—What goes alone: and what changes?

A.—The soul (like the sun) wanders alone. The mind (like the moon) undergoes changes.

Q.—What is the best of all enjoyment and happiness?

A.—Health and contentment.

Q.—What makes one beloved, and obviates repentance?

A.—By giving up pride one becomes beloved; by giving up anger he avoids repentance.

The above episodes may lead us to the time when, the term of their exile approaching, the Pandaus began to collect their allies for the great final struggle then impending with the

usurping Kuraus. But first the omens and portents of the
great war, as detailed in the Bhishtma Parva* may be given.
A few are as follows :—"Birds of prey stare at the elephants,
"and the sun is beset with 'kabundhas'—trunks of men
"without heads. Circles across the sun. Stars in a blaze [a
"dreadful omen!] The noise of boars and cats fighting in the
"sky. Gnats with iron-like trunks bite the horses. Locusts.
"Dust, flesh, and iron falling from the sky. Asses associate with
"cows. Monsters howl with gaping mouths. Eggs produce
"young starlings, cocks, and owls. Elephants make unpro-
"pitious shrieks. Women produce litters of children. Comets.
"Lilies grow on trees. Mars or Jupiter in retrograde is tor-
"mented by the sun; and Jupiter's second satellite, like fire.
"Cows' milk like blood. Fire proceeds from arrows shot with
"fine ghee. Beasts and birds shrieking on all sides. Birds
"with one eye and leg cry terribly in the sky at night. Showers
"of dust. Earthquakes in Himôdi. High winds and light-
"nings. Conchs sounding on the left."

Vyâsa said, "Such omens, O Vaisanpayána (Son of Dit-
"râshtura), portend great wars and death of princes!"
Vyâsa ended by recommending peace with the Pandaus.

After such portents we may anticipate that the great war
is not far distant, and we may accordingly proceed to narrate
a few particulars and legends of the great battle of Korau-
Khét (or Kúrú-Kshétra), so often alluded to in the preceding
stories, and around which indeed so much of the Mâhâbârât
mainly clusters.

Before proceeding, however, to narrate the details as we find
them in such portions of the great epic as the Bhishtma Parva,
the Drôna Parva, &c., it may be permitted us to picture to
ourselves the arena on which the great field was fought, and
the aspect of the opposing hosts as they appeared in · arms
about March 1367 B.C. We must draw largely on the imagination, although indeed some tradition of the arms and array
of the ancient warlike Aryans has in part come down to us.

* A section of the Mahabharat.

The hour may be supposed sunrise ; the time of year just that period when the cold season of northwest India is beginning to give way before the approaching summer. The sun rises over the vast plain of Thanésur, still covered with the verdure of spring, and dotted here and there with smiling crops, but from which the slight hoar frost and mists of the preceding night have scarcely lifted. The loom of the distant Himalaya mountains, crowned with snow, is just visible in the horizon. The crisp, cool air of morning braces the nerves. As the rival hosts approach in the distance, the wild pig, disturbed in their haunts of sugar cane and reedy brakes along the river bank, are seen whiffling through the long grass toward the lower spurs of the Seváliks, their mountain home. The wild cry of the sairas-crane, and of the koolen, flying north from their feeding grounds on the banks of Sárásváti, is heard high overhead in the morning sky. The harsh crow of the francolin partridge, and the whistle of the quail as they whirr out of the long jungle grass is also heard around. Presently, in the distance, barbaric music heralds the approach of the Pandau army, descending through the passes of the Seváliks, fresh from victory in the mountains. The growl of the long iron trumpets of the highlanders from Thibet and the south-eastern mountains of Himáleh, forms a hoarse monotone to the clash of kettle-drums and conchs. Shouts of invocation to great Siva sound on all sides. The Hindoo war-cry, "*B'hùm, b'hùm, Mahadeo! B'hùm, b'hùm, Mahadeo!*" fills the air, as they march toward the foe. Soon the Pandau army debouches on the plain, raised above the ground in mid air* like the heavenly host of King Indra! The pennons flutter in the lifting breeze of dawn. The lion, the monkey, the crocodile or alligator, the royal fish, the wolf, the lotus, and many other emblems appear upon their banners, and are described in the chronicles.

---

* This is no mere figure of fancy: the author has himself more than once seen troops of the *Army of the Punjaub* thus matamorphosed by the mirage of early morn.

The rival Kings — Duryodhana the Kúrú, and Yûdishtír the Pandau, raised high above the rest on lofty elephants, survey their respective hosts.   The principal chiefs or champions in war-cars or chariots, each conveying two, the driver and his chief.   The lesser chiefs on horses housed with glittering trappings.   Their followers on foot, chiefly armed with spear and bow, and sword and mace, and orbed shield.

How shall the wandering stranger describe the glittering lines of warlike Kshatriyas drawn up in battle array facing each other, ready to join issue in the deciding throw for empire.   Not to the pen of the wandering Cimmerian is it given to recount in fitting strain the high emprise and lofty deeds of semi-human champions, enacted in the 14th century before the dawn of Christianity on earth.

The poet might tell of deities of the Hindoo Pantheon— Indra, Varûna, &c., hovering around and above the combatants in the sultry air; and the Stars and Constellations in their courses trembling for the issue of the great event which shall confer a sovereign on the sunny land of Ind!   He might tell of the thunder of the war-cars, of the shouts of the contending heroes, the shrieks of elephants and of horses taught to battle for their riders; of the air darkened by flights of arrows, as spikes of thistle-down floating in the wind; of the plunge of fire-rockets in the surging grass, which taking fire involves the combatants in flame and smoke; of the cruel aspect of the victors, the agitation and despair of the conquered!

In the distance, on the walls and towers of Hustinapoora, the mothers, sisters, and wives of the Kuraus stand, anxiously expectant of the issue; whilst Ditrashtura, the aged father of the Kuraus, sitting in his palace gate, awaits tidings of the great battle from his Suta (charioteer) Sandjaya.

*   *   *   *   *   *

The hosts approach each other, and halt when a bow-shot apart.   Silence!   The leaders are seen to pause.   The chiefs gather round them and confer.   What hinders them instantly to close in battle? But one thing—the *consanguinity* of the contending factions! Still silence! At length an aged chieftain of the Kuraus (Bhishtma) sounds the challenge, and great Arjûna, the Pandau, impatient for the fight, answers by a blast from his heaven-bestowed conch-shell. Alone he advances in front of the two armies; then observing faces of his kindred in the opposing line, he pauses and consults his charioteer—supposed great Krishna. His soul is softened: he argues the question of the war of kindred, with his god-like Suta (charioteer). Too late! The die is cast: to fall or conquer is the Pandau's high emprise; and soon the battle joins.

Here we must pause, and reverting to the written records of the Cave,* and to the ancient chronicles above alluded to, content ourselves with the bald legends they present to us of the fabled deeds of a few heroes of the war, conspicuous for their birth or prowess, or the part they enact in the great drama of the Wars of the Kuraus and Pandaus, as related in the Mâhâbârât.

II.

The Battle of Korau-Khet, B.C. 1367.

IN the month of Kartik, K.Y. 2268, when the moon was near the full, brave Bhîma, commander of the Pandau army, advanced from Kedar-Khûnd across the Sevâlik mountains, and marched adown the sandy Sârâsvâti stream towards Thanésur plain. Soon he discovered the Kurau host under the command of aged Bhishtma in his front, drawn up on the plain of Thanésur (afterwards called Kúrú-Kshétra), covering their capitol city, Hustinapoora. The army halted. Silent the warlike Kshatriyas stood in arms—their arms and war-cars resplendent in the sun. Brave Bhîma paused a space, then communed with Yûdishtíra,† here called Dhurm Raja, "King of Justice." Arjûna "of the sounding bow," and the "twin sons of Mâdri"—Nakoola and Sâhâdeva—also join the

---

* See foot note, page 137.

† *Yudhi*—battle, and *sthira*—firm = Unflinching in war. Dhurm-Raja = King of Justice or Religious Virtue.

council. They consult the omens; Markandhya, with wise
Vyâsa is standiug nigh.

Say, O Kartikáya, God of War! the names of heroes and
of godlike chiefs on both sides! But are they not narrated in
the Bhisthma-parva, and in the Drôna-parva, and in the other
chronicles of the Varna-purana, written by Markandhya the Sage!

First, Bhishtma — surnamed also Devavráta — sounds the
challenge. Arjûna, whose Suta (charioteer) was great Krishna,
sounds the devadatta couch-shell in reply! then advancing to
the fight he recognises so many faces of kindred in the opposing line that he pauses, and communes with Krishna whether
he be justified in engaging in such a fratricidal strife. An
extraordinary mataphysical argument ensues, which ends in
Krishna assuaging his scruples, and convincing him of the
justice of his cause in accepting wage of battle. Arjûna, the
"rider of white horses," then again advances, and the battle
joins. He "recites formulas" as he shoots his arrows from
the Gandiva bow, whilst Késava loudly blows the Panchajanya
war-horn. Arjûna overthrows the "Monkey Standard" of
Dhánajaya, and drives on triumphant; and at the very outset
Bhîma slays King Bhágadatta. Various flags are described.
In the battle, Sikhandi, aided by Arjûna, kills the driver of
Bhishtma's car, and captures his flag. Yûlishtír then concentrates the Pandau army, and falls on Bhishtma (son of
Ganga); and so the battle goes on till the tenth day, when
Bhishtma falls by the hand of Arjûna. He remains on the
field "wounded to the quick." A great destruction of the
Kuraus eusues. The dying Bhishtma "hears cheering voices
from the sky." Geese from the holy lake Manâsa circumambu-
late the hero as he lies; and fan him with their pinions till the
sun and moon are in a happy position ; then Bhishtma sends
for Arjûna, and "takes water from him." Arjûna recites a
mantra (or hymn) over the fallen chief, who dies recommending
peace with the Pandaus. The death of Bhishtma closes the
first period of the great battle.

On the death of Bhishtma, the Kuraus proceed to elect a successor in chief command. *Karna* refuses to take command before Drôna (Acharya), his preceptor in arms, who accordingly is chosen to succeed Bhishtma. He immediately leads an attack in the "châka-vyûka" formation—apparently an échelon —on the Pandau array. Abhimanya, son of Arjûna, assails the échelon, and discharges arrows at Karna which "cut his armour as a snake enters an ant-hill." He commands the Pandau van. He is opposed by the Kúrú Dûhsasâna, who, however, is wounded and carried off the field; but at length, after achieving vast success, Abhimanya is himself wounded by Subhadecoss, a brother of Karna; but still he holds the field and wages fight. The Kuraus are at length repulsed; "their faces parched, their eyes rolling, their bodies covered with sweat, the hair of their bodies standing on end, intent on flight, bad in the bowels," so says the charioteer Sandjaya to his master the aged Ditrashtara, sitting on the walls of Hastinapoora. Their flight, however, was for the present arrested by the fool Lackshmána, who soon pays the penalty of his temerity, and is killed by Abhimanya; but Abhimanya at length himself is slain, and falls "with his face to the foe." Arjûna then advances and "recites formulas" as he plies the Gandiva bow. Drôna hurls a spear and disables Yûlishtira's car-steeds. The King is hurled from his chariot, but is saved from Drôna by his brother Sâhâdeva (Sediva), whose chariot he mounts. He rallys the Pandaus, and concentrates for a final charge on the partly successful Kurau host. The hero *Alambásha* then makes head, but is utterly destroyed by Bhima: "he fell like a heap of black collyrium and the flame tip of the red kinsúta tree in bloom." *Kritavarna* alone confronts the victorious Pandaus, and puts them to temporary rout, but is at length killed by Satyâki, who, following up his success, rides on and achieves great success : he is one of the chief Pandau heroes.

Thus the battle fluctuates. At length the great Kúrú hero

Drôna, who has performed prodigies of valour, falls by the hand of *Dhrishtáp-yumna:* Arjûna had tried in vain to save him.

At one period of the fight the Pandaus are worsted. During the rout *Ashtokthána* seeing Vyâsa "the compiler," thus humbly addressed him: "Bho! O mûni, what is this? What "defect have I?" He is comforted by Vyâsa, and resumes the fight. The Pandaus, moreover, are rallied by Yûdishtira, the "firm one" in battle; and finally, as we have seen, achieve a mighty victory.

In the Bhishtma-parva the Kuraus are finally described as "terrified, confounded with fear as beasts at the roaring of a lion, *bad in the bowels!* utterly disorganized and routed, and all their leaders slain."

Then we have the spectacle of the mothers, sisters, wives of the slain Kuraus, streaming across the plain from Hustina-poora, and settling on the dead as screaming sea-fowl on the sea-washed shores of Abûsín—"Father of Waters"—as narrated in a former story,* which, together with the incidents there related, forms the *closing* scene of the great battle ; wherein, moreover, Duryodhana, the usuper, having despaired of success, swallows poison on the field, leaving absolute victory to his rival, King Yûdishtír, surnamed "The Just."

*   *   *   *   *   *

So ends the great battle, and it may here be remarked that the conditions of warfare amongst the ancient Indian Aryans appear to have been essentially humane, and many passages might be quoted where clemency towards the enemy is inculcated and practised ; and often do we meet with the appeal to the Kshatriya's oath "To spare the fallen foe who says 'I yield me!'" an honourable act of grace which seems to have been scrupulously observed by the brave Aryan warriors of ancient times ; and a large humanity is clearly recognizable through all the monstrous fables and myths which involve their chronicles, and with which the heroic march of their great epic the Mâhâbârât is clouded.

---

* See page 104, "Bhima,"

Krishna & the Siege of Math'ra.

T HE readers of the preceding tales will have noted that the semi-human champion Krishna played no inconsiderable part in the Wars of the Kuraus and Pandaus: he was in fact the cousin of the latter.

The "Hárivansa"—written by Vyâsa the son of Parásara and Satyavâti—and the "Prem-Ságur" (or ocean of love), both give us a mythic history of his life, differing in many respects, but both claiming him as an avátar of Vishnú or Hári; and his brother Bálárámá as an avátar of Séshnâg or Ananta. Their exploits are of course mythic, or at least fabulous; and the Hárivansa contains also a mythological account of the genesis and geodesy of creation of which Hári was the fabled primæval exponent—the "dweller in the lotus" of life.

A quasi-historical account of his deeds on earth is given in both works, whilst the Prem-Ságur—a comparatively modern work in Hindi—relates adventures of a most grotesque and fantastic nature—warlike and amatory. They may be dismissed with a very few words.

Krishna's birth is stated to have occurred at midnight, on Wednesday the 8th day of the dark half of the month Bhádon: "all nature rejoices," but Raja "Hans" or "Causa," the enemy of the house of Vasondéva, orders the destruction of Brahmins, Vaishnavas, Jôgis, Jâtis, hermits, suniásies, bhairâgis, and other votaries of Hári, in hopes of destroying him; in fact, the history of the dangers encountered by Krishna in infancy are somewhat analogous to those of the classic Jupiter at the hands of Saturn. His mother's name according to the Prem-Ságur was Rohini, who gave birth to him "amidst the cows" in the Land of Braj; and, according to the same authority, his youth comprehended some rather remarkable exploits, of which the following—amongst many more—may be mentioned as examples :—

148   KRISHNA

"Pútána," a she-demon, is sent to destroy Krishna at Gókul, his birthplace, but is herself exterminated, and the young hero's parents are comforted. Next a "serpent-shaped demon" devours Krishna and certain cowherds, his friends, but the former swells to such a degree that "the serpent's belly is burst and he falls." Krishna's brother Bálárámá vies in prowess, and slays Dhénuk "a demon in form of an ass"; whereupon Krishna, not to be behind, disposes of the great water-serpent Káli, who dwelt in the river Yamâna.

Krishna, seeking to reform society, abolishes the worship of Indra, and builds the mystic mountain "*Goverdhun,*" where he and Báláráná "dance the circular dance" with cowherdesses beneath the moon.*

The tricks of Krishna are innumerable and far from edifying; and his frolics with the fair and frail gópies (cowherdesses) of the "Land of Braj," must be pronounced, I fear, reprehensible. In those days the "circular dance" beneath the merry moonlight seems to have been their principal pastime in the "Land of Braj." Meantime, continued attacks by Hans, the Enemy, continue : Krishna's steed Nand is seized by Varûna, but is rescued by Krishna, who further slays three demons in form respectively of a bull, a horse, and a wolf, sent against him by Hans ; also the elephant Kubalaya, two gigantic *wrestlers*, and finally Hans himself.

Such exploits, amongst many others, go to prove—as explained in the Prem-Ságur—that Krishna was born for the express purpose of saving Math'ra from the tyranny of Raja Huns or Cansa as aforesaid.

Báláráná then slays the demon Prálamb, and wages war with "Dubid the Monkey," whom he slays by pronouncing the mystic word "*Hún,*" and releases twenty thousand captive kings, amongst them King *Vrij* "the lizard of the dry well." He further slays the Titanic Jálab, son of Láb, with one of the swords called "dhop," with which his army is armed.

___
* This fantastic myth of Goverdhun seems a prototype of the "raised hills" so often met with in Scandinavian fairy mythology.

Generally both the brethren (like the classic Castor and Pollux) enact the part of *Rescuers* and *Preservers* from evil.

But apart from, and underlying, these fantastic myths, we seem to approach a quasi-historic element in the history of Krishna, and we arrive at the period when the warlike brethren take part in the war of the Kuraus and Pandaus, which forms the subject matter of the foregoing sections of this little work.

It appears that Kunti, the mother of the three elder Pandaus, was Krishna's paternal aunt. He determines to assist their cause, and sends the virtuous Akrour as his ambassador to Hustinapoora to ascertain the state of things. Akrour returns and reports the exile of the Pandaus, whereupon Krishna allies himself especially to Arjûna, and with his son Pradyumna, accompanies him to the wars, which culminate in the great battle of Kurau-Khét, as already related.

It seems doubtful whether the war of which the *Siege of Math'ra* was the climax—about to be related—was prior or subsequent to the great war of the Mâhâbârât. On the whole, I am inclined to consider it as subsequent to that great event, for we find the brethren, Krishna and Báláráiná, resorting to Yudishtir's great sacrifice after his restoration to the throne, at which Sisupál is dissatisfied, and inveighs against Krishna, whereupon his head is cut off by the quoit "Sudarsan," but a mystic light emanates from his body. It appears that this arch-enemy, in previous stages of existence, had been first Hiranya-Káshipu, second Ráwun, third Sisupál.   The Titan *My* then builds a palace for King Yûdishtír.

Further, the warlike brethren visit the field of Kúrú-Kshétra to view an eclipse, and there, at the request of their mother, recover from Hades their six elder brethren slain by "Hans." These events naturally lead up to the great event,

THE SIEGE OF MATH'RA.

THIS great quasi-historical event which caused the removal of Krishna and his tribe of Jadous to the western seaboard is alluded to in the chronicles of the Mâhâbârât, the Hárivansa, and the Prem-Ságur.

In its bare outlines it may probably rest on a basis of historic fact; though of course embellished by mythic exaggerations: the following are the primary circumstances as related by some of the chronicles.

Krishna, having overcome his arch-enemy Raja Hans or Cansa, places his Ally and friend "Ougrascin" on the throne of Math'ra, and calls a grand council of war. Vasondeva; Satyaca, Daronca; Bhôdia; Vêtaráca; Vicondára; Prince Bhayésáka; rich Viprithon; Babhron, the treasurer; Satya Varmon; brave Bhowritedjas, King of Math'ra (son of Ougrasein)—all children of the Jadous—band themselves together and repulse no less than 17 attacks or invasions by Raja Djarasandha, King of Magadha. It appears that Swâpti and Prâpti, daughters of Djarasandha had been the wives of "Hans" or Cansa, the deposed King of Math'ra; Djarasandha accordingly marches to avenge Cansa against Ougrascin whose cause is supported by Krishna, aided further by 30 Kings, whose names are given; amongst them the Rajas of Karouncha, Daulavaktra; Tchédi; Kalinga; Budri (bravest of the brave); Sâmereli; Késica; King Bhîchmaka and his valiant son Roukmin (rival of Arjûna in battle); and others.

Although repulsed 17 times, Djarasandba (or Lucifer himself according to some accounts) instigates certain Mlechchas* (barbarians) to attack Krishna, who retreats across the mountains towards Dwar'ka on the Sea.

Djarasandha then advances with 23 armies—each army consisting of 21,870 chariots and as many war elephants, 109,350 foot and 66,000 horse, such it appears being the prescribed number of the *Akshanhini* or corps d'armée of ancient India. The Prem-Sâgur adds that 30 millions of "very unclean and frightful barbarians, whose arms and necks are thick, teeth large, aspect filthy, eyes red," &c., &c., under

---

* These Mlechchas or barbarians are often alluded to in Sanscrit chronicles, and were apparently Scythians, or Medians from Central Asia. India was more than once overrun by hordes of them, especially on the overthrow of the Median Empire, B.C.

Djarasind, drive Krishna into the mountains, and at length capture Math'ra."

There is probably a basis of historical truth in this exaggerated fable, as doubtless the seat of the Jadou's power was removed from Math'ra to the seaboard under overwhelming pressure, and it is stated that on the side of Krishna and Ougrasein only Djanadhana and his Vrichnies at last remained.

    *   *   *   *   *   *

Behold therefore great Krishna at length retreating : The Brahmans recite the daily prayer, the *Sâvitri* in his behalf. In his perplexity Krishna implores the Gods his ancestors. Bálárámá's evening prayer is also given corresponding with the (quotidien) evening prayer of Krishna, Baladeva, and other great ones—" That I may be preserved by Brahma and " the Gods ; by the 5 elements ; by the 11 Rudras ; the 12 " Adityas ; the 8 Vasous ; and the 12 great Aswinis—By Hri, " Sri, Lakshmi, &c.—That I be preserved in the 4 Seas, in " the Ganges, Sârâsvâti, &c.—By the 3 Fires; the 3 Veds ; " the rock Costoubha ; the horse Out d tchêhsrâvas ; the " Amrit; the Cow ; the wise Virgins ; the blue Chattah, &c.

    *   *   *   *   *   *

During the retreat across the mountains our friend Krishna is found at his old tricks: he marries the beautiful Rukmini, whom he carries off on her marriage-day from a temple. She was the daughter of Bhishmak, King of Kandalpur. She became his principal wife—the others being Jamaváti (ever jealous of Rukmini), Satyabhana, Kalnidi, Mitrihindi (his cousin), Satya (for whom 7 bulls were slain) ; Bhádra ; Laksmani ; each wife had 1 daughter and 10 sons ; but according to the Prem-Sâgur Krishna had other 16,108 wives ! !

On the other hand Bálárámá is constant to one wife—the virtuous Rewâti,—whom he married at Krishna's request.

Arrived at Dwarka or Dwaravali, Krishna was welcomed by the Bhojas, Vrichnies, and Andacas, and "dwelt in Majesty;" and his entry is described in glowing language. He would seem to have soon renewed the war : the Hárivansa relates

that after the great " Sacrifice of Káshyapa " he declares war
against the Dánávas and giant Daityas ; Arjuna the Pandan,
and'Krishna's son Prâdyâmna accompany the Hero to the war.
They conquer Vadjranabha, but the " Swans " persuade his
daughter Poôbhavâti to marry Pârdyûmna and peace is made.
The loves and marriage of the young couple with their court-
ship "by moonlight" is dwelt upon, and forms a romantic
episode---but war is soon after resumed, and terrible deeds are
enacted.   At its conclusion the " General " Anâdhrichti
reproaches Krishna with the deaths of Asolomân, Poulomán,
Nisounda ; also of Naraka, Sôbha, Sahoa, Ménda, Dwirida (a
Monkey,)* and great Hayagriva killed in the war.   Krishna
" blowing with the power of an elephant " replies " General !
It's false ! "   He then becomes furious ; attacks Djwâra (who
ever he may be) and fights Siva himself, and his son Kartikaya
(the war god) into the bargain ; but Durga, in form of Kotâvi·
the "naked woman," interposes her golden lance between the
combatants and forbids the fight.   Krishna exclaims : " O
Goddess, go back ! Go back ! stay not my arm."

Then our old friend Krishna (who, however, scarcely appears
in so amiable a light as when first introduced to the reader,)
here appears to pass into final beatitude ; and from Chapter·
182 of the Hárivansa we are presented with the *Dream of
Markandhya*, containing an extraordinary cosmogony and mythological genesis of Hári or Narryan—of whom the earthly
Krishna was considered the avatar—ending with the Wars of
the Titans, the defeat of Madhou by the "Man Lion," and
the final overthrow, of "Tripoma," the flying city of the Assurs.

To enter on this would be a work in itself, and foreign to
the subject in hand, which only purports to be "Tales of the
Pandaus" and their friends, of whom the earthly Krishna was
chief.   The poet adds—"O, Sonaca ! I have now told thee of
"the ancient virtues, and foretold the vices of the coming ages ;
"what more can I tell thee?"

---

* Probably an aboriginal chief.

The Last Days
of Krishna and the Pandaus.

———o:o———

IT will have been gathered from former sections of this work that the Pandaus, having overcome and all but exterminated their rivals the Kuraus at the great battle of Kuru-Kshétra, had regained their ancestral throne.

Under the sway of Yûdishtíra "the Just," who reigned at Hustinapoora (or Ayodhya) with patriarchal mildness, the kingdom enjoyed peace and prosperity for more than thirty years, during which period *Aryavarta*—the Holy Land inhabited by genuine Hindoos—may be held to have realized the visions of an oriental Arcadia, as depicted in the Râmâyânâ during the reign of the virtuous monarch Dasarátha, the father of Râma, the hero of the great epic.

It may perhaps be interesting to introduce a few paraphrases of that noble poem, as typical of the civilization and social life of ancient India.

> On pleasant Sarju's fertile side
> There lies a rich domain,
> With countless herds of cattle thronged,
> And gay with golden grain.
> There, built by Manu,* Prince of men,
> That saint by all revered,
> Ayodhya, famed through every land,
> Her stately towers upreared.
> Her vast extent, her structures high,
> With every beauty deckt,
> Like Indra's city, showed the skill
> Of godlike architect.
> Or like a bright creation sprung

---

* Manu was the first prince of the Solar dynasty.

From limner's magic art,
She seemed too beautiful for stone:
  So fair was every part.
Twelve leagues the queenly city lay
  Down the broad river's side,
And, guarded well with moat and walls,
  The foeman's power defied.
Her ample streets were nobly planned,
  And streams of water flowed
To keep the fragrant blossoms fresh,
  That strewed her royal road.
There many a princely palace stood
  In line on level ground;
Here temple, and triumphal arc,
  And rampart banner-crowned.
There gilded turrets rose on high
  Above the waving green
Of mango-groves, and bloomy trees,
  And flowery knolls between.
On battlement and gilded spire
  The pennon waved in state;
And warders, with the ready bow,
  Kept watch at every gate.
She shone a very mine of gems,
  The throne of Fortune's Queen :
So many-hued her gay parterres,
  So bright her fountains' sheen.
Her pleasure-grounds were filled at eve
  With many a happy throng,
And ever echoed with the sound
  Of merry feast and song.
For meat and drink of noblest sort
  In plenty there were stored :
And all enjoyed their share of wealth,
  Nor heaped the miser's hoard.
At morn the blossom-scented air
  The clouds of incense stirred,
And blended with the wreath's perfume
  The sweet fresh smell of curd.
Streamed through her streets, in endless line,
  Slow wain and flying car :
Horse, elephant, and merchant train,

And envoys from afar.
Her ample arsenals were filled
  With sword, and club, and mace :
And wondrous engines, dealing death,
  Within her towers had place.
Nor there unknown the peaceful arts
  That youthful souls entrance,
Of player, minstrel, mime, and bard,
  And girls that weave the dance.
There rose to heaven the Veda-chant,
  Here blent the lyre and lute :
There rang the stalwart archer's string,
  Here softly breathed the flute.
The swiftest horses whirled her cars,
  Of noblest form and breed :
Vanayu's mare that mocked the wind,
  And Vahli's fiery steed.
There elephants, that once had roamed
  On Vindhya's mountains, vied
With monsters from the bosky dells
  That shag Himaleh's side.
The best of Brahmans, gathered there,
  The flame of worship fed ;
And, versed in all the Vedas' lore,
  Their lives of virtue led.
By penance, charity, and truth,
  They kept each sense controlled,
And giving freely of their store
  Rivalled the saints of old.
Her dames were peerless for the charm
  Of figure, voice, and face :
For lovely modesty and truth,
  And woman's gentle grace.
Their husbands, loyal, wise, and kind,
  Were heroes in the field,
And sternly battling with the foe,
  Could die, but never yield.
The poorest man was richly blest
  With knowledge, wit, and health ;
Each lived contented with his own,
  Nor envied other's wealth.
All scorned to lie : no miser there
  His buried silver stored :

The braggart and the boast were shunned,
The slanderous tongue abhorred.
Each kept his high observances,
And loved one faithful spouse ;
And troops of happy children crowned,
With fruit, their holy vows.*

It may be stated generally that two seats of ancient empire, ruled over by descendants of Satyavrâta the seventh Mânû— during whose life all living creatures, except himself and his family, were destroyed by a deluge—are recorded as having existed in upper India; one at Ayodhya (Oude), ruled by a scion of the *Solar* race, and another at Pratishtâna, ruled by the *Lunar* race; whilst another kingdom was afterwards established at Magadha (Behar) by a governor appointed by a prince of the lunar race. Besides these, moreover, in the south of India were three other ancient kingdoms—*Pandya, Chola*, and *Chera*. Madura was chief city of Pandya, and its king's name, *Pandion*, is mentioned by Pliny, Arrian, and Ptolemy. The name Pandion suggests that this kingdom may probably have been an offset of the Pandau (or lunar) empire of Upper India, of which the great Yûdishtíra was chief; and for practical purposes we may perhaps assume Yûdishtíra to have ruled the Empire of India, or at least to have exercised sway as suzerain over most of the provinces or minor kingdoms composing it. In the story of "The Wanderings of Yûdishtír" it has been so assumed, and in it we have endeavoured to imagine a few of the progresses of the "Just King" towards various outlying portions of his empire ; these are, however, purely imaginary, as also are most of the romantic legends attributed to him or his brethren in the "Tales of the Pandaus" already ventured on. No hint of such things is to be found in the chronicles of the Mâhâbârât or elsewhere. It is generally assumed that the Pandaus, after their victory, dwelt at Hustinapoora in happiness and honour.

The last section of the great epic, however, brings us to a

From the "Ramayana," by R. T. H. Griffiths, M.A., of Benares.

time when, owing to the misfortunes which overtook Krishna
and the great tribe of Jadons—the chief allies and supporters
of the Pandaus—a political crisis in their affairs was brought
about, and King Yûdishtíra was led to contemplate the abdi-
cation of the throne, having previously endeavoured to reconcile
conflicting interests by establishing for his successors—as
king and ministers respectively—representatives of the various
possible claimants to power, associated also with a female re-
gent or guardian of the kingdom in the interests of the young
Prince Purrojit, grandson of Arjûna.

From these fragments and hints the historical novelist might
build a fabric of romance, and introduce much calculated to
interest readers in the probable march of affairs in the great
Aryan Kingdom of the northwest during the period of the
Pandaus' ascendancy; dramatic scenery might be created; and
the characteristics of the great king himself—Yûdishtíra the
"just one"—supported and advised by his four brethren, all
remarkable for various forms of prowess—present suggestive
pictures and interesting studies of Asiatic character; their attributes, indeed, in some aspects would almost seem intended to
represent the types of the abstract quality by which each was
distinguished—Strength, Valour, Wisdom, Beauty. Such
traits suggest also didactic teachings, religious developments,
and high-flown moral sentiments. Such a view of the subject must be left for future research or fancy. In this place,
dropping *imaginary* fable, we will at once proceed to the
closing scenes of the great drama, as presented to us in the
Mâhâbârât; wherein, amidst a maze of metaphysical obscurities involving ceremonial and ethical teachings, the Pandaus
approach the end of their career; and whereby, indeed, some
support is given to the theory above suggested, in the extraordinary death of the five heroes in succession whilst ascending
the mountains of Himôdi—abode of snow—so often the arena
of their wanderings and adventures in life, now the scene of
their transmigration or apotheosis from earth.

Without further preface then we proceed to narrate the "Last Days of the Sons of Pand," as given in the concluding section of that portion of the Máhábárát translated into Persian by the Mahomedan Nékheib Khan, in comparatively modern times.

* *
*

Krishna dwelt at Dwârka amidst his tribe of Jadous (perhaps Magi) with his aged father Basdeo, and his brother Bálúrámá. Santek and Kerretburma were his grandsons. Disputes, accusations of theft, and jealousies occurred amidst the kindred chiefs, and a general slaughter ensued. Bálárámá, from distress of mind, then retires into the forest and there dies. Krishna goes in search of him, and witnesses his death; having already beheld the bodies of his sons Pardáman, Samba, and Chardepas, with others, slain in the tumult. Krishna, whilst in the forest, is himself wounded by a hunter in the heel of the foot by an arrow, whose head is found to be the mystic thunderbolt swallowed by the fish, and recovered on the salt sea shore by the hunter in his nets. Krishna is "translated!" and all the celestial spirits, the Eleven Rûdras (weepers), Assurs, Deotas, and Seraphs, convey the soul of Krishna to paradise.

* * * * * *

The news of these sad events is conveyed by Nárok, the charioteer, to Yûdishtír and the Pandaus at Hustinapoora, who are plunged into great grief at hearing of the destruction of the tribe of Jadou.

Arjûna proceeds to Dwârka to advise and assist. He finds the city "like a widow sorrowing for her husband." The aged Basdeo, the father of Krishna dies ; Arjûna performs the funeral rites, and afterwards conducts the surviving family and wives to Hustinapoora. He, however, falls in with bands of robbers on the way, and his arm being weakened and arrows blunted with age and disuse, he incurs some loss, "his strength of arm to wield his bow having declined."

Arjûna finds the bodies of the slain Jadous lying along the

shore. He burns Pardáman, Santek, Kerretburna, and Ek-uror; and, finally, incremates Krishna and Bálárámá (or Bulbhuddur, as he is designated). He then advises and con-ducts a general emigration of the survivors of the tribe of Jadou to Hustinapoora. His adventures on the way are described. Many of Krishna's wives burn themselves (perform Suttie); others retire into the forests and become suniássies; the rest go to Delhi. Arjûna visits Vyâsa the Sage, whose advice he seeks, and then returns to Hustinapoora.

On hearing of the final destruction of the race of Jadou, Yûdishtír determines to abdicate the sovereignty: he sends for Hejis, the son of Ditrashtura and for Purrojit, the grand-son of Arjûna, and placed the diadem on the brow of the latter, appointing Hejis as his wuzzeer. Also he summoned Sephedra, the sister of Krishna and wife of Arjûna, and commended them both to her care. Then King Yûdishtír and his brethren re-paired to the Ganges and bathed, and announced to the people their determination again to go into exile. They set out on their journey followed by the people of the whole city, who, in tears, beseech them to remain; but, steadfast in their purpose, they pursue their journey. Many of the wives destroy them-selves: Abonni, wife of Arjûna, walks into the Ganges and disappears. However, at length the escort of people gradually drop behind and return to the city, and Yûdishtír and his brethren are left to pursue their melancholy journey alone, or accompanied only by their faithful dog. Arjûna throws his bow and quiver of arrows—being useless—into the lake Post, where also the "cháka" of Krishna had already been deposited.

In single file, at intervals between according to age, the Five Pandau Brethren pursued their melancholy journey up the rugged slopes of Himálch, Yûdishtír leading, then Bhîma, Arjûna, Nakoola, and last of all Sediva. As sorrowfully and painfully they wend their way towards the rugged upland, Sediva drops and dies. The brethren pause. "Alas! how should this noble youth succumb?" Yûdishtír sighs, "Alas! he was

vain and not perfect.   Brethren, let as proceed toward Kaiáls."
Next Nakoola falls.   "How is this, oh, just one!   The wise
Nakoola perishes!   Alas!" quoth Yûdishtír, "he trusted in
knowledge!   Proceed."   Then great Arjûna sinks on earth.
"His arrows were too keen and unsparing," said Yûdishtír.
"Onwards!"   Next brave Bhíma falls.   "Too much he trusted
in his strength.   Alas! my brother."   Yûdishtír, now alone left
alive of the Pandans, continues his solitary way, accompanied
only by the faithful dog.   At length great Yûdishtír himself
perceives the approach of dissolution, and falls; but Vishnu
himself supports him, and promises paradise.   The noble chief
exclaims,—"Not so, oh Yâma! except this faithful dog accompany : he has followed his master to the last, and possesses
the virtues of the best of men without their sins.   Let him
attain metempsychosis and attain to paradise.   My brethren
have already attained the reward of their virtues ; this faithful creature alone remains unrewarded."   Whereupon Vishnu
explains that in truth this generous animal is no other than an
embodiment of "Dharm"—charity, virtue, justice—who had
accompanied Yûdishtír in life, and now finds salvation with
him.   So ends the life of great Yûdishtír on earth.

*   *   *   *   *   *

His adventures in Purgatory and Paradise are narrated in
the Mâhâbârât, and are quite Dantesque in character, but are
of too metaphysical and fantastic a nature to merit detail.   They
are to be found in the concluding section of the Mâhâbârât, as
translated into Persian by the Mahomedan Nékhaib Khan; but
as many other metaphysical subtleties and rules of conduct
&c. are involved in portions of that great epic, and seem in
fact to be interpolations—some I should judge of comparatively
modern times—I prefer to end the Legend of the Pandaus,
as is indeed suggested in the text, in the heroic style the
occasion merits, and to say that amidst the glorified aspects of
nature, great Yûdishtír and his brethren, after a noble career,
closed their pilgrimage on earth in calm introspection of the
Past, and in sublime aspirations for the Future.

✦✛The Vision of Markandhya,✛✦
(The War of the Titans.)

TO such of my readers as have followed the erratic fortunes of the Pandaus, a few final words concerning their friends and allies—mythic and earthly—may not be out of place.

The doughty deeds of the champion Krishna have been given, but the sage "Markandhya," their chief adviser and historian, has been but briefly represented, although he, with his pupil Vyâsa, the "compiler," were the chief authors of the Mâhâbârât, the chronicle which narrates the Pandaus' deeds of arms, and they are in fact credited with inaugurating the mystic Brahminical Philosophy which ranks amongst the six or seven schools of Hindoo thought.*

The Hárivansa contains the account of the exploits of Hári on earth (or Krishna), epitomized in the last section of this little work, but the second part seems almost a rescript of the cosmogony of the Mâhâbârât (Book LXIV.), and may be considered as embodying the same vedanta or theory of creation, in which the genesis of Narryána or Hári (of whom Krishna was considered an avatar) is especially pronounced.

After a chapter or two of a metaphysical character, devoted to the "manifestation of Poushkâra," the author of the Hárivansa proceeds to the dream or "*Vision of Markandhya.*"

---

* The Schools of Philosophy, according to Hindoos, are—
   (1) The Atheistical Sankhya, attributed to Kapila; Materialistic, the plastic principle.
   (2) The Yogas of Patanjali and the Bhagavad-Gita.
   (3) The Parva-Mimansa, attributed to Jaimini.
   (4) The Vedanta, attributed to the Vyasa (compiler); Krishna Dwaipayana—the mystic Brahminical school.
   (5) The Nyaya of Gautama—the Logical Method.
   (6) The Vaisheshika of Kanada—the Atomic System.
   Some authors divide No. 2 into two branches, viz. (1) Emancipation by asceticism; (2) that of the Bhagavad-Gita, asceticism as applied to life—salvation by good works.
                                    N

From amidst the mythological subtleties which involve this strange myth, the following synopsis may be given as not without interest to the general reader.

But first let us imagine the Sage as he sits beneath the stars at his cäamah or cell in the forest of Rishyamukhi, where he has already been introduced to the reader (page 128).

Near there had lovely Uma, daughter of Himalaya, *Lady of the Mountain*, dwelt and practised austerity. Enamoured of the gloomy Siva, the maiden dwelt apart to try whether by pious austerities she might win the object of her love, whose virtues she appreciates. Her friends expostulate, and endeavour to dissuade her. The faithful Uma, in noble language, defends her love for Siva. She exclaims:—

> " 'Tis ever thus, the Mighty and the Just
> " Are scorned by souls that grovel in the dust;
> " Their lofty goodness and their motives wise
> " Shine all in vain before such blinded eyes ;
> " Say, who is greater, he who strives for power,
> " Or he who succours in misfortune's hour ?
>
>   *   *   *   *   *
>
> " She sent a maiden to her sire, and prayed
> " He for her sake might grant some bosky shade,
> " That she might dwell in solitude, and there
> " Give all her soul to penance and to prayer.
>
>   *   *   *   *   *
>
> " Her gentleness had made the fawns so tame,
> " To her kind hand for fresh sweet grass they came ;
> " Then came the hermits of the holy wood
> " To see the Vot'ress in her solitude.
> " In hermit's mantle was she clad ; her look
> " Fix't in deep thought upon the holy book ;
> " So pure the grove, all war was made to cease,
> " And savage monsters liv'd in joy and peace ;
> " Pure was the grove ; each newly-built abode
> " And leafy shrines, where fires of worship glowed." *

So fair Uma had fairly won the Gloomy Deity, and became his spouse—"Parhuttie"—the Lady of the Mountain. Their

---

* From Kalidasa's " Birth of the War God."

son was Kartikaya "or Skanda," the War God, who has figured in the preceding "Tales of the Pandaus."

Many legends cluster around the sacred shores of the great lake of Kûrû-Kshétra, mentioned, as formerly existing, by Varâha-Mihira. Here, at eclipses, during the days of "Parva" —full moon and planetary conjunction—the waters of all other lakes are supposed to unite, hence the bather obtains the merit of the combined snân or sacred ablution. Great are its virtues. Here Indra slew the Kshatriyas; his thunder bolts being of the horse's head of the mythic Dadhyanch supplied by the Aswinis.*

To this mystic spot had repaired King Yûdishtíra and the Pandaus to do penance for Kshatriyas slain. Mournfully the heroic brethren stood and sang the ode to Vishnoo and great Siva on the desolate shores.

In the sacred grove of Rishyamukhi—that elephant of saints—Markandhya the Hermit, had taken his abode.

After bathing in the sacred lake the Pandau brethren stood before him. "Bho! O Muni! Give us clean breasts: the blood "of Kshatriyas rests on us. Let the head escape from sin! "Aum!"

Yûdishtíra, the *Just*, cast his conch or warhorn of victory— *Ananta-Vijay*—before the sage. Bhîma, the *War-Chief*, let fall the warhorn *Pounda*, at the feet of Markandhya. Arjûna, the *Valiant*—"Lord of the Sounding Bow"—cast on earth the Panchajanya trumpet that so oft had scared the foe. Nakoola, the *Wise*, cast down the conch "Soogasha;" and Sediva, the *Handsome* one, his horn "Máni-poosh-páka."

Deep in thought the Hermit stood. At length he said: "O Chiefs! turn to the east, and recite the hymn to great "Bhowâni; but look not round!"

The Pandaus, with uplifted arms, invoked the silent Deity, and chaunted the sacred hymn to "the Avenger."

---

* (1) The Kimmeras, musicians of Kuvern, God of Wealth, are represented with horses' heads. (2) Indra's park, called Nandam.

"Now turn," exclaimed the hermit.

They did so. Lo! the warhorns had vanished from earth "Oh, children of Mânû," continued the Sage, "the sacri-"fice is accepted. Go in peace."

Vyâsa, the "compiler," saw the sacrifice, and wrote it on a pépul leaf.

This was in the years when great Yûdishtír dwelt at Hustin-apûra, and ruled the kingdom of his ancestors, whilst Purrék-chit, his grandson, was minister, and rich Vipron, treasurer of state. He it was of whom the weird and wise Hanumân had said, "Public officers are like obstinate tumours; until they "are squeezed, they disgorge not the inner substance of the "king!" so saying, he had laughed and vanished into the leafy shades; but King Yûdishtír only smiled, and bestowed a jewel on old Vipron.

   *   *   *   *   *   *

So the Pandaus had departed to Hustinapoora, and Mark-andhya, the sage, continued to dwell alone in the Rishyamukhi wood. There it was he pondered the wise words of the Mâhâ-bârât, which the Compiler Vyasa wrote on leaves of the sacred pépul. There it was the hermit wrested omens from the stars, and talked with seraphs, and saw visions of the past and future.

One night the sage sat beneath the canopy of heaven and deeply pondered on the origin of things. As the stars came out and glimmered through the leafy canopy of his sylvan home, in the month of Aswin, at the time of "Parva," in the planetary conjunction of Jupiter and Mars—when the moon was at the full—Markandhya saw the vision of the origin of earth and heaven—the genesis of Sank Narryána. He sang it to the winds of heaven, and Vyâsa, his pupil, wrote it in a book, and related it to Djanamedjaya and to Parikchet, his father, years after the five great Pandau kings had sought Kailâs. Markandhya chaunted aloud a hymn to Narryána from the Rig Veda, and soon he saw a vision.*

---

* See "Hymn to Narryana," page 168.

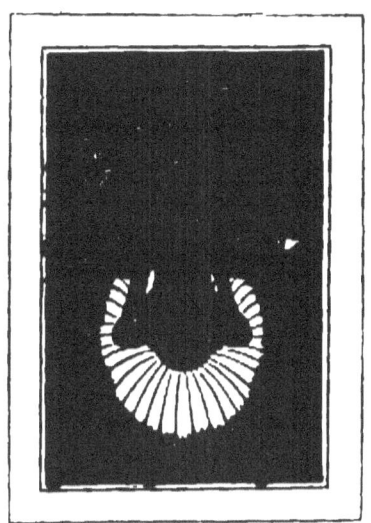

Nagyana, or Padmasan
(Son of the Golden Lotus).

From a Native Picture.

𝕿𝖍𝖊 𝖁𝖎𝖘𝖎𝖔𝖓 𝖔𝖋 𝕸𝖆𝖗𝖐𝖆𝖓𝖉𝖍𝖞𝖆.

Floating as a babe on the primæval ocean of chaos, Narryána was addressed by Markandhya:—" Who art Thou, Lord?"
" I am Narryána, son of the golden lotus!"

From the bosom of darkness (tamas) a great Assur of
darkness named "Madhou" arises, and another named "Kit-
âbha,"—"born from the bosom of passion (radjas)." They are
destroyed by Brahm, and Manâsa, Brahma, Bhowrah, and
Iswâra are created. Then ensues the contest of Narryána—
or Vishnoo the "Preserver"—with "Madhou," his eyes yellow
as honey.* Madhou falls into lake Poushkâra; "its hills with
their metallic veins resemble clouds lit up by lightning."
The "churning of the ocean" is then described. The formation of the "egg of the world," and the avatar of the Boar,
who roots up the dry land of the earth with his tusks.
Indra is raised to the throne of heaven.

*   *   *   *   *   *

"At the time when the mountains had wings"—during the
War of the Titans—arise the great Giants (Assurs) "Hiranya-Kasipû, Hiranya-Garbha, and Hiranya-Yaksha. They
are slain by Narryána in form of the "boar," or by the "Man
Lion," in which form he especially overcomes Hiranya-Kasipû,
king of giants. The War of the Giants, who are at first
triumphant, is particularly described in Chap. 226 et seq. of
the Hárivansa. "Indra and his marouts draw off in retreat."
Universal terror prevails.   "The howls of Cródhavâsas,
"Kalakéyas, Angapontras, Bâhonsalins, Vêgas, Vêgalâyas,
"Sênhikeyas, Samhrâdêjas (of loud voices), the Vidwéchas;
"of Capila, "Son of the earth," resound on all sides; the
shrieks of Vyâghrakchas, "Birds, Infants of the Night;"
Inhabitants of Hell, are heard; and "the Rudras—"whose
eyes are like the suns"—groan aloud."

---

* A play on the word Madhou—honey.

At length Hiranya-Kasipû, "armed with thunder and a trident," is slain by the Man-Lion.

Praise of the Man-Lion (Chap. 233).

During the War of the Titans the following champions are "told off" to fight in pairs:—Sâvitha v. the Rakshas Bâna, Bala v. Dhronva, Poûlomân v. Vayon, Namoutchi v. Dhara, Hayagriva v. Pouchan, Sambava v. Bhaga, Sarabha and Sallabha v. Soma, Bela—brother of Krita ("of the honey yellow eyes") v. Mrigrayadha; whilst the "horrible Rehon" (of one hundred heads and one hundred stomachs)," is confronted by Adjeeapâd.

Such were a few of the champions enumerated as engaged in the great final battle between the Devs and Assurs, in which the latter appear to have been victors. It may be added that many of these names have meanings in the original more or less grotesque.

The Chief of the Assurs—"Kondjambha—flaunts on the field of battle like a storm at the ending of the ages." Indra, with his Marouts, draws off the field in retreat; and Bâli—the King of the Giants—surrounded by his army, "was com-"plimented by his friends, and shows to all eyes with the "majesty of Hiranya-Kashipû."

The reign of the Assurs is established, and the Giant Bâli reigns as king in their flying city, "Tripoma."

But now, at last, the Gods appeal to Brahma, to whom they address prayer by voice of Kasyapa; they also address Vishnoo, the "Preserver," who intervenes in favor of Indra and the host of heaven. Soon the eternal Brahma appears with the Saints Poulastya, Poulaha, Mantchi, Brighon, &c., chaunting the Vedas, "especially the hymns of the Rig Veda and Sama." The clouds disperse; all nature recovers; and Bâli (Chap. 257—261) is relegated to hell; and the great war of the Gods and Titans ends with the destruction of "Tripóma," the flying city of the Assurs; whilst Indra and the deities of the inferior Hindoo Pantheon at length reign supreme in heaven.

Such, in brief, is the "argument" of this strange cosmogony and mythic genesis of creation, as enunciated by Markandhya and his pupil Vyâsa; and which, as before explained
(page 161), in itself forms a school of Brahminical mystic
philosophy. It is difficult to reconcile the pure and beautiful
monotheistic hymns of the early Vedas with this strange
legend ; one such hymn has been put into the mouth of Markandhya, and appears at the end of this section, but it forms
only the original poetic thesis of Hindoo cosmogony, and was
probably written ages before the era of Markandhya and the
Mâhâbârât.

We have now examined, however imperfectly, a few of the
legends which cluster round the life of the errant Pandaus
on earth. or illustrate their apotheosis.

The dust of ages which covers these time-worn chronicles
has somewhat sheltered them from the view of the "Wandering
Cimmerian," and dimmed his vision and guage of their mythic
value ; nevertheless, having ended his labours in the "Cave,"
he now ventures to offer his "Tales of the Pandaus" to the
indulgence of a romance-loving public.

Hymn to Narayana.

" **S**PIRIT *of spirit, who, thro' every part*
Of space expanded and of endless time,
Beyond the stretch of lab'ring thought sublime,
Bad'st uproar into beauteous order start,
"*Before Heaven was, Thou art!*
    *   *   *   *

" *Wrapt in eternal solitary shade,*
" *Th' impenetrable gloom of light intense,*
"*Impervious, inaccessible, immense,*
" *Ere spirits were infused or forms displayed,*
" *Brahm his own mind surveyed.*
    *   *   *   *

" *Leap'd into being a shape supremely fair!*
" *Primœval Maya was the Goddess named.*
" *First an all-potent, all-pervading sound,*
" *Bade flow the waters—and the waters flowed,*
" *Excelling in their measureless abode—*
" *Diffusive, multitudinous, profound,*
" *Above, beneath, around;*
" *Then o'er the vast expanse primordial wind*
" *Breathed gently, till a lucid bubble rose,*
" *Which grew in perfect shape an egg refined,*
" *Till from its bursting shell, with lowly state,*
" *A Form cerulian fluttered o'er the deep—*
" *Brightest of beings, greatest of the great,*
" *But heavenly-pensive on the Lotus lay,*
" *That blossomed at his touch and shed a golden ray.*
" *Hail, primal blossom! hail, empyreal gem!*
" *Kamul or Padna, or whate'er high name*
" *Delight thee.**   *   *   *   *
         " *Forth from thy verdant stem*
" *Full gifted Brahma, rapt in solemn thought*
" *He stood, and round his eyes far-darting threw;*
" *But whilst his viewless origin he sought,*

---

* Called also "Venamali, Pertamber, Padmanabha, &c.

" *One plain he saw of living waters blue,*
" *Their spring, nor saw nor knew.*
" *Then in his parent stalk again retired*
" *With restless pain for ages ; he enquired*
" *What were his powers, by whom and why conferred :*
" *With doubts perplexed, with keen impatience fired*
" *He rose, and rising, heard*
" *Th' unknown all-knowing word,*
" *Brahma ! no more in vain research persist ;*
" *My veil thou can'st not move.   Go, bid all worlds exist.*
" *Hail, self-existent in celestial speech,*
" *'Narayana,' from thy wat'ry cradle named !*" *   *

A Hymn to Maya, from the Rig Veda.

" *Omniscient Spirit, whose all-ruling power,*
" *Bids from each sense bright emanations beam,*
" *Glows in the rainbow, sparkles in the stream,*
" *Smiles in the bud, and glistens in the flower*
        " *That crowns each vernal bower ;*
" *Sighs in the gale and warbles in the throat*
" *Of ev'ry bird that hails the blooming spring,*
" *Or tells his tale in many a liquid note ;*
        *   *   *   *
" *Breathes in rich fragrance from the sandal grove.*
        *   *   *   *
" *In air, in floods, in caverns, woods, and plains ;*
" *Thy will inspirits all, thy sov'reign Maya reigns.*
" *Blue crystal vault and elemental fires*
" *That in the ethereal fluid blaze and breathe*
" *Thou, tossing main, whose snaky branches wreathe*
" *This pensile orb with intertwisted gyres*
        " *Mountains whose radiant spires*
" *Presumptuous rear their summit to the skies,*
" *And blend their em'rald hue with sapphire light,*
" *Smooth meads and lawns that glow with various dyes*
" *Of dew-bespangled leaves and blossoms bright,*
        " *Hence ! vanish from my sight ;*
" *Delusive pictures ! unsubstantial shows !*
" *My soul absorbed One only Being knows,*

"Of all perceptions one abundant source,
" Whence ev'ry object ev'ry moment flows.
"Suns hence derive their force,
" Hence planets learn their course,
"But suns and fading worlds I view no more;
"God only I perceive; God only I adore!"

NOTE.—These Hymns are from the Rig Veda, Vol. XIII. of Sir W. Jones' Works.

Printed by BRANNON AND SON, Newport, Isle of Wight.

www.ingramcontent.com/pod-product-compliance
Lightning Source LLC
Chambersburg PA
CBHW030553040726
47497CB00008B/2709